COVENANT
CHILD

The Women of Faith Fiction Club presents

COVENANT CHILD

TERRI BLACKSTOCK

W PUBLISHING GROUP™

www.wpublishinggroup.com

A Division of Thomas Nelson, Inc.
www.ThomasNelson.com

Published by W Publishing Group, a division of Thomas Nelson, Inc., P.O. Box 141000, Nashville, Tennessee 37214, in association with the literary agency of Alive Communications, Inc., 7680 Goddard Street, Suite 200, Colorado Springs, Colorado 80920. All rights reserved. No portion of this book may be reproduced, stored in a retrieval system, or transmitted in any form or by any means—electronic, mechanical, photocopy, recording, or any other—except for brief quotations in printed reviews, without the prior permission of the publisher.

Scripture quotations in this book are from the *New American Standard Bible* (NASB) © 1960, 1977, 1995 by the Lockman Foundation. Used by permission. All rights reserved.

This is a work of fiction. Names, characters, places, and incidents either are the products of the author's imagination or are used fictitiously. Any resemblance to actual persons, living or dead, events, organizations, or locales is entirely coincidental and beyond the intent of the author or publisher.

Library of Congress Cataloging-in-Publication Data

Blackstock, Terri, 1957-
   Covenant child / Terri Blackstock.
     p. cm.
   ISBN 0-8499-4301-9
   1. Title.
   PS3552.L34285 C68 2002
   813'.54—dc21   2002016799

Printed in the United States of America
02 03 04 05 06 PHX 9 8 7 6 5 4

Other Books by Terri Blackstock

Cape Refuge

Evidence of Mercy

Justifiable Means

Ulterior Motives

Presumption of Guilt

Never Again Goodbye

When Dreams Cross

Blind Trust

Broken Wings

Private Justice

Shadow of Doubt

Word of Honor

Trial by Fire

Seaside

Emerald Windows

For Love of Money: Sweet Delights Anthology

With Beverly LaHaye:

Seasons under Heaven

Showers in Season

Times and Seasons

Web page: www.terriblackstock.com

This book is lovingly dedicated
to the Nazarene

ONE

There's a question that haunts me in the blackest hours of night, when wasted moments crowd my dreams and mock the life I know. The question is this: How could a child born of privilege and promise grow up with nothing?

I was Somebody when I was born. Lizzie, my twin, says we were heiresses all along. "Our grandfather was a billionaire," she says. "Just *think* of it, Kara!" There were newspaper articles about us when we were three. They called us the "Billion Dollar Babies."

But these Billion Dollar Babies wore Goodwill hand-me-downs. We ate dry cereal most nights for supper, right out of the box, picking out the raisins to save for our school lunches the next day. In my memory, we never formally observed a birthday, because no one around us considered that day worthy of celebration. We were worthless no accounts to most of the people in town.

But all along we had an inheritance that no one told us was ours.

I sometimes try to remember back to the days before we were three, but my memories are tainted with the lies I've been taught and the pictures I've seen. I can't quite sift out real recollections from my faulty assumptions, but I do know that the things I've laid out here are true. Not because I remember them, but because I've studied all the sides, heard all the tales, read all the reports . . . and a few things have emerged with absolute clarity.

The first thing is that my father, Jack Holbrooke, was the son of *the* Paul Holbrooke, who did something with microchips and processors, things I can't begin to understand, and amassed a fortune before he was thirty. My father, Jack, got religion in his teens and decided he didn't want to play the part of the rich son. He became a pilot instead, bought a plane, and began flying charter flights and giving lessons. He disowned himself from the Holbrooke money and told his father that, instead of leaving any of it to him in his will, he preferred that he donate it to several evangelical organizations who provided relief and shared the gospel to people all over the world.

My grandfather tolerated his zeal and noted his requests, then promptly ignored them.

My mother, Sherry, was a teen runaway, who left Barton, Mississippi, at fifteen to strike out on her own. She wound up living with a kind family in Jackson, and she got religion, too.

She met my father in Jackson, when he put an ad in the paper for some office help at his hangar, and they fell in love around the time she was nineteen or so. They got married and had Lizzie and me less than a year later.

She was killed in a car wreck when we were just weeks old. Our father raised us himself for the next three years. I've seen pictures of him, and he looks like a kind, gentle man who laughed a lot. There are snapshots of him kissing us, dunking us like basketballs in his father's pool, chasing us across the lawn of the little house we lived in, reading us books, tucking us in. There are three birthday photos of our father lying on the floor with two cake-smeared redheads tearing into boxes of Barbies and Cabbage Patch dolls.

Sometimes I close my eyes and think hard, trying to bring back those moments, and for a while I convince myself that they are not just images frozen on paper, but they're live events in my head somewhere. I even think I can smell that cake and feel my father's stubbled face against mine. I can hear his laughter shaking through me and feel his arms holding me close.

But in truth, my memories don't reach that far back.

I don't even think I remember Amanda. Lizzie says she has more *impressions* of her than memories, that the snapshots just bring those impressions into clearer focus. I guess that's true with me, too.

But I wish I could remember when she met our father and us, how she wound up being his wife, how she was widowed and robbed of her children, and how she spent her life trying to keep a promise she had made to him . . . and to us.

But, according to Lizzie, truth is truth, whether it lies in your memory banks or not. So I'll start with Amanda's story, the way it was told to me, because it is very much the beginning of mine.

TWO

My father was playing guitar the first time Amanda saw him. He sat on a metal folding chair at the corner of the crowded rec room, watching the animated faces and soaking in the laughter around them as he strummed some tune that she didn't know. She would later tell that her eyes were drawn to the red hair that was in dire need of a cut; the open flannel shirt, its tails draping down along the sides of the chair, a plain white T-shirt beneath it; jeans that looked as if they'd been washed a dozen times too many; and torn, dirty tennis shoes that spoke of age and overuse.

Her best friend, Joan, who'd attended the Bible study for single professionals for several months, told her he was a pilot. But Amanda knew little else about him.

When the group had been called to order, people found places to sit along couches and rocking chairs in the big, rustic room. Amanda chose a spot near the guitar player and sat on the floor with her arms hugging her knees. He smiled at her and kept strumming.

The leader turned the meeting over to him, and he began to lead the group in praise songs and rock-revved hymns, and she finally heard the voice, deep and gentle, unadorned, as it brought them all into worship. When he'd finished singing and playing, he put the guitar down and took a place beside her on the floor. His presence birthed a sweet homesickness inside her for something she couldn't name. She had known right then that he held some treasure that belonged to her, one she longed to unearth and possess.

When the meeting was over, he held out a hand. "Name's Jack."

"Nice to meet you, Jack." She shook his hand, feeling the guitar calluses on his fingertips against the bottom of her hand. "I'm—"

"Don't tell me. Let me guess." He held tight to her hand. "I once worked at a fair and did this for a living."

"What? Played guitar?"

"No," he said, "guessed names. Now don't tell me. I can do this. I'm psychotic, you know."

She laughed. "You mean psychic?"

"Yeah, that, too." He winked as he gazed into her eyes. "Let's see. I'm getting an *A*."

Her eyes widened.

"An *M*."

She snatched her hand from his.

"Amanda!" he blurted.

"How did you know that?"

"I told you."

"I know. You're psychotic. But really. How?"

Grinning, he picked his guitar back up. "I asked somebody when you came in."

Her face grew warm as he rose, took her hand, and pulled her to her feet. He was a good seven inches taller than she.

"So how do you feel about chocolate milkshakes?" he asked.

"Tell you the truth, I haven't given it a whole lot of thought."

"Well, you should. Now aren't you grateful I came along to get you thinking about it?"

"Are you asking me to go have a milkshake with you?"

"I was trying to be a little more suave than to ask straight out, but yes," he said, "I was asking you for a date."

Though he'd charmed her quickly and thoroughly, he grew more serious over their shakes as he showed her pictures of Lizzie and me. Her heart sank that a man so young already had the baggage of divorce to drag around. "So how did you get custody?"

"Custody?" He frowned, then his eyebrows arched. "Oh, no, you don't understand. I'm not divorced. My wife died."

The smile on her face collapsed. "I'm so sorry."

"It's okay." His voice was soft, and he swallowed as if the memories still went down hard. "It happened three years ago, when they were just babies. Car accident. I've gone through all the textbook stages of grief. I'm in the acceptance stage now."

Though his words sounded flip, she could see in his eyes that they didn't come easily.

"So you've been raising the twins alone ever since?"

"That's right. But they're doing great."

Quiet beat out the seconds between them, and finally, he said, "So how's the shake?"

"Everything I hoped." Her face grew warm, and she had to look away.

He took her back to the retreat center and held her hand as he walked her to her car. "If you'd agree to let me buy you dinner this weekend, I could introduce you to Stapley's Steak-on-a-Stick. It's the favorite of all your best amateur guitar players."

She was twenty-five years old, but felt as giddy as a fourteen-year-old with a crush. "I'd love to have dinner with you, Jack. And as good as the Steak-on-a-Stick sounds, I'd rather be introduced to your girls."

He laughed then. "No kidding?"

"Why would I be kidding?"

"Because they don't exactly make for a quiet, peaceful meal, if you know what I mean."

"I love children," she said.

"Okay, but you asked for it. Tell you what. You can come to my house, and the girls and I will cook dinner for you. How's that sound? We make a mean spaghetti."

She fished through her purse for something to write on. "Just give me an address and a time, and I'll be there. Only let me bring something."

"The girls would be downright insulted if you did. Besides, how can we impress you if we let you help?"

She started the car, still laughing under her breath. "All right. I'll see you then."

He wrote down the address and gave it to her through the door, then took her hand from the steering wheel and kissed it with Rhett Butler finesse.

She wore a silly smile as she drove away.

That night, she lay awake in bed thinking about this man with two little girls whom she hadn't expected to enter her life. He wasn't the kind of man she was looking for. Her checklist of "Mate Traits" did not include a previous marriage or three-year-old girls. But here she was, her mind and heart lingering on him, keeping her from a moment's sleep.

She couldn't wait to thank Joan for taking her to the Bible study.

"It'll be a good boost for you, Amanda," Joan had said. "It's kept me grounded for a long time now, and it's fun. You need to get out and meet some people, get your mind off of your problems."

Amanda's problems weren't that easy to put behind her, however. They were significant, and lingering, and there were times when she found herself sinking into a mire of depression. Her lifeline had been the Scripture passages she had committed to memory.

"When you pass through the waters, I will be with you; And through the rivers, they will not overflow you. When you walk through the fire, you will not be scorched, Nor will the flame burn you."

Isaiah 43:2 had proven true in her life, just as Deuteronomy 31:6 had: *"Be strong and courageous, do not be afraid or tremble at them, for the LORD your God is the one who goes with you. He will not fail you or forsake you."*

When she'd found herself going under, she had grabbed hold of those words, and they had slowly pulled her out until she could breathe and look up with gratitude, instead of down with self-pity.

The uterine cancer was behind her now. Surgery and six months of chemo had taken care of that. Her hair had grown back in just as thick and blonde as it was before the cancer, and it had finally reached a length that didn't advertise her condition. The color had returned to her face, and she no longer looked emaciated and sick.

But the effects of the disease remained. She would never have children, at least not of her womb. It was the one thing she'd wanted in her life—a real family of her own, one that could erase all the longings of her past and make her feel safe and part of things.

She was reconciled to adopting children when she was ready . . . but her fears remained. After all, what man would want to marry a woman who couldn't bear him children?

Her father tried to turn her plight into a positive. "Honey, this is a great filter for the men who don't deserve you. Either they love you the way you ought to be loved, or they hit the road. The Lord knows what He's doing."

Could it be that the Lord had a guitar-playing pilot with twin daughters in mind for her?

That question stayed with her for the next several days as she waited for Saturday to come.

∞

My father prepared us for her visit the way one would prepare a classroom for a visit from a queen. He told us that a "very nice, very pretty lady" wanted to meet us, and that she was especially fond of little girls with curly red hair.

By the time Saturday night came, we were ready and waiting, decked out in our best garb and all atwitter with anticipation.

She rang the bell fifteen minutes early.

My father opened the door, that trademark grin on his face. We stood just behind him, peeking through his legs at the woman who was everything he'd described. "Thank goodness," he said. "I forgot to ask for your phone number, so I couldn't confirm that you were coming. I figured you would have come to your senses by now and backed out, but I was praying you'd show up anyway."

Amanda pegged us right then as Anne Geddes material, with our big blue eyes and red mops of Shirley Temple curls.

Lizzie wore a Cinderella dress and a tiara on her head. My tastes were more eclectic: a straw fedora, a hot pink feather boa, a brown sweater, and cobalt blue leggings.

"They dressed up for you." My father had a laugh on the edge of his voice. "Lizzie's Cinderella, and Kara's some cross between Crocodile Dundee and Zsa Zsa Gabor."

She stooped down and got eye level with us. "Look at you," she said. "You look exactly alike. I'm glad you dressed up so I could tell you apart."

"We made ba-sketti." Lizzie grabbed Amanda's hand and pulled her inside. "Wanna see?"

"And we're off." My father laughed as he closed the door and followed our lead.

Amanda would remember for years how the bubble of delight floated up in her chest as she followed us into the kitchen. She saw one chair pulled up to the sink, and another to the counter. Lizzie climbed onto the chair in front of the sink full of suds.

"Lizzie likes to wash dishes," my father said with a wink, "so I have her washing these jars of spaghetti sauce. Not that we used them, you understand."

"No, of course not."

"And Kara likes to stir. They're both very helpful." He smiled a little too brightly and crossed his eyes.

I leaned a little too far, and the chair began to scoot away. My father dove to rescue me as I fell. I didn't miss a beat, but went back to stirring my salad.

"I'm impressed," she said. "How many rescues like that do you handle at each meal?"

"Oh, four or five . . . dozen." He winked at her and popped a piece of French bread into his mouth. "That's the beauty of a tiny kitchen. I can reach either of them without too much effort."

I've driven by that little house we lived in and watched the children who live there now run and tumble in the yard behind it. The neighborhood still looks safe and sweet, though age has tattered the homes. I'm told it was new when we were small, though. With only two bedrooms, I suspect the house was adequate for our needs. In the pictures I've seen of us in that house, the place was always clean and neat, though unimpressive. One snapshot tells the story of our brief art careers. Finger paintings and silhouettes and little construction paper butterflies covered the refrigerator, and two pairs of tiny little tennis shoes sat beside the door.

I study those pictures with sadness, because it truly looked like a home.

That night, we fought over the plates in our special twin language that no one else understood, and our father called out, "Talk English, girls."

Amanda gave him a curious look.

"They have this unique language they use to talk to each other," he said. "Lots of twins do it, but I try to stop them when I hear it."

"It must be amazing having twins."

"It's interesting; that's for sure."

Amanda—the nice lady who looked like the princess we'd expected—gave us each two plates to settle our argument. She watched as we arranged them in a three-year-old style that would have chafed Amy Vanderbilt.

As we shoved the silverware around, my dad turned back to Amanda.

"So, how are we doing? Are you ready to run away screaming just yet?"

"No," she said, a giggle bursting out of her, "they're absolutely precious. And you're doing such a good job with them."

We beamed and worked harder to get the table set just right.

"Well, I understand rebellion kicks in in another few years, so I have a long way to go."

We had set three plates so close together that they were touching, and one was alone across the table. "Daddy, that's yours," I announced.

"They want to sit by you," he said. "You don't know how lucky you are. Shame you wore white pants. I'd better get you a towel."

He insisted she put the towel over her lap to protect her from our soiled little hands and sauce splashing from carelessly slurped noodles. We always slurped with great gusto.

But Amanda didn't worry about spaghetti sauce on her clothes. She was flattered that we liked her enough to want to be close to her.

∞

Amanda recalls that we went to bed early that night. My father hosed us down in the bathtub while she cleaned up the dishes, and then we ran in to say good night in our bare feet and flannel pajamas, dragging battle-weary blankets behind us. She followed him into our little room to kiss us good night and watched as we debated over which bed to sleep in—Lizzie's or mine—because we always slept together. We curled up together, legs entangled and arms flung over one another. We had that uncanny twin closeness that scientists find fascinating. Sometimes we dreamed the same dreams as we lay together, like two halves of the same body. Neither of us could ever sleep alone.

When Amanda speaks of that night, she gets a catch in her throat. According to her, my father wore a soft, vulnerable expression when they returned to the living room. He dropped down next to her on the couch. "Bet you never thought you'd have a date like this."

"It's been fun. I love being around the girls."

"That's good, because I kind of hate being away from them." He leaned back, resting his head on the back of the couch. Looking over at her, he said, "So tell me about you."

"What about me?"

"Everything. Starting with how your parents met."

She laughed too loudly. "You're kidding, right?"

He shifted to face her. "What? You don't think a man could be fascinated with you?"

His eyes were serious, like they'd been when she'd first seen him strumming that guitar. "My parents met in the emergency room after a Fourth of July picnic that went bad."

"Fireworks accident?"

"No. Potato salad accident. My mother's cooking, actually. She almost killed half the town."

"So your father had a thing for dangerous women?"

"Actually, no. Not right then. But she felt so guilty that she took phenomenal care of him until he was better. *Then* he fell in love with her. Her cooking did improve, eventually."

"Great story." He shifted his body to face her and set his elbow on the back of the couch. "So . . . then you were born and grew up into a beautiful woman who would catch my eye at a Bible study."

The grace in that statement made her heart swell, and by the time the evening was over, she was head over heels in love with my father, and counting the blessings that seemed enough to last for the rest of her life. And ours, too.

THREE

I find it hard to believe that my father didn't kiss Amanda until their seventh date, which happened to be a week after that dinner with us. But Amanda swears it's true. She'd had a crash course in our dad and found herself distracted and miserable whenever they were apart. The kiss, which she'd been anticipating to the point of madness, seemed to seal her destiny.

"So . . . ," he said, his breath marking the word on her skin, "are you extremely attached to your sanity, or is it something you could do without?"

It wasn't quite what she'd expected after the first kiss, but his fingers still lingered on her face, and his lips hovered so close . . .

"Why do you ask?" she murmured.

"Because it occurs to me that the idea of marrying me might cost you your faculties."

She later said that if hearts really melted, hers would have puddled around her toes. "It would cost me more to say no," she whispered.

"Then don't say it."

It was then that the realities she had avoided for the last several days began to flash like a neon sign in her mind. He didn't know everything about her. She had expected to have more time, to break it to him slowly . . .

But it couldn't wait any longer.

"Jack, there's something I haven't told you yet. Something that might change the way you feel."

"Nothing," he whispered. "Nothing could change it."

She cleared her throat and backed away from him, looked down at her belt buckle, absently ran her hand along the chrome. "I still need to say it."

"Okay." He waited, his face open to whatever she was about to reveal.

"I'm not able . . . to have children. Not ever."

His slow frown held more compassion than disappointment. "Why not?"

"Because I had cancer."

His expression went from compassionate to fearful. "You what? When?"

"Well, I had a hysterectomy a year ago. The cancer's in remission, and the doctors say my prognosis is excellent."

He reacted as if he'd just received a death sentence and a reprieve, one right after another. "Thank You, God." He grabbed her then and pulled her against him, held her close. "I wish I could have been there for you. I'm so glad you're all right."

"Me, too." His response left her with a lump in her throat, and well it should. My own throat gets tight when I think about the kind of man it took to react that way.

"But, Jack, did you hear what I said?" She touched his face. "I can't have children."

"You certainly can." He tipped her face up to his. "You can have mine. Lizzie and Kara already love you."

She started to cry then, big, rolling tears that she couldn't control. "Oh, Jack, I love them, too. I'd count it such an honor to be their mother . . . to take care of them for the rest of their lives, to love them like my own." She sucked in a sob, then whispered, "God is so good."

"Yes, He is." Jack kissed her again. "Yes, He's very good, to bring you to me . . . to us . . ."

And I suspect he meant every word.

He held her for a while, letting her cry against his shirt. She says it felt so natural being in his arms, knowing his love for her, feeling his heart beat against her face. Sometimes when I close my eyes and concentrate hard, I think I can remember that feeling.

His own revelation followed close behind hers. "I have a confession to make, too," he whispered. "There's something I have to tell you before I marry you."

He could have told her he was wanted in three states, and it wouldn't have mattered. "What?"

He drew in a deep, foreboding breath, like a man about to

share the worst news of his life. "It's about my family. Actually, my father."

"What about him?"

"It's just that . . . he's . . . Paul Holbrooke. The billionaire."

"*The* Paul Holbrooke?" Her jaw dropped, and she gaped at him. "You've got to be kidding me."

"No, I'm not." He looked like a man whose skeleton was out of the closet. "And I would love it if I never had to tell you because I don't want it to change anything about us. I don't live off of his money. I love my father, but I got rid of the trappings of his money a long time ago. I don't like for people to know who I am because it too often changes the way they treat me. I'm not going to inherit his money. None of it will ever be mine."

She squinted at him, trying to follow his speech. "Jack, you act like this is bad news. I'm not really seeing a downside."

"I thought you'd be mad that I didn't tell you right away."

"Why didn't you? It's not like it's some terrible thing. There aren't many women who'd be upset that they're marrying a billionaire's son."

"I wanted you to love me for me. I wanted to know that it has nothing to do with the money."

"Well, I hope you do know that."

"I do. That's why I want you to marry me. But are you okay with never having a dime of my father's money?"

"Of course," she said.

"I'm serious. In the event of his death, I want him to give my portion to charity. I've told him that."

"That's fine, Jack. I understand."

He leaned back on his couch and pulled her head to his shoulder. Kissing her temple, he said, "I was hoping we could elope. I don't want to deprive you of your fairy-tale wedding, if that's what you want, but it's not going to be easy. If we have a wedding, my parents will take over, and they'll invite ten thousand of their closest friends, and the paparazzi will take a sudden interest in you, and I'll never again get to live in this town as plain old, ordinary Jack Holbrooke, the pilot and father of twins."

"I don't care about a wedding." She touched his face with her fingertips. "If you want to marry me, I'm already in my fairy tale."

That serious look on his face melted away, and he lifted her off the ground and swung her around. "Doing anything tonight?"

She caught her breath. "Tonight? *Tonight?*"

He set her down and looked into her eyes. "If I'm moving too fast, just tell me. I don't want to scare you to death. It's just that . . . I don't think I can wait. Amanda, I never thought I could feel this way again. Truth is, I want to marry you tonight because nights are so long without you. And because you smell good. And because I'm so in love with you that I think I might not make it until some far-off wedding date. My heart starts racing when I hear your voice on the phone, and I get weak at the sight of you. It's painful. Two weeks would be far off to me."

Her eyes twinkled as she took in the words. "Me, too."

"I could call the Guerreros, who baby-sit the girls sometimes, and just ask them if they could stay all night. Then we could have our wedding night to ourselves." His thumb drifted across her bottom lip. "What do you say, Amanda? Are you crazy enough to marry a billionaire's disinherited son on a moment's notice?"

"I didn't fall in love with a billionaire's son. I fell in love with a guy who plays guitar and wears flannel shirts and is crazy about his babies . . ." She reached for the phone and handed it to him. "Call them."

He grinned at her breathless whisper and took the phone.

"And I'll call my dad," she went on. "He'd never forgive me if I didn't let him give me away."

"Will he be upset?"

She smiled. "No. I've already told him about you. He might be a little surprised by how fast things are moving, but he'll give us his blessings. You'll see."

∽

They got their marriage license just before the office closed that day, then were married in the little chapel attached to their church. My dad dressed us up in our Easter dresses, which thankfully still fit, and bought us little white baskets with rose petals in them. We celebrated as if Amanda married *us* instead of him. He told us she would be our new mommy because she loved us so much that she couldn't stand to be away from us.

They tried to put one of us on each side of the happy couple for the pictures, but Lizzie and I didn't want to let go of each other. We were hams in the privacy of our home, but in front of other people, we often got bitten with the bashful bug. So we stood in front of them for the pictures, our white-gloved hands clasped tightly together.

Amanda's father was there to give her away and to welcome us into the family. Our grandparents, stunned but cooperative, arrived by helicopter for the event.

My grandfather would have showered our father and new mother with a limousine and mansion, but my dad only allowed his father to give them a night at a romantic little inn in Natchez. My grandparents took us home, where the Guerreros waited. Amanda and my dad went to Natchez, checked into the romantic little room, and a horse and carriage took them to the cozy restaurant, where my grandfather had reserved a private table for them. They talked of their future and their dreams, then hurried back to the honeymoon suite where they knit their souls and bodies together, becoming one in every sense of the word.

It was the most special night of Amanda's life, and probably mine and Lizzie's, too. It changed our lives in so many ways, even if it was for a very short time. I've learned that you can't deny those precious moments in your history just because you know how fleeting they were.

To Amanda, it seemed like those moments would last forever, each one better than the one before it. It's good that she didn't know what lay ahead of us all.

Later that night, as they sat out on the balcony of their room, gazing up at the stars, my father asked Amanda, "How does it feel to be a mommy?"

"It feels just right."

"It's nice to know I'm not the only one in Lizzie's and Kara's lives anymore. That if anything ever happened to me, you'd take care of them. You would, wouldn't you, Amanda?"

She sat up and looked into his eyes. "I promise, Jack. They're my children now. I'll take care of them for the rest of my life."

His own eyes grew misty. "I have perfect peace that that is a promise you'll keep."

But looking back, I see the naiveté in that simple little promise. If she had known what it would mean, I wonder if she would have made it.

FOUR

Amanda became our mother in almost every way. She quit her job to stay home with us and turned into some kind of Betty Crocker clone who spent her days wiping faces and hands and dirty tables. Happiness had the face of twin toddlers who shadowed every move she made, it sounded like my father's laughter, and it felt like his arms. The family she'd thought she could never have became the joy she thought she'd never lose. Pictures of those days don't show stress on her face, but a brilliant joy. In all of them, we're laughing and running and bouncing and chattering. Sometimes when I sleep, I think I can hear the sounds of happiness in my head. Laughter whipping up on the wind, my father's gentle teasing, Amanda's soft delight . . . and our endless giggles, as if the joy would never end.

But it did. Suddenly, cruelly, in one of those twists of life that leaves its irrevocable imprint on you.

My father's cousin was getting married, and he had planned to fly his parents and us to the wedding in Southern California. That morning, I got sick, and Amanda decided to stay behind with Lizzie and me and nurse me back to health.

My grandparents waited at the airstrip when Amanda dropped my father off. He nuzzled our necks, reducing us to screaming giggles. Then he kissed Amanda and hugged her tight.

Amanda stood with us, pointing to the sky and the plane growing smaller and smaller in the clouds.

"Wave bye-bye," she whispered to us. And we waved, mesmerized, our eyes following the spot that grew smaller and smaller, until it entered a cloud and vanished entirely.

"Do it again, Mommy," Lizzie said.

Amanda laughed in that lilting way of hers. "I can't do it again, honey. Daddy's gone." She didn't know how true those words were.

I have a dream at night. I've had it for years. It's of that same plane with me on it, rolling down the airstrip, faster and faster, then leaping into the air. I'm standing on the tarmac watching it grow smaller and smaller, knowing I'm somehow outside it and inside it at the same time. I hear a woman's voice next to my ear, whispering, "There he goes. Wave bye-bye."

And I wave at the plane, and I see my own face looking out, sad and stricken, like I know something that no one else knows.

And then the plane disappears into the clouds.

I always wake up feeling sweaty and anxious . . . and frightened, though for the longest time I didn't know why. The disappearing plane shouldn't be a frightening dream, not like the other dreams of monsters or ghosts or people chasing me.

I now know that it wasn't just a dream, but probably a bona fide memory. That my father never got to that wedding, because his plane went down in a grove of trees.

When we kissed him good-bye that day, we were kissing him for the last time.

FIVE

Amanda got the call while we were napping that afternoon, and she snatched us out of bed and raced to the hospital, carrying both of us on her mad race. When she got there, she learned that my grandparents had died instantly. My father was still alive and in surgery.

I picture her sometimes, appeasing us while suffering the misery of waiting. I picture her with one whining child on each hip, pacing back and forth in front of the double doors to the operating room, assaulting each doctor who emerged with tearful questions and frightened demands. "You've got to *do* something," I picture her saying. "Don't you give him up! I want heroics!"

But heroics didn't matter, not that day. My father died one hour after his parents, leaving everything unfinished—so many things undone—and thrusting my sister and me down a long, lonely road that took us to places we did not want to go.

Amanda has told us that she ran from the news down the long, cold corridor of the hospital, clutching one of us on each hip. The hall smelled of alcohol and Clorox, scents she would forevermore associate with death.

We screamed out our own fear as she fled down the stairs and out to the parking lot. She placed us into our car seats, knowing that her tears and her haste frightened us. But she was helpless to stop them.

∞

The sun was going down as she drove home, hiccuping sobs, but when we got there, she couldn't go in. The house was just as we'd left it earlier, but it wasn't the same. She took us out of the car and tried to pull herself together. "Let's not go in," she said. "Let's go to the playhouse."

"Whatsa matter, Mommy?" I asked on a whisper.

Amanda couldn't answer. "Mommy just . . . got some bad news. I just need to sit in the playhouse. But don't worry. It's going to be all right."

We took her word for it and bounced around to the back lawn, to the playhouse my father had built us just three weeks before. We had helped him hammer, and the wood siding bore the scars of our work. The paint was blotchy and uneven, where we had "helped" again. He and Amanda had planned to paint over it when there was time.

But there was never time.

I'm told we went in and began playing with the plastic kitchen appliances my dad had put in there for us, next to the beanbag chairs and the bucket of Barbies on the floor.

Amanda sat out on the little porch he'd built on the play-house, in the cracker-barrel rocking chair he'd bought her the week before. And before she could head it off, the devastation caught up to her. She buried her face in her hands to muffle the racking anguish.

She speaks of that moment with a white face and misty eyes. He couldn't be dead, she told herself. He had just left a little while ago. She had hugged and kissed him good-bye, and he had promised he'd see us in a couple of days. He would never have accepted death that way. He wouldn't have left us without a fight.

"Excuse me. Mrs. Holbrooke?"

She started at the voice and looked up to see a man who had come around the house looking for her. He was a tall, thin man in a black suit and held a briefcase in his hand.

"Who are you?"

He came toward her. "Mrs. Holbrooke, I'm Robert Eubanks. Paul Holbrooke's attorney."

"Haven't you heard? He's dead." She knew the words were cruel, but she didn't have the energy to couch them in courtesy.

"Yes, that's why I'm here."

She got up then and walked out into the yard, turning her back to him. "I don't want to talk to you. I . . . can't right now."

"I'm so sorry for your loss. I know how hard this must be."

She wanted to shove those words back into his mouth and tell him he didn't have a clue. "Please leave. My children are in the playhouse, and they haven't been told yet."

"I understand and I won't keep you long. I just wanted to explain something you might not be aware of."

"There's got to be a better time."

"Actually, it can't wait, Mrs. Holbrooke. The press is going to be here soon, and you need to be told first. You see, you are the heir to the Holbrooke fortune."

"The *what?*" She choked back her tears. "That's ridiculous. I'm not the heir to anything. My husband might have been once, but he had them take him out of the will."

"They didn't take him out," the lawyer said. "I understand that Jack asked for that, but his father didn't comply. And Jack very clearly left all he owned to you, specifying that you are to raise his children in the event of his death, even though the adoption hasn't gone through yet. When the Holbrookes died before Jack, their son inherited everything they owned. Legally, it doesn't matter if he survived them by one minute or one hour or ten years. The moment Paul and Anne Holbrooke died, the estate belonged to Jack. And now that Jack has died, the estate passes to you."

"I don't want it! He wanted it to go to charity. Just sign it over to a Christian ministry. There are plenty of them who need it."

"Well, you're perfectly free to do whatever you choose with the estate, but you do have children to consider. I'm the one who drew up Jack's will shortly after the two of you were married. Jack didn't leave his estate to the children because he trusted you to handle things."

"Jack never meant for any of us to live off of his father's money."

"I understand that. But the fact remains that the inheritance is yours. Mrs. Holbrooke, I know you're not in any position to think clearly right now. Might I advise you not to make any decisions until you've gotten legal advice? Thousands of employees will be impacted by your choices. Even though the estate wasn't left to the children, you and I both know that Jack left all he had to you with the expectation that you would provide for the children for the rest of their lives and give them their portion when they're older. If you turn that inheritance away, they might resent you when they're older. They *were* Paul's grandchildren."

She wanted to scream and break something, wanted to crawl into her bed and cover her head, wanted to climb into a plane and follow Jack into eternity.

"I know it's a lot to take in, ma'am. This is a hard thing for me, too. But you're about to become a very wealthy woman. You own his mansion, his cars, all of his collections. HolCorp was a privately held company. You own that, too, now."

The declaration that might, for someone else, have eased the blow of death only left her rabidly angry. "None of that will bring my husband back!"

He looked down at his hands, and his voice softened. "No, it won't. I'm sorry, Mrs. Holbrooke. Can I just . . . contact you later about all this?"

"I guess."

He pulled a card out of his pocket. "Ma'am, I hope you don't mind my suggesting that you get some security around you. Once word gets out, your life isn't going to be the same. Mr. Holbrooke has people who could protect you and take care of the arrangements . . . Please call if you want to get in touch with them."

"I'll bury my husband." The words sounded too final, like someone had stamped *The End* onto the fairy tale of her life. "I might need help with his parents."

"Certainly," he said. "I'll take care of it."

When he had gone, she went back to the porch and sat down on the floor, her back against the wall. She began to weep again, long, deep, racking sobs that rose on the breeze. Lizzie and I peeked out the door. "Mommy?" I asked.

Amanda reached for me and pulled me against her, then Lizzie came, too. She held us both and wept against our curls. "It's okay, sweetie. It's okay." I think I remember the way she held us that day. It's deep in my mind, buried under years of clutter. A sensation . . . a homesickness . . . like the way Amanda said she felt when my father sat next to her the night they met. I've had enough awareness of it to know I was missing something . . . all those years later, when I couldn't remember a thing.

SIX

I can just imagine the day my maternal grandparents, Eloise and Deke Krebbs, showed up at our front door.

It was the day of the funerals, and the Krebbses looked like hillbillies who'd tried to dude up for the occasion. Eloise wore a blonde, curly wig that never seemed to sit right on her head, and her massive body was stuffed into a dress two sizes too small. Deke's scrawny body reeked of cigarette smoke, and his leathery face was that of a man who had lived too hard and aged early.

They came to the door while Amanda still had a houseful of funeral company. She was numb and exhausted and weary from well-wishers, but someone found her in the bedroom and urged her to go to the door.

She faced the Krebbses with a look that said she didn't have the energy for one more condolent platitude. "We're the children's grandparents," Eloise said in a saccharine twang. "We heard about their father's death and came as soon as we could."

"*What?*" Amanda stared. "What do you mean, their grandparents? Their grandparents were killed . . ."

"Their other grandparents," Deke cut in. "Our daughter, Sherry, was their mother."

She caught her breath. "Oh."

Until that moment, Amanda had never given our mother's parents a thought. My mother had been a teen runaway and, according to our father, had remained estranged from her parents. Our grandparents had never even met us.

"I'm Amanda Holbrooke," she said.

"Eloise and Deke Krebbs here." The woman offered her fingertips for a tentative handshake.

"It's not really a good time to see the girls," Amanda said. "It's been a long day. Do you think you could come back tomorrow? They're confused right now, and I haven't had the chance to explain all this to them. I appreciate your wanting to meet them, but—"

"We're not here to meet them." Eloise's sniff was clearly indignant. "We're here to make arrangements to take them back with us."

Amanda's eyes flashed. "You can't take Lizzie and Kara back with you. They're staying with me. They need things to be as normal as possible."

"You ain't their mother," the old man said. "*We're* their next of kin."

A dull ache started at the back of her neck. "I *am* their

mother. They call me *Mommy*. I'm going to adopt them. My husband's will states that I am to raise them."

"But the adoption can't go through without our consent. You're only their stepmother, and we've come to take them back."

"Well, you can't have them!" She drew in a deep breath and forced herself to lower her voice. "I'm sorry. You can visit them. You can get to know them, but you're not taking them anywhere."

Buzz, Amanda's father, heard the commotion from the kitchen and stepped up behind his daughter. "Is there a problem here?"

She turned her twisted face to him. "Dad, tell them. The children are mine. They think they can come and take them away from me because they gave birth to their mother."

"We got ourselves a good lawyer," Deke said. "He tells us that the girls belong with us, not with you."

"You *can't* be serious." Buzz stepped around Amanda and looked hard into Deke's face. His age and limp were eclipsed by the anger in his eyes. "Their father's wishes were clear."

"No court's gonna give them to a stepparent over blood relatives. The children need to be with *family*."

"But I've been with them for six months!" Amanda cried. "I'm all they have left that's familiar. You can't do this."

"We can, and we will."

"I think it's time for you to leave, pal." Buzz grabbed Deke's arm and turned him around. Deke jerked his arm away and looked as if he might fight back, but Buzz wasn't intimidated. "Leave, or I'll call the police."

"Fine!" Eloise lifted her chin, the picture of haughty arrogance. "We'll go, but you ain't heard the last of us. Expect a call from our lawyer."

"My daughter has a lawyer, too." Buzz ground the words out. "And I'll see that she spends every penny of her inheritance to fight you people, if she has to. But you're not taking those girls."

"Hide and watch," Deke called from his car. They got in and drove off, their faces smug.

∞

That night, Amanda sat between our twin beds as we slept and wept her heart out for her husband and the simple life they had known. She cried out to God, pleading that He would intervene and stop this downhill spiral of madness. Everything seemed out of control, and she couldn't stop the descent.

She wept long into the night, then sat on the bed we'd slept in that night and prayed over us. It was hard to tell where Lizzie's hair ended and mine began, or which legs were hers and which mine. We slept as if we were connected somehow, and of course we were. Lizzie and I, though separate, seemed conjoined at the heart.

Finally, Amanda lay down on the empty twin bed, unable to go back into the bedroom where she had slept with her husband, for she couldn't yet accept that he wasn't in that bed.

She could hear her father's gentle snoring from the couch

in the living room and, lulled by that sound, she fell into a rest-less sleep.

∞

Through the fog of her mourning, Amanda took special care in explaining death to Lizzie and me. We're told that we cried for him often during the first few weeks, and threw several tantrums, which usually ended in sad, hiccuping sleep. Amanda didn't leave our sides. She slept with us at night, comforted us when we woke with disturbing dreams and distressing thoughts, and often she explained to us how the angels had come to get our daddy and taken him up to be with Jesus.

She later said that, in the privacy of her own thoughts, she raged at any angels who would fulfill such a task, and won-dered why God had not ordered them to rescue our father out of the crash.

I've seen snapshots of us during that time of grieving. Amanda's smiles look laced with sorrow. She grew thin and pale, and her eyes bore dark circles that spoke of sleepless nights.

When Lizzie's and my sadness turned to the resilient childish laughter and fun that hit between our moments of grief, we ran around flapping our wings like the angels who had taken our father away.

Amanda talked to us of heaven and read to us from Revelation, how the streets there were made of gold, with a sea of glass and the colors of every precious stone, and gates made of enormous pearls. She told us how we would see our daddy again when we went to heaven, that he was there because he believed in Jesus. And she told us that, if we believed, we would see him again, too. So we busied ourselves with coloring pictures of Jesus and the cross, and lying in the grass looking up at the sky for glimpses of Jesus or our daddy, and wondering when we could join him.

As she buried herself in her family, Amanda kept her phone unplugged and stopped answering the door. She planted a security guard in her front yard to keep media and gawkers away. Her father stayed there with us, returning calls about the grandparents, who had already filed papers to get custody of us, and talking to the lawyer about the obscure lawsuits filed by distant Holbrooke relatives who wanted portions of the inheritance.

As the weeks went by, healing came for us, though the pall still held over Amanda.

She would later say our laughter was a healing balm for her soul, and when we napped or slept at night, she would hide herself in the Word, soaking it up like the living water promised to the Woman at the Well. It filled her spirit and her soul, and she found herself dwelling often on the day she would go home to heaven and see Jack once again, dressed in a flannel shirt, playing guitar, with his favorite sneakers on his feet and a chocolate milkshake in a plastic cup beside him. She anticipated God's perfect reason for her pain . . . some unfathomable purpose that made her sacrifice worth it.

But the thought of Eloise and Deke Krebbs, and the threat they were to us, never left her mind, and she knew that more heartache could be just over the horizon.

SEVEN

When a court date was set to decide our custody, Amanda went to see Robert Eubanks, the lawyer who had visited her on the day of my father's death. He didn't offer her the hope she wanted.

"The truth is, you have no legal right to Lizzie and Kara."

Amanda stared at him. She had gone to his office in hopes of getting closure on both the custody and the adoption. It was just a matter of paperwork, she'd told herself. The Krebbses *couldn't* have a right to us.

"Whose side are you on?" she asked. "Those are *my* girls. They call *me* Mommy. I'm the only mother they've ever known, and the only parent they have left. I promised my husband that I would take care of them for the rest of my life."

His compassionate eyes rested on her, and she knew her words did matter to him. He rose, drawing in a long sigh. He was a tall, lanky man, who looked awkward in his own skin.

"If you'd had them since birth, there might be a chance," Robert said gently, "but you've only had them a few months."

"But can't we prove those people are unfit to take them?" She clutched the edge of her seat so hard that her knuckles turned white. "I got a cold feeling just looking at those people, even before I knew why they were there. Maybe they heard about the inheritance and they think they can get something out of me." Her eyebrows shot up at the thought. "In fact, take some of that money I'm supposed to have and bribe them. Offer them a settlement to drop the suit."

"That might work," he said, "*if* we had access to the money. But until probate—"

She sprang up out of her chair and stormed across the room. "How could any right-minded judge wrench those children from their home? Their only security? Especially when my husband's will named *me* as their legal guardian? And after he started the adoption process himself?"

"The Krebbses do have the blood rights, and since the adoption wasn't final—"

"I want to hire a detective." There was resolution in her voice. She could endure anything if she had a plan. "I want to know everything about these people, where they live, where they work, what they eat, who they know. I want to know if they have any past history of criminal behavior, or if they've even had a parking ticket. I want to know if they drink. I want to know what kind of parents they were to their daughter. She ran away when she was fifteen, you know. She was taken in by a Christian family in Jackson and she met Jack there when she was nineteen."

"That doesn't speak well for them," Eubanks said. "Maybe we can get some mileage out of that."

"They're *not* getting my children," she said, leaving no room for debate. "Robert, do everything you can. Get every scrap of information you can find. We've got to show the judge that they're better off with me."

But it didn't really matter who we were better off with . . . since our best interests were up for grabs. It was all about the Krebbses' legal rights—the blood connection that meant nothing to us, the greed that drove them.

And Amanda knew it could go either way.

EIGHT

As it turned out, Deke and Eloise Krebbs had no criminal record.

There were only a few parking tickets and some hunting violations. There was no documentation to prove their daughter—our mother—had run away at fifteen. No one had ever filed a missing persons report, and while the detectives had found the family who had taken her in, their testimony that she was a troubled teen and a drug abuser before she'd come to them didn't help in proving that her parents had driven her away.

Panicked, Amanda drew closer to us as the prospect of losing us neared. She thought of fleeing the country, taking us with her and raising us in France where our grandparents couldn't reach us.

But her father needed her in Jackson.

Buzz had already suffered one mild stroke, and she could

see the fatigue and the paleness of his features when she visited him each day. She knew traveling to another country would be too hard for him, and she didn't want to take him from the friends of his old age. And she didn't know what would become of him if she left him to fend for himself as he declined in health.

The night before that final day in court, Buzz limped into our home. His face was paler than Amanda had seen it before and he had a tremor in his hands. Lizzie and I slept soundly, blissfully unaware that tomorrow might be one more cruel turning point in our lives.

"I'm sorry for the way things have turned out for you." Buzz sank down on her couch. "I always thought I'd prepared you for life," he said, "but I never counted on the kind of things you've been hit with here lately."

"Neither did I," she whispered. Tears came into her eyes and she tried to blink them away. It disturbed him so when she cried. She didn't want to upset him.

He cleared his throat and looked between his knees to the floor. "When your mother died, I grieved for two years. I thought it would never go away, but I had you. I could see her in your face, your mannerisms, the way you spoke, even your approach to life." He touched her cheek. "You are the only thing that pulled me out of it. I had hoped the girls would do that for you."

She could hardly manage to speak. "I had hoped that, too."

"You had options." He leaned forward. "You could have left the country and taken them where the law couldn't reach you. But you stayed because of me, didn't you?"

She didn't want to admit that, so she got up and walked across the room to the mantel where a picture of my father and us sat. She fingered the frame, then turned back to him.

"It just didn't seem necessary. I always thought the court system would come through for me. Don't they always say that people with money get what they want?"

"You're changing the subject." His smile was soft, tender, filled with a pained compassion. "Amanda, I always knew that you would be here for me. But the truth is . . . if it means losing those girls, I'd rather have you far away. I have plenty of people here who can tend to me."

She couldn't hold back the tears as she looked at the man who had been such a precious part of her life.

"I have a buddy who's a pilot," he said. "I had him rent a jet, and if you want, you can pack up those girls and carry them away tonight. Any place you want to go. The farther, the better."

She gaped at him. "Dad, how could you afford that?"

"I have my retirement. I was saving it to leave to you, but it doesn't look like you're going to need it. I can't think of a better way to spend it."

For a moment she thought of running to the back, throwing a few things into a bag, and grabbing the girls. They could be in France by court time tomorrow. The Krebbses would not have the resources to track her down and find her.

But that would mean she wouldn't see her father again. And what if she won in court tomorrow? What if the judge had the good sense to leave the children where they were?

Then fleeing the country and this home she'd shared with Jack would be unnecessary.

"I can't go tonight, Daddy."

"Why not?"

"Lots of reasons. What if the judge comes through for me, and I can have the best of both worlds? You and the girls."

He waved a hand at her as if dismissing such a ludicrous thought. "Go with the sure thing, Amanda. Take the girls and leave. I'll come visit you."

"But you can't. It would be too hard on you. Besides, the girls need to be in their own home. I don't want to leave Jack's things, or the little playhouse he built in the back." She reached out and took his hands. "I want them to grow up knowing you."

He sighed and touched her face. "All right, then. But tomorrow, if the judge rules that those terrible people should get the girls, I want you to be packed and ready. We'll have the plane loaded, and before they can come and pick them up, you'll be on your way to France."

The idea sounded feasible. "All right. I'll go pack right now."

She hugged her father, then pulled back and kissed him on the cheek. "I don't want to leave you."

"I know." His ragged whisper nearly broke her heart. "But you promised Jack you would take care of the girls. They need you, Amanda. You can't chance losing them."

Feeling hope blossom in her heart like a delicate rose, she dashed to her room and began to pack.

NINE

The road in our lives turned that next day, when the judge made his ruling.

As we played "kitchen" in our little playhouse with our babysitter, Mrs. Guerrero, watching over us, Amanda sat rigidly in court. She felt as if a fist had rammed through her sternum, crushing her heart, as the judge ruled that we must be given into the custody of the Krebbses by two o'clock that afternoon. Amanda let out a strangled cry.

"Mrs. Holbrooke—" the judge looked at her as she collapsed in her grief—"I don't doubt the quality of home that you would be able to offer these children, and I commend you on your care for them to this point. But as much as I tried to find some legal basis for allowing the children to stay with you, I wasn't able to. I can't deny their only living relatives their right to custody."

She couldn't even hear the words as the judge seemed to ramble on, trying to explain and justify this horrible thing he'd just ordered. She managed to get to her feet and vaguely realized that a celebration was going on, on the other side of the room. Deke and Eloise Krebbs were hugging and laughing as if they'd just won the lottery.

"Your Honor!" Amanda's voice barely functioned. "You can't do this to them. They've already lost their mother and their father, and now they're going to lose me, too? *You can't do it.*"

"I have no choice," he said. "Please sit down. I'm not finished."

"But, Your Honor, this makes no sense!"

He drew in a deep breath, then banged his gavel. "Mrs. Holbrooke, I can't help but think that a woman of your means might do something drastic, such as taking the children away."

"I don't *have* any means," she said. "The estate is in probate. I've been living off of life insurance."

"Still, I order that a marshal accompany you to your home to make sure you don't try to flee with the children."

Her hopes crashed like plate glass on concrete. "But, Your Honor! That's ridiculous! You don't have to send a babysitter home with me. I haven't done anything wrong! I simply want to be alone to say good-bye to my children."

"The marshal will give you the time you need."

Before she knew it, court had ended and the grandparents of her children began to hoot and holler like inebriated fans at a college football game.

She fell into her father's arms.

"You should have left last night!" His fierce whisper echoed her own thoughts. "Maybe it's not too late. Maybe we can distract the marshal, get you out of there before he even knows you're gone."

"Oh, Daddy, do you think so?"

"Let's just go home and get the girls ready. I'll let you know when the coast is clear."

TEN

Much of our things had already been packed the night before as we slept. Amanda tried to listen to what was happening out in the front yard. Her father gave the marshal a tour of the yard, trying to keep him busy so she could get away. But he hadn't yet sent the signal that it was all right to go ahead. She paced back and forth across our room, back and forth, back and forth, until I finally looked up at her.

"What's the matter, Mommy?"

"Nothing, sweetie. Everything's okay." She later said that she searched her mind and heart for what to do. Should she be explaining to us why we were being taken away from her? Should she prepare us in case her plan didn't work? Should she tell us that she would always love us no matter what happened, that she hoped we would never forget her, and that she would never stop trying to get us back?

No, she thought. Somehow this had to work.

She went to the window and saw her father limping toward the playhouse. Buzz had engaged the marshal in some deep conversation, probably about his war days in Korea. The marshal was smiling and nodding his head. She saw her father turn back to the house, and nod toward the window.

Was this his signal? She wasn't sure, but time was running out. She couldn't take the chance of missing the opportunity.

Suddenly panicked, she turned back to us. "Girls, we have to go somewhere. Quickly. Come with Mommy."

"Where we going?" Lizzie asked loudly.

"Shhh. Just come with Mommy. It's a surprise. I'll show you when we get there. Be real quiet, now."

She grabbed us both up, one on each hip, and hurried to the front door. She quickly got us into our car seats, started the car, and carefully pulled out into the street.

Hawkins Field . . . that was where the jet was. Her father had laid a map of back streets on the passenger's seat. She trembled as she picked it up and glanced down at it.

She looked in her rearview mirror as she left her yard. The marshal turned around, saw the car pulling out of the driveway, and started to run toward her.

She felt sick as she realized that they wouldn't get away with it.

Still, she gripped the wheel and stomped the accelerator, wondering if she'd just made things unbearably worse . . . or if there was still a chance to escape.

She turned down the back road on her father's map, took

another turn, then another. Chances were, the marshal wouldn't think to go this way. He would head to Jackson International, not Hawkins Field. By the time he figured out his mistake, maybe they could be gone.

"Mommy, we're going fast!" I said, looking out the window with glee.

She crossed a dirt road to get to another street, her heart racing. The airport was about five minutes away—if we didn't get stopped.

Five minutes seemed an eternity. She looked in the rearview mirror, didn't see anyone coming after us. Maybe she had, indeed, lost him.

In moments, she found the small private airport and drove right onto the tarmac. She saw the jet waiting, ready to go.

"Girls, we're going to take an airplane ride." She got out of the car and threw open the back door. "Would you like that?"

We probably had visions of getting into a plane and flying off into the clouds, just like our daddy had done. We probably imagined going to join him in heaven. So we started to cheer and tried to get out of our seats. She unhooked us and lifted us out.

Then we heard it. A siren behind us.

"Policeman!" Lizzie shouted, and Amanda looked back to see the lights flashing. She started to run, but knew she wouldn't reach the plane before they caught up to her.

It was all over.

Before she could decide what to do, she was surrounded. With all the vicious crimes being committed in the world, she couldn't fathom how so many in the police force could have been called to stop one woman trying to save her children.

"Ma'am, I'm going to have to take the girls now," a woman in a business suit shouted, and I started to scream.

"I want my lawyer!" Amanda held tight to us, though the woman tried to fight us away. "I want to talk to my lawyer now!"

"Ma'am, this isn't about you. It's about them. You can talk to a lawyer about your own arrest, but I have a court order to take these girls and I'm going to do it now."

Horror sank deep into her heart as they tried to wrench us out of her arms.

I don't remember Amanda or Buzz, my father or my mother. I just know what I've been told. But I do remember people grabbing us, someone screaming, me shrieking out for help. I remember the horror of being ripped from the fabric of my own life, of strangers holding me and running toward a waiting van . . .

"Please. Just a few minutes. They don't understand!"

I remember my sister's anguished cries, my own efforts to break free and run back. I remember a van with blackened windows, doors slamming, wheels screeching.

Our own cries echo through my dreams sometimes, and I remember that sense of falling off a cliff into a never-ending drop . . . with no one there to catch me.

I now know that Amanda was arrested moments later. She waited at the jail, pacing back and forth across the holding cell until her father could reach her lawyer. She decided they would have to lock her up forever to restrain her from going after her children.

The door flew open and her small father stood at the threshold, Robert Eubanks at his side. Amanda flew into her father's arms.

"Oh, Daddy, where are they? Have you been able to stop them yet?"

"I'm sorry, sweetheart." His shoulders slumped. "I was so busy trying to get you out of here. And I didn't know where to go after them."

"*I'm* not what matters!" He didn't deserve to be shouted at, but she couldn't help it. "Those people have my children by now. I've got to *do* something."

He was breathing hard, she noticed, and his right hand came up to rub his shoulder. "They said there was paperwork," he got out. He stumbled and almost fell. She leaped toward him.

"Daddy, are you all right?"

Beads of sweat broke out above his lip and across his brow. He stared into space for a moment, blinking as if he couldn't see . . .

Then he collapsed onto the floor.

"*Daddy!*"

Robert ran out to get help.

She cradled his head in her arms and screamed out, "He needs an ambulance! Somebody *help!*"

Within seconds, several of the guards had come to his aid. One knelt over him, pumping frantically at his heart.

But once again, it was too late.

The ambulance came, but there was no hurry.

"I'm sorry, Mrs. Holbrooke," she was finally told, "but your father is dead."

ELEVEN

I can't imagine why I have so much trouble remembering the pleasant things of my life, when the memories of our ride home with the Krebbses is so clear. I remember Lizzie and me holding hands in the backseat of that car that smelled of wet dogs and fast-food bags. We had never ridden in a car without our car seats, and Eloise and Deke had not fastened our belts. Lizzie had found one end of a seat belt and pulled it limply across our laps, as if that would give us the security that had been snatched from us.

"Told you this was a fool idea!" Deke yelled over our cries. "Screaming brats and two more mouths to feed."

"They'll learn about the screaming," Eloise said. "And don't you worry about the money. We got us a gold mine."

"It's a hard way to make easy money." Deke had permanent scowl lines on his face, like he'd frowned one too many times and his face finally stuck that way. "Shut 'em up, Eloise."

Eloise turned around in her seat and swatted at our bare legs. "I *told* you to stop that squalling!"

Our wails rose an octave as we pulled our knees to our chests and tried to back as far as we could from her.

"Shut up now!" Eloise made like she was going to hit us again. "*Hush!*"

We tried to hold back our cries, clinging to each other. Confusion weighed down on me. There had been a terrible mistake, I thought. These dreadful people had taken the wrong pair of twins! If they just realized it, we could go back. "I want my mommy!" I squeaked out.

"Your mama's dead. You're *mine* now, so straighten up or I'll get Deke to stop this car and spank you hisself."

Twisting our faces in an effort to hold back our cries, we huddled together against the door. Eventually, Lizzie fell asleep, but I was too frightened.

I wondered if it was true that Mommy had died just like Daddy. Had the angels come for her, too? Why hadn't they taken Lizzie and me?

I looked up through the window, to the stars that Lizzie and I had lain under so many times talking about heaven and Jesus and Daddy.

I wanted to go home.

I heard a snore and jumped. The old woman was asleep, with her head back on the headrest, her mouth wide open. Her yellow wig was slipping off of her head, revealing matted, cropped gray hair underneath.

Next to her, the old man held a cigarette in his lips, and

the smoke almost choked me. The car turned off of the highway and took several turns. "Wake up, Eloise. We're home."

I caught my breath and got my knees under me so I could rise up and look out. Home meant only one place to me, and I longed for it. I wondered if Mommy would be waiting there.

But the house I saw was nothing like my own home, with the little flowers in the front yard and the playhouse in the back. Instead, I saw a little brick house with a dirt driveway, and nothing familiar.

I nudged Lizzie. "Wake up," I whispered.

She stirred and, realizing where she was, began to cry again. "I want to go home!"

As if offended, Eloise got out of the car, flung the back door open, and jerked both of us out. She popped our bottoms, as if that would stop our tears. We tried to hold our cries in until we got inside.

The house smelled of dirty shoes and grit. It was dark, until Eloise turned on an old lamp in the corner of the living room. Shadows loomed around the room, monsters mocking and threatening us.

It was hot in the house, so the woman went around opening windows. When she threw open the side door, two dogs leaped through.

Lizzie shrieked.

"I *told* you, I can't *stand* that squalling," Eloise said. "You can muzzle it right now, or I will!"

We clung together, our eyes squeezed shut against the dogs

sniffing us and the shadows stalking us and the woman yelling at us.

Eloise kicked the dogs away. "Deke, you get them dogs out, and I'll take care of the young'uns."

When Deke came back through with a cigarette hanging from his mouth, she grabbed up our hands and jerked us into the next room. It was as tiny as our daddy's toolshed. It had only one twin bed, and barely enough room to walk around it.

"I won't have this crying and carrying on." Her eyes were two bitter slits in her face. "If you can't shut up, I have ways to teach you to."

Lizzie covered her mouth to muffle the sound, but she couldn't stop the wail. "Momm*meeeeeeee!*"

The woman jerked her hand again, threw her into the closet, and closed the door. Lizzie's screams echoed through the little house, making me shiver and gape up at Eloise in terror.

"I'll be good!" I backed against the wall, tightening my body against her. "I won't cry. Lizzie will stop! Then will you take us home?"

The woman lifted me at my waist and stormed out into the hall and back to her own bedroom, where she threw me into another closet.

Agonizing darkness smothered me, and I screamed murderous, heart-wrenching screams that fell on deaf ears.

And I began to despair of anyone ever rescuing me.

TWELVE

I picture Amanda standing alone at her father's grave, a lone figure in black on a bright green manicured lawn, autumn trees whispering around her in blazing colors of orange, yellow, burgundy, and red.

I imagine the inside-out grief sucking her under, her limbs feeling heavy and sluggish as she went back to the car, moving like she walked under water, with the world floating slowly and out of control around her.

I imagine it because that is one of my own disjointed dreams. That drowning, plodding journey under treacherous waters, with no source of air or escape.

She told us later how she went back home and sat out on the cracker-barrel rocker on our playhouse porch. The sky grew dark and the stars emerged, bright and clear, against velvet black.

The beauty and peace of it enraged her, as if it provided some mocking counterpoint to the turmoil within her.

"Where *are* You?" she demanded of God. "What are You doing?"

But there was no answer in the brilliant stars or the whispering wind.

"Why do You hate me so much?"

The words sucked the breath out of her, and she sat there and wept. As angry as she was at God, she did want answers. And she had always known where to find them before.

She went into the house, tears chapping her cool face, and grabbed Jack's Bible from the bed table. The order of worship the Sunday before his death was stuck in Isaiah, and she opened the book and pulled it out. He had folded the front page of the bulletin back, and her eyes swept over the program. She tried to remember sitting close to him, their shoulders brushing, their fingers entwined, as the pastor had preached from Isaiah 49.

Funny, but she couldn't remember a thing the pastor had said. That sermon hung somewhere at the back of her mind, less prominent than the tender feelings that had always pulsed through her whenever Jack was near.

She glanced down at the open Bible, to Isaiah 49. Mechanically, she scanned the verses, until she came to verse 20.

"The children of whom you were bereaved will yet say in your
    ears,
'The place is too cramped for me;
Make room for me that I may live here.'

Then you will say in your heart,
'Who has begotten these for me,
Since I have been bereaved of my children
And am barren, an exile and a wanderer?
And who has reared these?
Behold, I was left alone;
From where did these come?'"

Thus says the Lord GOD,
"Behold, I will lift up My hand to the nations
And set up My standard to the peoples;
And they will bring your sons in their bosom,
And your daughters will be carried on their shoulders.
Kings will be your guardians,
And their princesses your nurses.
They will bow down to you with their faces to the earth
And lick the dust of your feet;
And you will know that I am the LORD;
Those who hopefully wait for Me will not be put to shame."

She wasn't sure what the words meant, or why she had turned to them. But they seemed to hold a promise. Was God telling her that He did care about her situation? That He was still in control?

Was He telling her that she would get her children back, if she was just patient, and waited hopefully?

I will not fail you or forsake you.

Joshua 1:5, she thought, as the verse reeled through her

mind. It was the first verse her parents had taught her when she was a child. Now they were gone . . .

But that promise remained.

No one could take that from her. Clinging to it like it was God's own hand, she curled up under the covers and waited for morning.

THIRTEEN

The doorbell woke her the next morning, and Amanda realized she had slept in the dress she'd worn to her father's funeral. A quick glance in the mirror showed her hair was tangled and disheveled, and smeared mascara darkened the circles under her eyes.

She opened the door a few inches and saw Robert Eubanks. "I don't want to talk about the inheritance. So unless you have news about the children—"

"I do have news, Amanda. Please, can I come in?"

She opened the door wider and slumped against it, and he stepped inside. "Amanda, I know you've been through a terrible time. I can't tell you how sorry I am."

She turned on a lamp and watched the morning shadows vanish.

"I wanted to tell you that Eloise and Deke Krebbs filed a

lawsuit this morning on behalf of the children. You'll be served later today."

"Of course they did," she said in a dull voice as she dropped onto a chair. "I told you that was why they wanted them. They smelled money all the way from Barton."

He sat down across from her. He was too tall for his chair, and his knees were higher than his body. His large bony hands webbed over his thighs.

"I'm afraid you were right, but they don't have much of a case."

"Just give it to them." The words came out flat, unconcerned. "I don't want it."

He leaned forward, clasping his hands. "Amanda, that money is the one negotiating tool you have. As long as it's yours, the Krebbses' plan won't work. If they don't get something out of their custody of Lizzie and Kara, then chances are they'll return them at some point. But if you surrender the estate to them, you may never get the girls back."

Amanda stared at him for a moment, turning his words over in her mind. "I probably won't get that inheritance anyway since all these little suits have been filed against the estate."

"Those are groundless. None of them are a real threat. They're just slowing the process down a little, because the money's not accessible to you until everything is settled. But the Krebbses *are* a threat because the suit is on behalf of the children."

"What if we offered them a settlement? Make them rich in exchange for my children?"

He considered her words for a moment, then nodded. "It's a possibility. We'll try it. But if they decide to go for the whole pot of gold, I strongly recommend that you fight them. I know you don't want to. I realize you don't have the energy or inclination. But it's critical that you fight."

When I think what she went through, how everything she loved had been taken from her, I can imagine how impossible those words must have sounded. "I don't know if I have a fight in me. Not over money, anyway. It won't bring my family back. No amount of money will do that."

He sighed. "Amanda, this estate is my last official job before I retire from the firm I've worked for most of my life. I want to see that it's taken care of. Out of respect for your husband, I want to fight for you and make sure that the estate eventually passes to his children. I'm a Christian, as I know you and Jack were. Since the Holbrookes' deaths, the company's leadership has taken it down some roads that would make Paul roll over in his grave. I would love nothing better than to see you get at the helm of that company to root out that evil. The current leadership will run it into the ground. Someone of character needs to be in charge."

She felt a sick churning in her stomach . . . how long had it been since she'd eaten? "I worked as a paralegal before I met Jack," she said. "I don't know anything about running a mega-corporation."

"I believe that you're the one God wants there." He said it like a prophet proclaiming the truth. "He picked a shepherd boy to be king of Israel. Why is it so hard to believe that He could pick you to run HolCorp?"

"God hasn't picked me for anything! The whole idea is crazy. There's no purpose to any of this."

"I believe you're wrong. Someday those children will grow up and they deserve to have what is rightfully theirs. You may have lost control over their youth, but you can protect their future. You might be the only one who cares enough about them to do that."

She got up and went to the window, looked out on the backyard. Memories played through her mind like the tattered photographs I've seen. "Why do you have so much faith in me? I can't even keep the most basic, simple promise! I promised my husband I would take care of Lizzie and Kara for the rest of my life. That they would be my first earthly priority. He died believing I would do that."

"You can still keep that promise, Amanda. You've lost touch with them for now, but someday they'll be back in your life. You can fight for this estate and keep Eloise and Deke Krebbs from getting it, or the people who are running the company from changing it entirely. Preserving HolCorp and the estate for the girls would be a way to keep your promise."

She stared at the window sill, wishing there were answers there. How could she juggle the problems of a billion-dollar corporation, when she couldn't even remember to shower in the morning?

But if it was a way to keep her promise . . . to take care of the girls in the best way she could . . . then maybe this was her obligation.

She drew in a deep, cleansing breath, but it didn't restore her strength. "All right. I'll fight."

He smiled then, the first time she had seen that since she'd met him. "You've made my day."

FOURTEEN

Just a few days into our stay with the Krebbses, Lizzie and I had the same dream. Hands groped and grabbed, and I clung tightly to something I couldn't see. I was sure those clawing hands belonged to death, the same death that had taken my daddy. If it wasn't death, it hurt my heart just the same.

I clung with all the strength of my arms and legs, but those pulling hands were winning, prying me away, fighting to take me.

My own screams echoed through my head . . .

I heard Lizzie hit the floor and I jolted awake. I was soaked in sweat and urine and tears. Darkness blinded me, and I didn't know where I was, but I reached for her in a desperate struggle to save her from those hands.

"I'm scared!" She was screaming. "The hands . . . I want to go home!" I came to my senses as I realized that Eloise and Deke might wake up. "Shhh. They'll wake up and come."

"They're not here," Lizzie said. "I heard them leaving."

"We're by ourselves?"

"Yeah, but I'm glad."

Lizzie pulled away from me and got up then and stood on her toes to turn on the light. It came on with blazing intensity, squinting my eyes. Lizzie's hair was rumpled and tangled, and her face was pink on one side.

We got brave and went into the living room and sat on the couch, trying to calm ourselves with *Gunsmoke* reruns.

We both dozed on the couch to the comfort of the TV voices.

The night had given way to daylight when I heard the car tires crunching the gravel driveway.

I got up and looked out the window. Deke and Eloise Krebbs were getting out of their car, staggering toward the house, looking as if they'd been in a fight.

"Come on, Lizzie, we have to go to bed!"

Lizzie woke up, groggy, and slid off the couch.

"Hurry! They're coming."

Before I could get her to move out of her sleepy stupor, the door burst open and Eloise and Deke marched in.

"What are you doing up?" Eloise bellowed. "It's five-thirty in the morning."

"We got scared," Lizzie whispered.

"Go back to sleep," Eloise ordered. "I ain't got any patience for you today."

We hurried back to our room and huddled on the bed together, listening as Eloise ranted in the next room. "I told you tonight wasn't a good night, but no, you had to keep on putting the money down. What's the matter with you, Deke?"

"I'll borrow some tomorrow. There ain't a bank in the area that wouldn't give me money, knowing that I've got the Billion Dollar Babies. We'll borrow the money and win every bit of it back tomorrow night. You just mark my word."

I fell asleep curled up with Lizzie, and the hands came back, groping and clawing and pulling . . . tormenting my rest and pumping fear through my veins like life itself.

I wondered if the hands were those of that monster, death, or if they were the angels who had taken my daddy. As much as I wanted to be with him or Amanda, I feared them. I began to hate those angels we used to lie in the grass and look for, the ones we dressed up like, the ones who, in my dreams, smelled and sounded like Deke and Eloise Krebbs.

FIFTEEN

Lizzie and I decided that we would have to find our own way home and we thought we had a plan. There were woods behind the Krebbses' house . . . and there were woods behind our house at home.

To our three-year-old minds, we figured they were the same woods and that, if we entered them, we would come out in our own backyard.

It took us days to get the courage. We were afraid of those oppressive trees and the bushes that grabbed and scratched and the tangled branches and vines. But we didn't see another way.

While Eloise and Deke slept off another casino night, we held hands and ventured into that frightening place . . . but we found it less frightening than the house where our grand-parents held us hostage.

Birds crowed overhead, and animals made noises from their

hiding places. We had no reference point for the things around us, except for Disney books and fairy tales in which trees spoke and birds smiled and Bambi romped.

Our fear soon lifted as we went deep enough into the trees to lose sight of the Krebbses' house. We walked and walked, and branches and thornbushes tore at our legs. The sounds of the animals around us grew more hostile.

I remember stumbling through those woods, searching for the opening that would take us to the other side—only there was no opening. Finally I began to wonder if there really was another side.

I sat down in a bed of muddy leaves and started to cry, and Lizzie stood helplessly over me.

"Where is Mommy?"

Lizzie's voice was flat, resolute. "They said she was dead like Daddy."

"I want to go home." My wail was high-pitched and frightened, wafting over the trees and hushing the forest sounds.

Lizzie sat down next to me, weary and dirty, and put her arm across my shoulders. "It's okay, sweetie," she whispered, echoing Amanda's comforting chant.

And then we heard it. A man's voice, yelling from some distance away.

We got to our feet, our grimy, tear-streaked faces lighting up with hope. I'm not sure what we'd expected—our daddy, back with a team of angels to whisk us off with him; or Grandpa Buzz and Mommy, ready to take us home.

But the man who made his way to us was gruff and scowling. He had dark, beady eyes, and his mouth was a straight slash across his face. He wore a thin, V-neck T-shirt and mud-covered jeans, and he carried a big blade in his hands, with which he whacked at the brush to form his path.

He stopped when he got to us and yelled, "What in the dog dickens?"

We got up and started to run away, but he dropped his blade and grabbed us both. Our screams rose to shriek level. "How in blazes did you get out here?" he yelled over our cries. "You those young'uns living with the Krebbses? They said they was red-haired twins. The Billion Dollar Babies."

We kept fighting to break away, but he put an arm around each of our waists and lifted us like we were sacks of potatoes.

"Hush up, and I'll take you home!"

The words somehow shot through our terror, and my sobbing slowed. "Home?" I asked, but Lizzie still shrieked.

"If you'll settle down, I'll take you!"

Lizzie tried to stop, so he finally set us down and bent down low. "You don't have to be scared of me. I got grandkids my ownself. I wouldn't want them wandering around in here during hunting season. You could be shot."

His voice wasn't threatening like Eloise's and Deke's always were, so we just stood there, waiting for him to lead us home. Our tormenter had suddenly become our savior. "Just follow behind me now."

He picked his blade back up and whacked at vines and bushes, held back branches, and got us to a path someone had already forged. We followed closely, thinking it would all be over soon, that he would take us straight to our little house with the playhouse in the yard, that our mommy wouldn't be dead but waiting for us, ready to take us in and put us into a bubble bath, feed us macaroni, and tuck us into our own beds. I could almost smell the scent of fresh-mown grass and the jasmine climbing the little arbor on one side of the yard. I could almost hear her voice . . . see the delight on her face.

Which one of us would she scoop up first?

It's okay, sweetie . . .

She would take off these nasty clothes we had worn for days, wash us and dry us with the fluffy towels that felt soft against our skin, then curl up in our bed with us on clean, fresh sheets . . .

"Almost there now," the man called behind him, and we picked up our step and began to run, run, run toward the light in the opening of the trees.

But the sight stopped us cold.

It was only the Krebbses' house. We were right back where we'd started.

Lizzie started to cry again, but I just stood there staring at that house, feeling kind of numb and very, very tired.

Deke opened the back door.

"Take your young'uns, Deke," the man said. "I found them wandering through the woods. They're just babies, man. You need to take better care."

Deke looked aggravated at the disturbance and grabbed both of our arms. "In the house! Eloise!"

She waddled toward us and swatted our behinds. "Where

you girls been? Don't you know your grandma's been looking all over for you?"

I was pretty sure she hadn't been looking for us. I figured she didn't even know we were gone.

We went to our tiny room before they could chastise us. Lizzie crawled under the bed, as if Deke couldn't get to her there, and she cried quietly. I joined her, and we curled up together, our hearts broken that our escape had failed. We wept together with gasping sobs as the disappointment seemed to smother us like some kind of gaseous fog.

Finally, I fell asleep and dreamed about coming out of that forest again . . .

Only this time, I saw our pretty little house with the flowers and the playhouse . . . arms to run into . . . and hugs that tickled us . . . love that smiled on us.

It lasted all the way until morning.

SIXTEEN

I remember the day the big box came to the house. I didn't think much of it when Deke signed for it at the door, but then he opened it and began pulling out the wrapped boxes with pretty bows and cards taped to each one.

"What is it, Deke?" Eloise asked.

"It's from *her.*" He uttered the word *her* as if it were a piece of gristle at the back of his throat. "Birthday presents."

"Oh, that's right." Eloise jerked the box away from him. "They're four today."

"Us?" I asked, looking up at her. "Are those for us?"

Lizzie, who had taken to sucking her thumb more than ever before, pulled it out of her mouth and looked up at the gifts. "Can we open them?"

Eloise and Deke didn't say no, so I bolted forward and tore into the paper of the biggest box. A lifelike baby doll lay inside it. My heart swelled as I gently pulled it out and held it against me, as carefully as if it were real.

"Kara, look!"

I looked at Lizzie and saw that she had a baby, too, wrapped in a soft blanket and cradled in her arms.

Eloise grabbed up the next gift before we thought to open it and tore into it before we could. It was a pair of pink sneakers. Deke snatched the next one, ripped into it, and found a frilly wedding veil attached to a plastic tiara. Lizzie gasped and reached for it.

Deke held it up out of her reach. "These are expensive things, Eloise," he said. "You reckon we can get anything for them?"

"The dolls, anyway. They're some of those collectors' dolls. We could hock them down at the pawnshop; get a couple hundred dollars, maybe."

Lizzie had sat down with her baby and was rocking her body back and forth and whispering to the doll. "Shhh. It's okay, sweetie. I'll take care of you."

I wanted to go off by myself and tell mine that she was going to be okay, too, that I would be her mommy and dress her and feed her and rock her to sleep at night.

But Eloise stalked across the room and jerked her from my arms. I yelled out my protest and flung my body at her, but she shoved me away.

"It's mine!"

But she sneered and held the doll over her head. "It ain't yours," she said. "Nothing's yours until I *say* it's yours."

Deke went for Lizzie's, but she screamed and tried to run. Eloise grabbed her by the arm and wrenched the doll away.

Lizzie's cry shook the house, and Deke's hand came down across her jaw. I grunted as if he had hit *me*. She fell to the floor, shrieking and gasping. He picked her up by one arm and jerked her back to his closet, threw her in, and slammed the door shut.

I threw myself at him, kicking and beating with my fists. But he threw the dolls down and picked me up, wrestled me into the other closet, and locked me in.

"Shut up, both of you!" His voice roared over our cries. "Else I'll throw one of them mutts in with you and let him tear you apart. You hear me?"

I bit my lip in the dense, smelly darkness of the closet, sobbing out my pain and childish rage.

That was how we celebrated our fourth birthday.

SEVENTEEN

Probate meant nothing to us, and we weren't aware of the newspaper articles or the label they had stamped on Lizzie and me. We learned to live our lives as quietly as we could and to stay out of Deke's way. It wasn't too hard, since he and Eloise spent most nights at the casino, then slept all day.

As the probate court date approached, though, they spent more time at home, talking on the phone to the lawyer handling their case. We didn't understand any of it then, but Amanda offered them settlement after settlement, enough to make them millionaires many times over, if they would drop the case and return us to her.

But their lawyer had visions of getting the whole estate for them and a commission check for himself that would have set him up for life.

The night before court, Mack, Grandpa Buzz's dearest and

closest friend, invited Amanda and her friend Joan to a barbe-
cue at his house. The old man was stiff with arthritis, but he had
set up their table outside so that they could talk and breathe the
sweet Southern air and try to put things in perspective.

Amanda was pensive and brooding, anxious about what the
next day might hold. "Tomorrow could be my last chance to get
the girls back. If I win, they're bound to regret not taking a
settlement. Then I can offer them a consolation prize, in exchange for custody of Lizzie and Kara. I know they'll take it."

"And if they win?" Mack studied her face.

"If they win, maybe I can still convince them to give the
girls back. They'll have gotten what they wanted and won't need
them anymore. They'd have to retain legal custody just for the
sake of the money, but maybe we could work out letting them
live with me."

Mack pushed his plate away and leaned on the table, his
concerned gaze resting on Amanda. "Honey, I hope it works
out for you that way. Maybe it will. But if it doesn't, I want you
to start trying to accept it."

"I *can't* accept it. How can you say that?"

"Because those girls aren't hidden from God. He knows
where they are and who they're with. He loves them more than
you do."

"Then He'll bring them home. He knows they're better off
with me."

Mack took her hand and kneaded it in his. "I just don't want
you suffering anymore. There comes a time when you have to

accept God's will and then ask what He wants you to do. You have to realize that He has some greater plan that you might not ever understand. But whatever it is, you can endure it."

She couldn't get angry at the sweet old man who loved her almost as much as her father. "I know. But I believe that God told me they would live with me again. He led me to Isaiah 49, and it talks about the children coming home."

Mack shook his head. "But He didn't say when."

"I don't understand why He had to take it all away."

"You may never understand," Joan said. She was a tiny woman with big brown hair and huge round eyes. She had the voice of a preteen, but Amanda knew her well enough to take her seriously. "None of us may ever understand. Will the girls be in court tomorrow?"

"I doubt it," Amanda said. "Robert said they don't have to bring them, and that they probably won't. It wouldn't help them to have the judge see them crying for me." She rubbed her tired, red eyes.

"Your whole life could change tomorrow." Mack got up and stirred the charcoal in the grill. They had stopped glowing and now were crusted in ashes. "Or nothing could change at all. Let's pray for a while, so you'll be strong going in." He came back to the table and reached for both their hands.

And as they prayed, Amanda tried to lay her burdens at the foot of Jesus' cross.

But she wasn't sure that she had the strength to leave them there.

The next morning, Joan and Mack went with her to court and sat at the back of the courtroom, their presence giving her a bit of peace.

Eloise and Deke were already at their table with their lawyer. They had left us with some woman in town who kept a dozen children in a tiny, cramped house.

Amanda would later say that she had searched their faces for a sign of empathy, a sign of gentleness, for she prayed each day that we would look up to smiling faces. But she saw nothing good in the Krebbses' faces.

The judge came into the room, and the court session began.

As the hearing progressed, it looked to Amanda as if the Krebbses' character was glaringly obvious to the judge. Part of her wished he would realize their greed and their misuse of us for their own personal gain and order the custody switched back to her. But this was not a custody hearing. It was only about money.

When both sides were argued, the judge left the room, and they broke for lunch. But she could not make herself eat a bite.

"Honey, you need your strength," Joan said in that adolescent-sounding voice. "Please eat."

"I'll be sick if I do." She pushed her plate away. "Mack, do you really think they'll lose?"

"I really think you'll win," he said.

"Then that means I can approach the Krebbses afterward and offer them some money. I might even get the girls back today." The weakness of her hope was reflected in her voice.

Still, the thought kept Amanda going as she went back into the courtroom to hear the judge's decision.

He put on his glasses, clasped his hands, and looked down at the paperwork in front of him. "This has been a very difficult decision." He took the glasses back off and rubbed his eyes. "I'd like to be fair to both parties, while still upholding the will of the deceased. Mr. Holbrooke clearly wanted his wife to have what was his. But he never knew that she would lose custody of Lizzie and Kara Holbrooke. It's an unfortunate situation, one that I don't think Mr. Holbrooke intended. But I'm only here to decide the matter of probate, not the custody issue."

He shoved those glasses back on and looked down at the papers. "And the fact is, I don't think Mr. Holbrooke had any intention of leaving his children with nothing. Their grandfather was a very wealthy man, and they deserve to share in that."

Deke Krebbs's hand came down hard on the table. Amanda jumped. She saw that he was already grinning.

"The court did give the Krebbses custody, and it's obvious that they aren't people of means. They probably do need financial help raising their grandchildren."

"You *bet* we do," Deke said.

The judge glared at him over his glasses, then took them off and leaned on his elbows. His face was clearly not at peace.

"I've decided to award Lizzie and Kara Holbrooke ten million dollars."

Deke sprang up out of his chair and let out a whoop.

The judge hammered his gavel. "I am not finished! If you can't be quiet, you can leave this courtroom!"

Deke sat down, still grinning. Amanda gaped at him across the room, wondering if he had any idea how much money he could have had in a settlement. Ten million was just a fraction of the whole estate.

"As I was saying," the judge went on, "I am awarding the children the amount of ten million dollars. Taxes and attorney's fees will be paid out of the lump sum, which should come to about half of the total. The balance will be paid out in annual installments of just over $300,000 per year for the next fourteen years. This is to support the children until they turn eighteen. The remainder of the estate will go to Amanda Holbrooke."

Amanda sat stunned, running the ruling through her mind, trying to decide if this was good or bad.

The media at the back of the room began buzzing and flashing, and some dashed out. Eloise and Deke Krebbs began to celebrate as if they'd just hit pay dirt.

Robert turned to her. "We did it. Congratulations."

"No!" Her mouth trembled as she got out the words. "This is terrible! The yearly installments will make them want to keep the girls so they'll keep getting the money. I won't have any chance of getting them back!"

"Amanda, you get the fortune. You get to guard it."

"I wanted my *children,* and you knew that. They're celebrating like they're rich. They'll never make a deal with me now."

"But at least the children will be cared for. They'll be able to live in a nice place, wear decent clothes, maybe have nannies that will take care of them. Their quality of life just improved. It's something, Amanda."

But it wasn't something to her. "They're *mine.*" She choked out the words. "This is all wrong." She grabbed his arm. "Robert, go over there and offer them twenty million for the girls. Tell them all they have to do is sign custody over to me, and they can have twenty, forty, a hundred million. Robert, give them all of it if you have to!"

"I'll talk to them," he said. "Why don't you just go home and rest, and I'll call you?"

"No! I'm going with you. Make the offer, Robert."

She followed him over to their table. Their attorney was the only one not celebrating their win. He listened as Robert extended an offer of twenty million dollars.

Eloise and Deke heard it and stopped celebrating, listened carefully, then told Amanda that they would consider it.

She went home with Mack and Joan at her sides and waited the longest hours of her life for the answer to come.

It sounds crazy to me now, and for the longest time I couldn't even believe that Deke and Eloise turned that kind of money down. It doesn't make sense. But they were suspicious of Amanda's offer and decided the whole thing was a trick to show the judge that it wasn't us they wanted, but the money. And they weren't going to play into her hands.

I chalk it up to stupidity and ignorance.

Then one of them got the idea that when Lizzie and I turned eighteen, we could sue again for everything Amanda and HolCorp were worth, and they would wind up sitting even prettier than they were with the ten million.

So they turned her offers down and held on to us with a vengeance.

That night, they came home from Jackson and got our dolls

from the pawnshop. They had them in the car when they picked us up from the babysitter's and told us that we were celebrating because we'd just come into some money.

I remember feeling such joy at the sight of my doll, soft and pliant in my arms. I imagined that she had been crying since they'd taken her from me. I pictured her lying on that shelf in that store, afraid and helpless, waiting to see what would happen next. But she was home now, back with me. And I could take care of her. Lizzie and I mothered our dolls together in our little bed as Eloise and Deke boozed it up with their friends in the living room.

Even with the noise and the laughter and the music blaring in the next room, I slept better that night, holding that baby in my arms, than I had since we'd been taken from our home.

EIGHTEEN

I'm sure that Amanda was inconsolable for the next few weeks. I've heard that she ate little, slept a lot, and refused to go out. Joan came over after work each day and tried to coax her from her despair.

One day, as they sat in her dark living room, Joan said, "Maybe this is how God feels when the world takes us away from Him. Maybe His heart is just as broken as yours is."

"Then why would He wish it on me?"

Joan got quiet and stared at the same spot in the air as Amanda.

"I made Jack a promise, Joan. I can't keep it."

"Yes, you can."

"How?"

Joan sighed. "You can take care of the girls financially. The only way I see that you can do that right now is to guard their fortune, clean up the company, and set your sights on their eighteenth birthday when you can give them everything that's theirs. Eloise and Deke Krebbs couldn't get their hands on it if they tried. *You're* the steward of it, and you can protect it and preserve it and even grow it for them. But that company has got a lot of problems, and I don't think you want to give it to them the way it is, or the way it might be by the time they're of age."

Amanda rose and went to the bathroom, turned the faucet on, and splashed some water over her face. She looked at her face in the mirror, puffed with misery. She hardly recognized herself. She turned back to the door and saw Joan leaning against the casing, her arms crossed.

"I hate this!" She scrubbed the towel too hard over her skin. "What am I supposed to do? Call HolCorp and tell them to clean me out an office?"

"Honey, that's exactly what you ought to do," Joan said in that childlike voice. "You call up there and you tell the acting CEO that you'd like for him to call a board meeting, and then I'll go with you."

Amanda turned around. "You'll be there? Why?"

"Because I'm quitting my job," Joan said, "and I'm hiring myself as your assistant."

Amanda almost smiled. "My assistant?"

"Somebody's got to do it, and it might as well be me." Joan came in and took her by the shoulders. "You're the best friend I've got, Amanda, and darn lucky if you ask me, since I'm the most efficient administrative assistant in town. You can ask any boss I've ever had. In fact, my boss, Mr. Miller, will probably throw himself across a railroad track and beg me to stay. But I'm committed to you."

"Would you really do that, Joan?" She set the towel down and stepped toward her. "Because it would help me a lot. I don't have any focus. I don't know which direction to go. I need somebody who has some skills."

Joan struck a *ta-da* pose. "I'm your girl."

Amanda finally gave in to that weak smile, and Joan pulled her into a hug. "You're gonna get through this, Amanda. And so are the girls. You're not alone, and neither are they. You have me, and they have each other. That's why God made them twins."

She accepted Joan's tight hug and dug deep enough in her heart to find her gratitude for her friend.

∾

That night, Joan slept in the room Lizzie and I used to share; she didn't want Amanda to be alone.

But when Joan was sound asleep, Amanda sat on her bed under the glow of the yellow lamplight, her legs folded beneath her, and paged through Jack's Bible, searching for some comfort.

She came to a yellow highlighted passage in Jeremiah 31. Jack had found it important, so she ran her fingers over the page as she began to read at verse 15:

Thus says the LORD,
"A voice is heard in Ramah,
Lamentation and bitter weeping.

Rachel is weeping for her children;

She refuses to be comforted for her children,

Because they are no more."

Thus says the LORD,

"Restrain your voice from weeping

And your eyes from tears;

For your work will be rewarded," declares the LORD,

"And they will return from the land of the enemy.

There is hope for your future," declares the LORD,

"And your children will return to their own territory."

She touched her mouth and leaned back on her pillows. God was speaking to her through Jack's highlighting pen. Once again, He was telling her to be patient. To wait. That it would be all right. That her children would someday return. She was to work now, in anticipation of her reward.

She started to cry again, but this time it was not from grief. This time her tears were of joy, for the Lord had mercy on her and had spoken to her in a clear voice tonight. He was telling her to wait, to trust, and to get up and move. He was telling her that He would give her the strength for whatever lay ahead of her.

He was telling her that He would be with her.

Christ knew of her suffering, for He, too, had grieved over His children. He had wept over Israel and said that He'd wanted to gather them like a hen gathers her chicks under her wings . . .

He had suffered grief and abandonment and tribulation. He had even suffered pain and death. He had felt forsaken.

But there had been joy to come.

For the first time since her whole nightmare had begun, Amanda thought ahead to that joy. God would not leave her nor forsake her. And so she made the decision, sitting there on her bed in the yellow glow of light, that she would trust His promise, no matter how long it took to fulfill.

NINETEEN

For the next few months, the money made life at the Krebbses' house a little happier for us, and we started to settle in. Eloise took to wearing hats and shoes that hurt her feet; Deke bought a brand-new Cadillac and opened a no-limit account at the casino down in Vicksburg.

They planned to buy a new house, but before they could find the right one, Deke lost most of the money in a poker game.

Things promptly got bad again.

They never did buy that house, so we continued sleeping in that tiny room on the single twin mattress, with sheets that hadn't been changed since we'd moved in. We learned that tears did no good, that they only got you locked in closets. We began to get food from the cabinets if it was in there when we needed it. Otherwise, we did without.

Eventually, when Eloise and Deke had lost so much money

that they couldn't pay their mortgage, we moved to an old trailer and waited for the next annual installment.

The woods behind our trailer became our personal playground, and the television became our teacher.

Kindergarten came with the same fanfare as our birthdays, which meant no one paid much heed to it. Some mornings, we got ourselves up on time and made it to the bus stop. Other mornings, we didn't. No one seemed to care one way or another. Eloise and Deke stayed at the casinos all night, leaving us to our own devices, with no supper or bedtime, no bath or homework.

When we got home from school each day, Eloise and Deke were usually sound asleep, their snores shaking the rickety trailer. At the barking dog or the closing door they would wake up and yell for quiet. Then, after a series of cigarettes and cups of black coffee, they would head out to the casino again.

As the days and years went by, we forgot that Amanda had ever existed. Our father remained some distant memory with as much mystery as that surrounding our mother.

We heard often about the money Eloise and Deke had won, but we didn't understand about inheritances or squandered fortunes. And on the rare occasions when we intercepted a letter addressed to us, Eloise would grab it and launch into a tirade about how Amanda had stolen the lion's share of our inheritance and was responsible for the way we lived now.

As we grew older, I learned to hate the mysterious woman who had robbed us of what was ours . . . this woman named Amanda Holbrooke.

TWENTY

The town of Barton was situated off of Highway 49, just south of Yazoo City. It was largely agricultural country, full of cotton crops, soybeans, and catfish farms. Two businesses employed most of the nonfarming residents of town: a paper mill and a chicken-processing plant. The air over the town was poisoned with the competing smells that clung to your clothes and blew through your windows, floated in the creeks, and blew through the vents of every building in town. It attached itself to our cars and our lawns and our trees.

We got used to it, though, and after a while didn't smell it anymore, except when the wind blew up just right and stirred the stink around. On the rare occasions when we could get far enough out of town to breathe clean air, the stench always surprised us when we returned.

The stench came in waves at our house. When Deke gave

the casino the last of the first installment of our inheritance, he went back to work at the chicken plant and came home daily smelling of rotten slime. The smell would never wash completely out of his clothes, and his shoes reeked so badly that Eloise took to lining them up on the front porch of the trailer to get them out of the house.

The woods behind our trailer became a place of mystery and adventure, from which an occasional moccasin or cotton-mouth would slither and torment us until Deke would go out with his deer-hunting rifle and blow its head off. Eventually, though, we overcame our fear of those snakes and ventured deeper into the woods.

We learned where all the paths had been cut by hunters trying to make easier passages to their deer stands, and we found that, by following them, we could get anywhere in the town of Barton. One path led to the library, where Lizzie and I spent many muggy afternoons. Lizzie loved to go for the air conditioning, but I loved to read.

One day when we were eight, Lizzie and I hung out at that library after school. She lay on one of the vinyl couches in the children's section, her feet hanging over the arm. I sat on the floor, deeply absorbed in *The Boxcar Children* by Gertrude Chandler Warner.

Lizzie stared at me. "Why do you like that book?"

"Because these kids are like us. Homeless, kind of."

"We're not homeless." Lizzie twirled her hair around her finger and flopped her feet off the end of the library couch. "We just *wish* we were."

"See, these kids are supposed to go live with their grand-father, only they're afraid of him, so they live in this boxcar and pretend that they have parents and people looking after them, when all along they do it for themselves."

"I'd be scared to live in a boxcar. Steve Crawley says there are rats in them."

I sneered. "Steve Crawley lies. Besides, this one doesn't have rats. They fixed it up like a real house. Where's your imagina-tion, Lizzie?"

"Not in some ratty boxcar." She got up and stood on the couch cushions and feigned a gymnastics dismount, without ever having mounted in the first place. She leaped down from the couch and waved to the invisible Olympics crowd. I went back to reading.

She lay back down. "I wish *Little Women* and *The Secret Garden* weren't checked out."

"You've read them over and over. Why don't you find some-thing new?"

"Ah . . . Ah *cain't*," she said, in some fake Southern accent that she'd heard in some television movie. She threw her wrist over her forehead and pretended to faint. I knew she was pulling a Sleeping Beauty, so I got up and kissed her on the lips. She started to giggle and pushed me away, and I wrestled her back down. "Oooh, you're so by-ootiful! Give Prince Charming another big smooch, why don'tcha?"

We were making too much noise, because Mrs. Hallitop came around the bookshelves and shushed us. "If you girls can't behave in here, you need to go on home."

So I checked out my book and we headed to our woods. One path led to the truck stop just near the highway, where we could watch strangers from out of town come and go with sour looks on their faces, probably from the smell of the air or the sour stomachs they had from eating the greasy food.

The path that crossed over the railroad tracks was our most frequented path, for we found that if we reached the tracks, we had a straight shot to downtown Barton, which consisted of a rotting hole-in-the-wall they called City Hall, a small strip mall with a Dollar General Store, an antique shop called Trash and Treasures, and a barbershop where unemployed men hung out all day shooting the breeze.

It was at that strip mall . . . on that very day . . . that Lizzie and I learned the art of shoplifting.

We hadn't meant to do it. It wasn't like we set out to become thieves. No one ever told us that stealing was wrong, but we knew it, just like you know that it's wrong to set someone's house on fire or bust them in the mouth.

We didn't know *why* it was wrong, and no one ever tried to tell us. But even if they had, I'm not sure it would have mattered.

What did matter was that when we made it home from the library that day, we saw that the dog had gotten hold of Lizzie's doll, which she had named Eliza, sort of after herself. The dog had dragged it by its dress into the backyard, and Lizzie found it facedown in a mud puddle. From her reaction, you would have thought she'd found *me* lying there, drowned in mud. She picked it up, cradling the muddy, ravaged doll in her arms, and began to wail with heartbreaking anguish.

I didn't know how to comfort her, so I picked up a rock, gritted my teeth, and threw it at the dog. I missed, but he cleared out of the yard, no doubt fearing more missiles aimed for his head.

Lizzie still cried, her nose running and her face red and wet, and I went to her and put my arms around her. "Shhh, it's okay, sweetie. Let's go in and give her a bath."

Through her tears, she nodded, and I escorted her in.

She brought the doll into the bathroom, and we ran a bath for it in the sink and washed the mud out of Eliza's hair and off of her soft little body. She was never meant to be bathed, not in the cloth part of her body, but we didn't know that. The mud and water stained her torso, tainting her beauty, and the dog had left teeth marks on her face.

Her hair stuck up every which way, like some kind of punk rocker. And the dress was ruined. The dog had chewed it and ripped its skirt to shreds.

Lizzie got under the bed and cried with that baby, keeping her voice real low since Deke always threw us in the closets when we cried. I don't know why she felt the need to get under the bed, except that it was some shelter from flying fists . . . and the mattress muffled the sound. It was dirty and dusty under there and made me sneeze. But Lizzie always grieved under the bed.

I got my baby, which I had named Missy, and thought of taking off her dress and giving it to my sister. But then my baby would have been naked. I considered the fact that it might make us even—that mine still had pretty hair, and hers would have a pretty dress. I knew it would have gotten Lizzie out from under the bed and made her feel better.

But I couldn't do it. The dog had come after her doll, after all, and if she hadn't left it where he could reach it, it wouldn't have happened. Mine had been under the covers of our bed. She should have put it somewhere safer, I thought. She deserved what she'd gotten, and I didn't deserve to have to suffer for her mistake.

Then I had an idea. "Lizzie, we can go buy Eliza another dress."

"I don't *want* another dress," she said, wiping her nose on her sleeve.

"But we can get one of those princess dresses they have at the Dollar General. Maybe it'll have a crown with it, and if it doesn't, we can make one."

She looked up at me. I knew that was a good sign that she was listening. "That pink one with the lace?"

"Yeah, that one. Come on out, Lizzie. Eliza doesn't like it under there, and she's already scared enough."

I finally coaxed her out from under the bed. She came out, and I gave her a dirty T-shirt to wipe her face on.

"I want the pink one with the lace," she said. We'd spent many hours in that store, dreaming over those pretty dresses and bathing suits and pant sets that would have fit our dolls. "But we don't have any money. How are we gonna buy the stupid thing?"

"We'll pick up Coke bottles along the way and sell them over at the recycling plant," I said. "Or even better . . . we'll go to the truck stop and look for change that's spilled out of the truckers' pockets. We always find change there, Lizzie."

"Those dresses cost ten dollars! Do you know how much change we'd have to find?"

I was really getting aggravated. "Well, if you want to be that way about it, just go back under that bed. But I'm going shopping."

Lizzie got all pouty-lipped, clutching her doll against her. "I'll come. And if I see that dumb, stupid dog, I'm gonna kick it right in the teeth."

"You do, and he'll drag you off."

Lizzie put her doll on the bed, carefully hidden under the covers in case the dog returned. Then we headed out to the woods and got on the path that led to the railroad track.

Lizzie's spirits lifted as we made our way down the tracks. She always liked to walk like a beauty pageant queen on the runway, waving at her admirers along the way. I had this thing I liked to do. I would run and leap, then count the crossties to see how many I'd crossed. I would get way ahead of her, then wait for her graceful gait to catch up to me. Then I'd run and leap again.

Today, she wasn't prancing or waving, and when I leaped and looked back, it took her forever to catch up. I hated that dog. He wasn't anything like a pet. He was some mutt that Deke had brought home for hunting. He didn't even have a name, just roamed around our muddy yard looking for something to tear up.

I hated to see Lizzie so sad.

"You want to go to the truck stop to look for change, or to the Dollar store and see how much the dress costs?" I asked her over my shoulder.

"I know how much it costs." She said it like I was the one who had chewed up her doll.

"Well, you don't have to be snotty about it. I helped you wash her off, didn't I?"

She didn't say anything, and we got to the place where the tracks crossed a road, and I made a big deal of jumping over the track, then tried a cartwheel, but fell on my bottom. She caught up to me.

"What if they sold it?" Her eyes grew wide and dark at the thought.

"They didn't sell it. We were just in there yesterday, and it was still there. They might have got some new ones, though." My eyes got big as I thought of the possibilities. "Maybe they got in one of those shiny gold kind, with shoes and a crown."

Lizzie looked up at me, suddenly interested. "Maybe."

We walked through the men standing out in front of the barbershop, smoking their cigarettes and smelling like sweat and Deke's shoes. We pushed into the Dollar General Store. The clerk was on the phone.

"She ain't fooling nobody. She's as pregnant as the day is long. I always expected that from her, didn't you? The apple don't fall far from the tree, and you know what they say about her mama . . ."

She never even looked up as we went in.

We found the toy aisle, and Lizzie pushed ahead of me and

rushed to the doll clothes. She flipped through the flat little boxes, looking for the one she wanted. The long, pink dress she'd had her heart set on was still there.

"Ten bucks," she said, waving it at me with I-told-you-so anger. "We don't have it, and we're not gonna get it."

"Who says we have to have money to buy it?" I asked in a whisper.

"Well, they're not giving them away."

I don't know what came over me right then. I wasn't all that brave, and I spent a lot of time worrying about getting in trouble or making Deke mad. But before I had the chance to talk myself out of it, I grabbed that box from her, pulled up my shirt, and stuck it down in the waistband of my pants. I pulled the shirt down, and you couldn't even see that I had anything under there.

Lizzie sucked in a breath. "Kara!"

"You want it or not?"

She thought about it for a moment, then looked back down at the clothes. She grabbed a red dress with matching socks and stuffed that into her pants.

Then we carefully walked back to the front, looking real innocent. The cashier had gotten off the phone and looked down at us, eyes narrowed. "Can I help you?"

I had to think fast, because I was afraid that she would see the guilt on my face, or that Lizzie might burst into tears and spill her guts. I grabbed a yo-yo out of the bin closest to me and held it up. "How much is this?"

"Dollar ninety-nine."

I acted like I was disappointed, just *crushed* that I didn't have the dollar ninety-nine. I put it back and in a sad voice said, "Come on, Lizzie."

Lizzie had her arms crossed over her stomach, looking very suspicious, so I opened the door and shoved her out. The girl behind the counter never knew a thing.

We didn't say a word to each other until we got back to the tracks, and when we were sure that no one had come running after us, we began to celebrate.

"That was easy!" Lizzie jumped up and down. "Eliza's gonna feel so much better."

"We'll share the red dress. It's only fair, since I took the pink one for you."

"Missy can wear it on Monday, Wednesday, and Friday, and Eliza can wear it on Sunday, Tuesday, and Thursday." Lizzie always liked to have things organized. She couldn't stand to have things uncertain.

"Maybe we could go back and get another one," I said. "Maybe we could get one for every day of the week."

Lizzie liked that idea and began to prance in her beauty pageant style, waving at her admirers. I leaped on ahead of her, feeling a whole lot better about that stupid dog and what he had done to her doll.

That was the beginning of our shoplifting career. It was like a door opening into a whole new world . . .

A door that beckoned us across its threshold, then shut to keep us from getting back out.

TWENTY-ONE

Around the time we were nine, something happened that all those scientists who study twins would have loved. I came down with chickenpox, so I had to stay home from school. Normally, Lizzie would have stayed home, too, since she never liked to go anywhere without me, but that day was picture day, and it was important to her to get her face in the yearbook where everyone could see.

She got all fixed up that morning, wearing stolen makeup that she didn't quite know how to apply and a glittery blouse she had taken from Wal-Mart a couple of weeks earlier.

"It's not fair." I scratched at my bumps. "I wanted my picture, too. I hate chickenpox."

"You can use my picture. We're just alike."

"Only I never would have worn such a flashy shirt. I was gonna wear that Western shirt with the fringe under the arms."

Lizzie gave me that poor-little-tasteless-Kara look. "It has a big stain right on the front of it. That's why somebody gave it away."

"I don't care. It wouldn't have shown in the picture. Now there'll be an empty place in the yearbook where my face ought to be."

"I'll tell them to put 'See Lizzie Holbrooke' under your name."

She bopped off to school, leaving me itching and feverish, while Deke and Eloise slept their gambling night off.

I was watching Jerry Springer about midmorning when I got this pain in my arm. I yelled out and clutched it. Don't ask me how I knew, but this awareness came over me, and I knew without a doubt that Lizzie had been hurt . . . that she was crying.

I ran out of the house in the T-shirt and leggings I'd slept in and tore through the woods until I made it to the school. A crowd was huddled on the playground, and I headed straight for it.

"Lizzie! Lizzie!" I pushed through the people and found her sitting on the ground, crying and holding her arm. It was clearly broken.

Her pretty shirt was stained and torn. I sat down next to her on the dirt. "What happened?"

"I fell off the slide. It hurts, Kara!"

"You're telling me," I said, because my arm still ached in exactly the same place.

"Kara Holbrooke, you're just infecting the whole school."

Our teacher, Miss Monroe, jerked me to my feet. "You get on back home now."

"What about Lizzie?"

"We're taking her to the emergency room. That arm's sure enough broke."

"I'm going, too," I said.

"No, ma'am, you're not."

I crossed my arms and tilted my chin. "Yes, ma'am, I *am*. And if you don't hurry and take her, I'm gonna tell Deke and Eloise to sue the school for pain and suffering."

I'd been watching too much *LA Law* and knew just enough about lawsuits to be dangerous.

My threat must have sounded real, though, because no one called my bluff. They just loaded us both into a car and took us to the emergency room in Yazoo City. We didn't have a phone at home, since the phone company had written us off as a bad risk, so they weren't able to reach Deke and Eloise. One of the janitors from the school went to our trailer personally to find them, but they must have been sleeping so deep that they never even woke up.

We had a big adventure as they casted Lizzie's arm, feeding us suckers and trying to keep the patients away from me so they wouldn't catch chickenpox.

When we got back home, Eloise sat at the sticky kitchen table without her wig, drinking black coffee.

"Lizzie broke her arm."

Eloise screwed up her face and examined the cast. "Girl, who put this on your arm?"

"A doctor," Lizzie said.

"*What* doctor?"

"Some doctor at the emergency room."

"You went to the *hospital?*" She got up and stormed back to get Deke. "Deke, get up! Them teachers took Lizzie to the hospital and ran us up a bill." She came back and stared down at us, like we'd just burned the house down or something. "What's the *matter* with you? We can't afford no emergency room."

"They couldn't find you," I said. "Her arm was real bad."

By now, Deke had come from the back, sleepy-eyed and clutching his head. "What fool thing caused you to break your arm?"

"I fell." Lizzie was in no mood for long explanations.

"Well, I'll tell you one thing. That school had better pay every penny of that bill, 'cause I ain't shucking out a dime. I can promise you that."

I ushered Lizzie into our room, and the two of us curled up on the bed as Deke and Eloise railed in the next room.

TWENTY-TWO

We celebrated our tenth birthday by stealing *The Boxcar Children* from the library and Lizzie's favorite necklace from the Wal-Mart in Yazoo City when we went with Eloise on one of her rare shopping trips. Because Lizzie feared that Eloise would find the necklace and keep it for herself, we set out to find a hiding place in our woods.

I thought of the perfect place. There was an old dead tree a few yards from the path that led to the railroad track. Weather must have split it in half, because no one would have chopped it six feet up, then left the trunk lying there on the ground. Lizzie and I used it often as our stage.

Lizzie would perform her talent competitions there, and I would perform my makeshift gymnastic routines as if it were a balance beam. The trunk of the tree had rotted down the side, leaving a hollow hole inside that only we knew about.

We named it the Secret Tree and anointed it our official hiding place. Lizzie hid her necklace there in a Ziploc bag she'd dug out of the trash at school after some kid had thrown it away in his wadded lunch bag. I wasn't ready to leave my book. Instead, I curled up on a bed of rotting leaves and read until the light got too dim, while Lizzie acted out an entire play she had made up on the spot, performing every part with as much passion as if she'd been on Broadway.

When it got too shadowy to read, we started home by way of the Goodwill bin on Fourth Street, where we occasionally found treasures that hung from the depository hole or were left in boxes on the ground outside it.

We found an old lace slip, and Lizzie acted as if she'd found a bolt of Parisian lace. "I can make a veil with this! Look, Kara. We can be brides."

I usually didn't get excited about the things that rang Lizzie's chimes, but I have to admit, I liked this idea. She draped the lace bottom of the slip over her hair, and I pictured myself in it. I dug into the box for more prizes and came up with a white, flowing lady's nightgown.

"Why would anybody want to throw this away?" I held the soft fabric against my face.

"Maybe it's somebody rich who got all new stuff."

I shot her a *yeah, right* look. "There's nobody rich in Barton."

We found a pair of high-heeled shoes with curled-up soles, an old sweater with fur around the collar, and a glittery handbag with some of the sequins falling off.

Delighted with our finds, we shook the contents out of a

garbage bag leaning against the bin, piled our treasures in it, and hurried back to our Secret Tree. We stuffed everything inside, then covered it with leaves so no one happening along would notice it.

When we got back to our trailer, we were in a great mood and singing "Happy Birthday" to ourselves . . . We came out of the woods and noticed right away that Deke and Eloise's car was gone, but another, ritzier car was parked on the gravel drive.

Curious, we went around the trailer and saw the woman standing on the porch, knocking on the door.

"Nobody's home, lady," Lizzie called out.

The woman swung around and caught her breath at the sight of us. You would have thought she'd seen two little red-haired ghosts wandering up, because she burst into tears. "Lizzie! Kara!"

I hung back, suspicious, but Lizzie took a tentative step up the porch steps.

The woman stooped down to get eye level with us and took Lizzie's hand. "Look at you," she said with a quivering voice. "You've grown so much."

Lizzie just gave her a blank look, and I inched up behind my sister. The woman reached for me. "Kara, you're so beautiful." She touched my long curls. "I'm glad they haven't cut your hair."

How in the world could she tell us apart? Eloise and Deke were always getting us mixed up. I frowned, trying to figure it out. "Who are you?"

"I'm Amanda," she whispered. "Don't you remember, honey?"

Amanda Holbrooke! I stiffened and looked at Lizzie, and she looked back with a pained expression, like we'd just walked into some kind of trap. We hadn't expected *the* Amanda Holbrooke, who'd stolen our fortunes, to look as pretty as this woman did . . .

Nobody in Barton dressed like her. She had on a bright yellow dress and a shiny gold chain around her neck. Her earrings had yellow and orange and red in them, and they dangled around her cheeks. Her hair was blonde and soft and swept down to her shoulders, and she smelled like heaven.

"It's your birthday," she said to both of us. "Ten years old." She dabbed at the tears in her eyes. "How did you celebrate?"

I didn't think we should tell her that we had stolen a book and a necklace, or dug through the Goodwill bin. For all I knew, she had come to trick us into confessing.

"I don't know," Lizzie said.

Amanda straightened and reached for a bag she had left beside the door. "I brought you presents."

Lizzie's eyes rounded, and she smiled over at me. She was so easy, but I knew better. I hung back, watching the bag for something cruel to jump out.

Amanda pulled out a package wrapped in glittery paper and tied with a shiny gold ribbon. She handed it to me, then got Lizzie's out and gave it to her.

I was nervous opening it, and I couldn't stop looking up at the woman and wondering how she knew that I was Kara and

Lizzie was Lizzie, and how she knew about our birthdays, and why she had come to bring us presents. But as suspicious as I was after all we'd been told, I couldn't resist the shiny package.

Lizzie got into hers first and let out a loud yell as she saw the Special Edition Barbie in a frilly, golden evening gown. "Wow!"

I tore into mine then and saw that I had another one, only with a different dress. I looked up at Amanda. "She's pretty." I didn't mean to smile at her.

I heard tires on the gravel then and turned around to see Eloise and Deke pulling into the driveway behind the woman's car.

Amanda's face changed. "I have to go." She bent down to look into both of our faces. "I love you, sweethearts. Happy birthday." She kissed us both and hugged us real tight.

Eloise jumped out of the car. "Call the police, Deke! That woman's trying to kidnap our children!"

Amanda just ignored them and started down the porch steps. "My phone number is on the cards in the bag. Keep it, girls. If you're ever in trouble, call me."

I stared down at her as she started to her car, trying to ignore Deke's hollering and Eloise's nasal accusations. Eloise was so upset that her wig had turned almost backward on her head. Deke started trudging toward Amanda, chicken slime making a sucking sound on the dirt as he walked. "We got a restraining order against you the last time you tried to kidnap these girls, woman!"

She seemed not to hear him as she got into her car. They

were blocking her in, so she put the car into drive and made a U-turn on our lawn, drove past both of them, and back out onto the street.

"*That's* Amanda Holbrooke?" I asked as Eloise raced into the house to call the police.

"That's her, all right," she said. "The woman who killed your daddy."

I looked down at the Barbie in my hands, but she wasn't as beautiful as she'd been a few minutes earlier. I didn't know why the woman who killed my daddy and stole my fortune would have given me a doll like this. All I knew was that I didn't want it anymore.

There was a big commotion in the house then as Eloise got the police there. They filed a report against Amanda Holbrooke.

Eloise didn't notice the presents Amanda had brought us, and even though I didn't want them anymore, I knew they might be of some use. Lizzie and I managed to keep them hidden until we could take them to the Secret Tree. I found the card the woman had mentioned, opened it, and read her cursive scrawl.

I'm always here if you need me, it said. Her number was written in big letters under her name.

"I thought she was nice," Lizzie said, combing her Barbie's hair. Mine lay on the bed, neglected and unloved.

"She's not nice, Lizzie, if she killed our daddy."

"She didn't look like a killer."

"They never do."

"Well, if she did it, then how did she do it? And why did she do it?"

"I don't know," I said. "But I'm gonna find out."

That night, when the police were gone and Eloise and Deke had finally settled down, I ventured into the tiny living room and asked the question that had been plaguing both me and Lizzie.

"How did she kill our daddy?"

Eloise rarely had time for our questions, but tonight she devoted her full attention to it. Deke joined her and sat down in his sock feet, still reeking of chicken guts.

"Truth be told, she killed your mama, too. Our precious daughter, rest her soul. And then she killed your daddy, and would have killed you, too, if the police hadn't stopped her."

Deke jumped in. "She was trying to get you on an airplane and take you to some country where they don't care if people kill kids."

I couldn't picture a woman who smelled like that trying to kill us. Fear shivered up my back at how close we'd come to being killed just this afternoon. "Why did she want to kill us?"

"Sit down, Lizzie," Eloise said to me, but I hardly noticed she'd mixed us up again. I was too stunned at the tone of her voice. It was almost gentle. "You, too, Kara," she said to Lizzie.

Lizzie came and sat down next to me on the torn-up ottoman.

"You girls are probably old enough to know the truth by now," Eloise said. "You see, your grandfather was Paul Holbrooke. He was a real rich man. Had billions of dollars."

"Practically lived in a castle," Deke added.

"That's right." Eloise nodded. "And he had a son named Jack, who was your daddy."

It sounded like a fairy tale in which I was a character. I hung on every word.

"So see, your daddy was rich. And he married your mama, Sherry, who was our girl. But just shortly after she had you, she died in a car wreck. Nobody ever proved it, but I've always known that woman Amanda killed your mama so she could finagle her way into your daddy's life. She wanted his money, see, and so she made him fall for her and she married him."

It took a moment for my mind to catch up with her story. "That Amanda lady was married to my daddy?"

"That's right. She married him, and lo and behold, next thing you know, your daddy turns up dead, along with your rich grandma and grandpa."

"Plane crash," Deke said. "Only we know that she did something to make it crash. Put a bomb in there or messed with the engine . . . we don't know what. All's we know is they're dead, and she gets all their money."

A strange sense of injustice swelled inside me, as if something important, something I *needed,* had been taken from me.

"Well, we come to get you as soon as we could." Eloise dabbed at her eyes, but I didn't see any tears. "We knew that the money rightfully belonged to you two girls, and that she'd just as soon kill you as look at you to make sure that nobody got in her way."

"We even went to court to try to get your money," Deke said. "By all rights we should be living in a mansion and driving limousines and flying to Paris once a week to shop. But that woman managed to finagle that money away."

Lizzie reached for my hand, and I leaned in against her. We listened carefully, our eyes darting from Eloise to Deke and back again, like spectators at one of the tennis matches over at the high school.

"We got some money, all right," Eloise said, "but it was just a drop in the bucket, and we only get one check once a year, and it don't hardly make ends meet . . ."

"But see, she knows that when you girls grow up, you'll have the right to sue her for her part." Deke spoke with more passion than I'd ever seen in him. "She knows you can pull the whole rug right out from under her. Then we'll *all* be billionaires and be sitting pretty, and she'll be the one out in the cold."

"That's why she wants you dead," Eloise explained. "If you don't never grow up, then you can't sue her for your part."

Lizzie squeezed my hand, and I knew it meant that she wasn't sure whether to believe them. That Barbie doll had really clouded her thinking. "She didn't act like she wanted us dead," Lizzie said. "She seemed nice."

"Are you calling me a liar, girl?" That gentleness in Eloise's voice was gone. "You don't expect her to have horns and a forked tail, do you? Of course she seems nice. But she acted all nice to your daddy, too, right up to the time she killed him. And if we hadn't come along, you two would be road kill."

I'd seen enough stiff cats lying on the side of the road to know that I never wanted to be like that. But I had a hard time being grateful that Eloise and Deke had rescued us.

"What did she say to you?" Eloise demanded.

"Just . . . happy birthday," I said quietly. "That we had grown."

I looked at Lizzie and saw that she had tears in her eyes. She held her eyes wide to keep them from falling. "She said we looked beautiful."

I might have known Lizzie would get hung up on that. Compliments just blew her away. If some dangerous killer came along and told her he wanted to strangle her, but that she really looked pretty, she would probably just stretch out her throat for him.

"Anything else?" Deke leaned close, real interested.

"She told us she loved us." I recognized the defiance in Lizzie's voice, and I squeezed her hand to silence her, but she went on. "She didn't act mean."

"They never do." Eloise got in her face, her eyes narrowing into slits. "Now you look at me, young lady. You promise me that if you ever see her again, you'll run. Do you hear me? You'll come get Deke or me, or you'll call the police and turn her in. If you don't, we could all wind up dead."

I was still trying to figure out the part about how we were rich. "You mean, when we grow up, we're gonna be rich?"

"Not if she gets her claws into you," Deke said.

"But if we stay away from her, we could have a lot of money and live in a castle?"

"Something like that." Eloise shifted her massive rump in her chair. "When you turn eighteen, we can get us a lawyer and sue the stew out of her. You can say that you were robbed of your inheritance, and yes, then you'll be rich and can buy me and Deke a mansion of our own, and dole out hundred-dollar bills like they were pennies."

"Will we be famous?" Lizzie asked.

"Of course you'll be famous," Deke said. "The Billion Dollar Babies? Darn right, you'll be famous."

I went to bed that night wishing I'd never taken the Barbie doll from that woman, wishing I'd spit in her face when she kissed me on the cheek . . . wishing I'd never gotten that scent in my brain. I took her card with the phone number and tore it up into little pieces and flushed it down the toilet. Lizzie wouldn't let me do hers, though. Instead, she memorized the number and kept the card so she could sniff it, because it smelled like Amanda's perfume.

I lay in bed for a long time, thinking about the mother and father and the grandpa and grandma she'd stolen from me, and all the money that we could have had. And I thought that if I ever saw her again I would kick her right in the shin and run.

I looked over at Lizzie before I went to sleep. She was curled up next to me under a dingy sheet, holding Eliza in one arm and that brand-new, decked-out Barbie in her other.

TWENTY-THREE

I never expected Lizzie to keep that phone number for so long, because I had flat forgotten about it. But she must have practiced saying it over and over in her head, as if it were some magical chant that would bring our fairy godmother.

When we were thirteen, Lizzie finally had cause to use it.

We hadn't known how the night would turn out when Steve Crawley and Teddy Malone, two sixteen-year-olds from the high school, asked us to go to the state fair with them. Lizzie and I had developed early, and we looked more like fifteen. The boys seemed to like our long, curly red hair, and I have to admit we got a lot of looks whenever we went anywhere. It seemed like overnight we went from being treated like little girls to getting instant attention when we walked through the truck stop to get a Coke.

And it suited me just fine. Lizzie said I was boy crazy, but

I just told her I was mature for my age. Most of the men who blew through town in their eighteen-wheelers grossed me out, and I wouldn't have given them the time of day.

But Steve and Teddy seemed pretty harmless and they were fun to be around. We had never been on a car date with boys before, and when they waved around a wad of money they'd earned mowing yards and said they would win us some stuffed animals and show us a real good time, well, how could we turn them down?

We picked a night when we knew Deke and Eloise would be at the casino, not because they wouldn't have let us go, but just because we didn't want them to come out snooping around for the money we would spend and find some way to trick Steve or Teddy out of it.

We drove the hour to Jackson and inched our way along the off-ramp near the fairgrounds, searching for a place to park. Teddy wasn't a very good driver. We'd had some close calls as we drove over the stack, where I-20 and I-55 crossed.

Once we got Teddy's rusty old car parked up on the curb along the ramp, we trekked around the fence to the entrance. The smells of corn dogs, cinnamon rolls, corn on the cob, and cotton candy wafted over the grounds, so unlike the air we breathed in Barton. The sun had already gone down, and we marveled at the way the double Ferris wheel lit up as it rolled over the city. From where we walked, we could hear the screams from the Matterhorn and the loud, competing heavy-metal sounds from each of the rides.

I thought I might burst with excitement.

I looked at Lizzie to see if she was prancing and waving,

but she was walking normally, gaping at the rides like we'd entered a whole new world.

"I want to ride the Ferris wheel first." She turned around and walked backward as she spoke, her face glowing. "And then the bumper cars. And I want one of those big Tasmanian Devils and a goldfish."

"I ain't buying you a goldfish," Teddy said. "I didn't come here to buy no goldfish."

"You don't *buy* them, genius," she said. "You win them."

"Yeah, but you got to pay about a hundred bucks to win one. And then how would you get it home?"

Lizzie looked disappointed, but I agreed with Teddy. There was no way we could get a goldfish home in one piece, and once we got it home, what did she think we'd do with the thing?

"I want cotton candy," I said. "Smell that, Lizzie. Have you ever smelled anything so nice?"

"We ain't eating all my money away." Steve Crawley tried to put his arm around me, but I shrugged it off. I didn't want to be too rude to him, since he was paying my way and all, but I didn't feel like being all lovey-dovey with some guy who was telling me I wasn't going to eat his money.

He got this insulted look on his face, like maybe this wasn't going to turn out like he hoped. "Hey, you're not going to act all seventh grade, are you?"

I threw up my chin. "If you're so worried about what grade I'm in, why'd you ask me to come?"

"Because you look better than any of the girls in my grade."

He said things like that all the time, which is why we hung

out with him. I don't mind telling you that it made me feel the slightest bit superior to those girls who looked down their noses at us because we were young or had less money. But I knew their daddies all farmed, or worked at the chicken plant or the paper mill, and most of them smelled as bad as Deke did when they came home from work each day.

We got to the entrance, and the boys shelled out the money for the ticket, and I had to keep myself from leaping and running along ahead of them.

They indulged us by taking us on the Ferris wheel first. I went with Steve and Lizzie went with Teddy, and when the thing stopped with us at the top, Steve tried to put the move on me. I elbowed him in the ribs and made him mad, and then I was sorry for it, because I had to sit there with him until the wheel rolled down again.

I looked behind us and saw that Teddy was kissing Lizzie. Her arms were crossed over her chest, but she wasn't resisting him. And she said *I* was boy crazy.

"Why are you so hostile?" Steve glared at me. "Here I am spending my life savings on you, and you take the first chance to crack my ribs."

"Oh, don't be such a baby. I was just playing."

"I don't know if I want to spend any more on somebody who's so hostile."

I started thinking that I didn't know if I wanted to spend another minute with somebody who kept holding that money over my head, like it was a big stick he was going to beat me with if I didn't act right.

"You know, Lizzie and I can get our own money. We don't *need* you." I looked back over my shoulder. Lizzie hugged the side of her chair and looked down into the crowd. I saw Teddy with his arms around her, coaxing her into a longer make-out session, and I felt like screaming for him to leave her alone.

But Lizzie was going to have to say it, and she didn't.

Finally, the Ferris wheel began to move, making me a little sick as it swept to the ground and back up again, the delicious-smelling wind blowing through my hair.

I watched a group go to the ticket booth and buy a roll of tickets. One guy in a red shirt took out a wad of money like Steve's and Teddy's and shoved it into his pocket. I got to thinking how easy it would be to take somebody's wallet in a crowd. I started wondering how it would be if we did that and found a stack of twenties in it. Then Lizzie and I wouldn't have to do anything Steve and Teddy said.

When we got off the Ferris wheel, I felt a little wobbly. Lizzie's clothes and hair were all disheveled, and she was in a real cranky mood.

I grabbed her and pushed her hair back from her ear so she could hear my whisper. "How about we ditch these guys and steal some guy's wallet? Then we can do whatever we want."

Lizzie looked at me like I needed a straitjacket. "How would we get home?"

"Well, maybe we can make up with them before they leave. Or find somebody else to take us home."

"I don't want to make Steve and Teddy mad and wind up walking home," Lizzie said. "But we could take a wallet, and then they wouldn't keep complaining about all the money they have to spend on us."

The guys started telling us that they needed for us to walk over to the coliseum with them, into the empty stables where they kept the animals for the agricultural shows. It was dark in there, and I knew what they wanted. But they kept hounding us to go with them.

"You guys go wait for us there," I told Teddy and Steve. "Lizzie and I need to find a bathroom. We'll be right over."

They looked doubtful that we could come.

"How would we get home if we lost you?" I asked Teddy. "What do we look like? Idiots?"

They seemed satisfied with that, and I realized that we would have to keep our promise to join them. We picked out a guy with a bulging wallet in his back pocket. We decided that Lizzie would bump into the guy from the front, distracting him, and I would grab the wallet and run.

We followed him into the most densely crowded area and watched as he tried to get through the people.

Then we made our move.

Lizzie ran around in front of him, then stopped suddenly, making him almost trip over her. I grabbed his wallet, but it didn't come out as easily as I thought it would.

His hand came back, and he tried to turn around, but before he could stop me, I got it out.

He grabbed my wrist. I yelled, and Lizzie started running. I managed to slip free, but he yelled behind us. "Catch her! She's got my wallet."

We ran together, dodging people and trying to lose him in

the crowd, but he was right behind us, running like a madman. He caught up to us, grabbed each of us by the hair . . .

And there we were, face-to-face with two cops who grabbed us and wrestled handcuffs onto us.

"I didn't do anything!" I cried. "He was chasing us for no reason!"

But the cop reached into my pocket, where I'd stuffed the man's wallet, and there it was, incriminating me like some kind of smoking gun. I was sunk.

"She was in on it, too!" The man pointed to Lizzie. "She bumped into me, trying to distract me. They're in it together."

"We didn't do anything!" I cried again, but it was futile. The two cops escorted us back to the gates and put us into their squad car.

∞

I had never been to jail before, so I didn't know what to expect. Since we had no identification and refused to tell them our names, the police assumed we were older and took us to the Hinds County Detention Center just a few blocks from the fairgrounds.

They took us through a heavy steel door that crashed shut behind us, then searched us in a garagelike room. Finally, they threw us together into a holding cell made of yellow cement blocks with bars over the glass.

"Nice going, Kara." Lizzie glared at me like I had just ruined her life.

"Hey, if you'd distracted him like you were supposed to—"

"I did the best I could. I didn't know you were going to fight him for his wallet! I thought you were just going to slip it out of his pocket."

I got up and went to the window. Through the bars, I could see into the processing room. A couple of deputies moved around in there, clearly unconcerned about us. "*Now* what are we gonna do? We can't call Eloise and Deke. They're not home. And there's no way to get in touch with Steve and Teddy."

"We can call *her.*"

I turned back and looked at Lizzie, knowing exactly who she meant. She was talking about Amanda, the woman who wanted us dead.

"Are you *crazy?*"

She stood with her face close to mine, daring me to protest. "She said to call her if we ever needed her. I know her number by heart."

"Why? Why would you know that by heart?"

"Because I thought I might need it someday."

"So you *planned* to wind up in jail for pickpocketing?"

Hot accusation burned in Lizzie's eyes. "I never planned to wind up in jail, *period.* But I'm here now, thanks to you. You got any better ideas?"

"Yeah. We can give them our names and tell them we're thirteen, and they'll realize we don't know better . . ."

"They'll put us in juvenile detention," Lizzie said. "I don't want to go to juvenile detention."

"You'd rather be in jail?"

"No. I want *out.* If we wait until Eloise and Deke get home, they might make us rot here. They sure aren't going to shell out any *money* to get us out of here."

"And she will?"

"She said if we needed her to call. Maybe she'll come."

"I don't trust her," I said. "Don't you remember what Eloise and Deke told us about her?"

"Maybe they lied."

"They didn't. That's the one true thing they've ever said."

"How do you know?"

"Because it makes sense!" I was losing my patience with Lizzie. Sometimes she could be so dense. "Why else would we be dirt poor and living with Deke and Eloise if our grandfather was a billionaire? She took all our money, that's why. She killed our parents and took our money."

"I'm calling her." Lizzie knocked on the glass. "You can get comfortable in here if you don't want to come, but I'm getting out."

"If you can figure out some way to get her to bail us out without our having to be alone with her, then okay. But I'm not giving her a chance to finish off our family."

When the deputies came to process us, Lizzie got to make her phone call. I watched her dial the number. Her face was pale as she waited for it to ring.

"Can I please . . ." She stopped and cleared her throat. It had gotten all raspy. "Can I please speak to Amanda Holbrooke?"

I waited a moment to see what would happen. I fully expected Amanda to hang up on her or laugh her head off that Lizzie had actually used the number.

They must have asked who was calling, because Lizzie said in a weak voice, "Lizzie Holbrooke."

Even though it was night and that was probably her home number, the person put her on hold. The deputy sat at her desk, typing information into a computer. We had finally given her our names, and she'd quickly discovered that we were thirteen. She'd allowed us the phone call, probably in hopes of turning us over to someone who could pay our fine, before she had to go to a lot of trouble figuring out what to do with us.

"Yes . . . ," Lizzie said, and I looked up at her again. "Hi. Uh . . . remember when you came on our tenth birthday? And you gave us the Barbies? And you gave us the phone number? Well . . . we're kind of in trouble . . . and I wondered . . ."

Her voice broke off, and I knew that Amanda woman was talking ninety-to-nothing, probably giving her an earful about her nerve in calling so late.

"Yeah . . . we're in jail, see . . . there was a misunderstanding at the fair, and some guy said we took his wallet . . . Hinds County . . . downtown . . . yes . . . We can't reach Deke and Eloise . . . Yes, Kara, too . . ."

It didn't seem that Amanda was laughing or chastising her at all. Lizzie seemed downright calm. When she hung up the phone, I gaped up at her. "What did she say?"

"That she would be here in fifteen minutes."

"Really?"

"Really. See? She's nice."

"No, she's not," I said. "She hates us and wants us dead, just like our parents."

"Well, she can't do it here, in front of God and the deputies and everybody."

"So how are we gonna get home?"

"We'll get her to drop us off at the fairgrounds. We'll find Steve and Teddy."

∞

Amanda got to the jail exactly when she said she would and managed to take care of our paperwork and bail us out.

She looked a lot more casual than she had when we'd seen her on our front porch. She was wearing jeans and tennis shoes and a rust-colored sweater that would have looked great with my hair. She burst into tears again when she looked at us.

"You're as tall as I am!" she exclaimed in a broken voice. "Oh, you're so beautiful."

Lizzie shot me a look that said I was way wrong about this woman.

She ushered us into her Park Avenue, gushing about how good we looked and how glad she was that we had called her.

"You can just drop us back at the fairgrounds," I said. "We can find our ride."

Amanda looked at me like I was too cute for words. "I can't do that, Kara. It's not safe for a thirteen-year-old girl to be at the fair alone on a Saturday night. I can't believe your grandparents let you come here in a car with boys who drive."

"They didn't exactly *let* us," Lizzie said. "They wouldn't have cared, though."

"Well, I care." The thing is, she sounded convincing. I figured she must have practiced it all the way over. "I'll drive you all the way home, and then I'll talk to them and tell them what I think of the supervision they give you."

"Hey, we're thirteen, okay?" Who did she think she was, talking about us like we were little kids who needed a baby-sitter?

"They should take better care of you. You could have been killed in a car accident on the way there, riding with boys who are barely old enough to drive . . . staying out until all hours—"

"I wouldn't say anything to Deke or Eloise if I were you," Lizzie said. "Deke might get his gun."

She was silent for a long time as we left the interstate for Highway 49. "How do they treat you? Do they hurt you?"

"They're okay," I said.

"But Deke . . . does he . . . do anything . . . inappropriate?"

Lizzie glanced at me, and I could see that she didn't understand the question any more than I did. "What do you mean *inappropriate?*"

Amanda swallowed and looked real uncomfortable. But the question must have been important to her, because she kept pressing. "I mean . . . is everything all right there?"

"It's fine," Lizzie said.

"I could take you home to my house if you're not safe there," she said. "It would take some doing, since there's supposed to be a restraining order to keep me from coming near you. But if we could prove that you were in danger there, or that your grandparents were abusing you in any way . . ."

I thought of the closets, but we hadn't been shoved in there in a while. Deke sometimes looked at us in that lustful way men had and got all nice and stuff, talking in a sweet, gentle voice that he'd never used with us in his life. When he came into our rooms at night, stroking our legs and talking that way, it always turned my stomach. But I could handle him.

Besides, the last thing I wanted was to wind up a sitting duck for Amanda Holbrooke. I kept thinking about that money, and how we would be able to sue her when we turned eighteen, and that we would be rich then and she would be the one left penniless.

The house was dark when she got us home, and since we wouldn't give her any information about abuse, she had to let us go in.

Lizzie held back at the car. "Thank you for helping us."

"Anytime." Amanda smiled at her. "Lizzie, I'm serious. Call me anytime you're in trouble. I'll always come for you. I mean it, now. Kara, do you hear me? Day or night."

I wondered again how she knew us apart. I was already halfway up to the house, and that big black mutt I hated came bounding up, jumping up on me with his dirty paws. I fought him down and got to the front door.

I turned back before going in and saw Amanda hugging Lizzie and planting a kiss on her cheek.

I felt a momentary, irrational surge of jealousy, but I went in and tried to shake it out of my mind. Lizzie came in moments later.

"See? She isn't like they said."

"She's *just* like they said!" I told her. "She just wants us to drop our guard."

"If she wanted us dead, she could have killed us on the way here."

"No, she couldn't. Not when the police had just handed us over to her. If we wound up dead, they would know who did it. She's just waiting for the right time." I sat down on the bed, angry at the way the night had turned out. "I can't wait to grow up and sue the stew out of her."

But Lizzie was quiet as she got ready for bed.

TWENTY-FOUR

I didn't see Amanda again until we were fifteen, though I know now that she had someone watching us a lot of the time, taking pictures and following us.

Lizzie and I were pretty wrapped up in our own lives and didn't notice. By then, we had both taken jobs at the SOS Truck Stop, where we made more tip money in one night than we could have stolen at the state fair. I was the first to drop out of school so I could work more hours, and shortly after that, Lizzie dropped out, too. The whole idea of sitting in class all day and listening to those Hitler-type teachers, whose husbands worked in the same chicken slop that Deke did, was just too much to take. I didn't like people looking down on me when I got something wrong and I didn't like being told what to do.

Rules and me just didn't get along. Lizzie wasn't crazy about them, either.

Deke and Eloise didn't care if we quit school, since we were going through one of our poverty periods when Deke had already lost all of the annual check in a crap game at the Isle of Capri Casino, way back in March. By September, when we wanted to quit school, they needed whatever money we could bring home to help with the rent and the light bill. We learned quick not to brag about our tips, because it was a sure bet that if we went to bed with money, we'd wake up with none. Deke would steal it and say he didn't, or Eloise would take it right out in the open and claim that we owed her for all the years she'd cared for us.

So we took to stopping by the Secret Tree on the way home from work and stuffing at least half of our tip money in there to be used at some later date. It wasn't like we were saving up for anything. It was mostly gone by the end of the month, as we used it to buy clothes or makeup or the occasional bottle of whiskey that our boyfriends couldn't afford.

It was around this time that Deke became a real problem. In the mornings, when he and Eloise came in from a night at the Isle of Capri Casino, he would come in our room. His hand on my skin would startle me awake, and I would smell his rancid, liquor breath as his beady eyes looked me over.

I would move his hand away and tell him to leave me alone, but he was awfully strong for looking so scrawny, and alcohol only made him mean.

One morning, when I found him sitting on the edge of our bed like that, I got mean myself. "Get out of here, Deke!" I pulled the covers up over me.

Lizzie woke next to me, and her hand closed over my arm.

I caught Deke's roving hand. "You touch me again and I'll break something over your head."

He grinned. "I don't mean you no harm, now. You know that."

Lizzie sat up in bed, her back against the wall. "Deke, if you don't get out of here right this second, I'll scream for Eloise."

Neither of us had illusions that Eloise would defend us, but we knew she didn't take it well when he looked at any other woman.

"Hush, now!" He stood up, his grin gone. "I told you I don't mean you no harm."

"You've *always* meant us harm," I said. "We'll remember this when we turn eighteen and get our money."

That did it. Deke held his hands palm out. "I'm leaving. You got me all wrong. All I've ever done is took care of you."

After that, we got Steve Crawley to put a locking doorknob on our door, and we locked it when we went to bed at night. It kept Deke away from us most of the time.

∽

By this time, Steve Crawley was pretty much my regular boyfriend, though I stepped out now and then with one of the younger truckers who came through town. Steve had also dropped out of school and taken a job at the paper mill. He thought he was hot stuff because he didn't get slime all over his feet, but he still smelled to high heaven whenever he got off work.

Our favorite thing to do was to go to the high school football games, boozing it up, just to face off against the authorities there, who had nothing over us since we weren't students. And the homecoming game was a perfect opportunity to thumb our noses at authority. There everybody was, all set for the dance—the girls with their fu-fu dos and their gaudy corsages, and the guys all moussed and ready. We loved to go and make fun of the homecoming court in their fancy gowns, riding around the field in convertible cars, waving like Lizzie used to do when she pranced down the tracks.

I always wondered if Lizzie was sorry she'd never gotten the chance to do that for real, to go out on that field and wave and hear her name announced on the loudspeaker. She might have made it, too. We were both as pretty as any of those tramps at that school and we knew most everybody in town.

But if Lizzie felt that way, she denied it. She said she wouldn't be caught dead doing that and she was glad that we didn't have to get all frilled up and go to that dance afterward.

We had already put away a fifth of vodka—Lizzie and Steve and a guy named Mick . . . and me, of course—when we got to the game. We were having a good time, mocking the homecoming court and prancing with exaggerated zeal, waving at the crowd and laughing our heads off.

And then I saw her—Amanda Holbrooke—sitting up in the stands and watching us with this look on her face.

I grabbed Lizzie and told her to look without looking. She was wobbling a little from the vodka, but she looked up in the stands and saw the woman staring at us.

"What does she want?" I asked.

"I don't know," Lizzie said. "But it's creepy, her just watching us that way."

"Let's leave." I worried that she was going to make her move and do us in. "Crawley and some of the guys got a hotel room near the dance. They've got a bunch of booze. We can party all night long."

Lizzie glanced back up in the stands. "I guess . . ."

I hated it when Lizzie got distant and pensive and gave such hazy answers. Any other time, she would have been anxious to get to the room and another bottle. Even the guys wouldn't have bothered her, because we had learned pretty much what it took to keep a man. We weren't prudes or anything, and we'd been around the block, if you know what I mean.

Plenty of men had taken advantage of us, and sometimes we just decided to take advantage right back. It was all in the way you thought about things, we'd figured out.

So we headed out to the hotel near the dance and partied to the sounds of the bass guitar from the live band in the ballroom nearby. We provided a place—for a fee, of course—for those bona fide students who got thirsty and restless to come and have a drink.

By the time the dance was over, we had enough money to do something crazy, so Crawley took us down to Vicksburg to the Isle of Capri. We knew that Deke and Eloise would be there, but we didn't much care. We weren't old enough to get in, but Crawley had figured out a way to get us fake IDs.

We divvied up the money and went in to lay our bets,

Lizzie and me at the blackjack table, Crawley and the others who'd come with us at the crap table. We won a little, then lost a little, and I finally saw the appeal it had for Deke and Eloise.

We were just about to lay down the last of our money when I saw Amanda again across the room. She stood in the doorway, wearing a baseball cap and a pair of sunglasses, watching us in that creepy way she had. I knew she didn't want us to see her—either that, or she didn't want to chance having Deke or Eloise see her.

The light glistened off of her face, and I was pretty sure it was wet. Had she been crying?

Over us? Did she cry because we were still around, destined to steal her fortune when we reached the ripe old age of eighteen?

I turned my back to her again and tried to forget she was there. I went on with what I was doing and wound up losing the last of my money.

When I looked back over my shoulder, she was gone.

TWENTY-FIVE

It wasn't long after that I turned up pregnant. Now, I'm not stupid, and I know about taking precautions and all that, but it wasn't something I exactly planned. It happened one night when I was a little high and I wasn't all that concerned with keeping things safe. Next thing I knew, I was puking my guts out in the mornings and tired all the time.

Lizzie had had a few close calls herself, and one time even thought she was, so when it was my turn she knew just what to do. She had already located an abortion clinic down in Jackson and she told me she'd go with me if we could find somebody to take us.

Don't get me wrong now. It's not like I don't like little babies. I do. And I really did have the secret dream of someday having one or two of my own. But I wanted to wait until I at least reached eighteen and sued Amanda Holbrooke, until I got the millions or billions due me. Then I figured I could marry a real high-caliber guy and shower my babies with everything I didn't have growing up. I had visions of moving to a place that smelled clean and fresh, maybe in the mountains somewhere.

I'm not one of those people in denial about abortion killing babies. I'm clear thinking enough to know that people have babies, not blobs of tissue, that whatever that suction hose took out of my womb was the beginning of a real live person.

So it wasn't an easy decision for me. I had known women who had done it before, women who had found out they were pregnant one day, bopped down to Jackson the next, and had it behind them in time to go out dancing that night. But I wasn't like that.

We got Crawley to drive us there, and Lizzie sat next to him in the middle of the seat, holding my hand. She felt bad for me, because she could tell it was a hard thing. I'd carried around Missy, my doll, until I got too old for her, but I still slept with her every night. You don't practice taking care of a baby your whole life and then not grieve over killing the first one you have the chance to have.

I leaned my head against the window for the hour's drive, wondering what kind of mother I would have been, how I would have supported her. I don't know why I thought it was a girl, but it just seemed like it was. It was probably because my dolls had always been girls, and I had practiced dressing them up and fixing little bows in their hair. I couldn't really picture myself having a boy.

Anyway, I was wondering what kind of mother I would be,

an orphan who'd never really known a mother's love—at least not that I could remember. Would I mother like Eloise? Yelling at my child to stop squalling, then throwing her in the closet until she got quiet? Or would my instincts kick in, giving me that maternal grace that made me nurture my child and hold her when she cried.

It's okay, sweetie.

It wasn't fair that I hadn't grown up with a mother, and now I wasn't going to get to *be* one, either, at least not to this baby.

I was ashamed when tears started rolling down my face. I felt like there was already a person that I could see and feel and smell growing inside me, and because of some mixed-up set of circumstances, I was going to have her ripped away from me.

Crawley must have heard me sniff, because he said, "For crying out loud, you're not over there blubbering, are you? It's not gonna hurt, Kara!"

"How do you know it's not gonna hurt?" Lizzie shot back. "You ever done this?"

"Of course not, but I do know—"

"Then shut up, why don't you?" She wasn't usually so grumpy, but she was really worried about me. "And leave her alone. You've already done enough damage."

"Hey, I'm driving her there, ain't I?"

"It's the least you could do," Lizzie said.

"Oh, because you think I'm the father. Tell her, Kara. You don't really know who the kid's father is, do you?"

"Shut up, Crawley." My voice was weak, distant. "Just drive."

It made me sick that he was right. I figured it was probably him, but there was one other guy I stepped out with around that time, and Crawley knew about him, so I couldn't say for sure. It didn't really matter though. In a few hours it would all be over.

I wondered if the baby would hurt when they did whatever they did. I wondered if she would kick and cry. And I wondered what they would do with her when they got her out of me. Was there some little graveyard for these babies? Or did they just wrap them up in a garbage bag and throw them in the dump?

I knew these weren't the thoughts I should have been thinking. They weren't helping matters.

When we got to the parking lot of the clinic, I saw a group of people standing behind a fence across from the building. They waved signs with pictures of aborted babies.

I had to look away.

We got out of the car, and I guess Lizzie could see what this was costing me. She put her arm around me. "Come on, Kara. It's gonna be all right."

Crawley got out and looked at me over the roof of the car. "Uh . . . I think I'll just drive around town or something. How long you think this will take?"

Lizzie shot him a condemning look. "Coward."

"Me? What did I do?"

"You should face this like a man and come in and wait for her, you jerk! She doesn't need to come out of this and have to wait for you to drive back up."

"Then I'll sit out here in the car," he said. "But I don't feel like going in."

I don't know why I didn't argue with him, but the truth was, I didn't really want him going in with me. I wanted to do this with some kind of dignity, and I didn't see any way he could contribute to that.

We started walking up to the clinic, and I heard those people behind the fence starting to yell things at me.

"Honey, don't do it! Don't kill your baby."

"The Lord loves that child you're carrying. There are other options."

"You're hurting yourself! You'll never get over this!"

Lizzie walked like a barrier between me and them, and she hustled me into the building. She signed me in, and they gave me some papers to sign. My hands were shaking so bad I could hardly write.

When we'd turned the paperwork in and paid the cash that I'd brought from my tip money, she sat down beside me again. "What are you thinking?" she asked.

"I was just thinking about all that money we're gonna have when we turn eighteen and sue Amanda Holbrooke. And wondering if this will hurt our case any."

"What do you mean?"

"If they find out I had an abortion. Maybe they'll think I don't deserve the money. Maybe they'll think I'm a terrible person."

Lizzie patted my hand. "This won't even be brought up," she said. "It has nothing to do with our inheritance."

"But if it did come out, would it change things? Would the jury decide that I'm a lost cause? A sleep-around dropout from

Barton, Mississippi? Would they decide I'm a lowlife who would waste all that money?"

"I don't even know if they have juries," she said. "Do you think they do?"

"I don't know. But if it was just a judge who decided, would *he* think it? Would it be on my record somewhere?"

"No, it won't. It's all private. They can't go around showing your records to people."

I thought about that for a minute. "Maybe they'd be right. Maybe I don't deserve that money. Maybe I'm just supposed to be dirt poor all my life. Maybe that's what I am . . . just dirt."

Lizzie's eyes filled with tears. "That's not true. We deserve what we've got coming to us. And no abortion is going to change that."

"But it seems wrong, Lizzie. Like I'm gonna burn in everlasting hell if I go through with this." She didn't say anything, and I knew that, somewhere deep in herself, she understood why I thought that. "What am I talking about?" I asked myself on a whisper. "I'm probably going to burn in everlasting hell, anyway."

Lizzie grunted. "Why would you say that?"

"Because I can't picture somebody like me in any better place."

The door opened, and the nurse called me back. I stood and drew in a deep breath, trying to make myself brave. When I got to the door, I looked back at Lizzie. She looked pale and a little sick, and I almost hated leaving her there by herself. But

I didn't want her coming with me, even if they would have let her. There are some things you just have to do alone.

∞

A little while later, I came back out, but Lizzie wasn't in the waiting room. "She's in the bathroom," the receptionist told me. "I think she was feeling a little sick."

When Lizzie came out, her face looked gray, and I knew she had been throwing up. It was that twin thing between us. When one of us got hurt, the other one felt it.

Lizzie walked me back out to the car. I didn't feel like crying anymore. Instead, I felt empty and numb, like they'd made a mistake in there and ripped out my heart instead of my baby.

The group by the fence started yelling at me again.

"Honey, please come over here and talk to us!"

"God loves you. He can forgive you for what you've done!"

I didn't want to go over to them, and let them tell me that I was pond scum, that I needed to get down on my knees and repent. I didn't want to hear about God or forgiveness or any of that stuff. I just wanted to get out of there.

Crawley was asleep in the car, his mouth hanging open, with a shiny piece of dribble on his bottom lip. He made me sick. Why had I ever let him touch me?

Lizzie opened the door and punched his arm. "Wake up, Crawley. It's over."

He squinted up at me. "She okay?" He was too much of a wimp to address me directly.

"She's fine." Lizzie stepped back to let me get in first, but I didn't want to be near him. I didn't want to be near anybody. I got into the backseat and pushed aside a coat and two ratty shirts that had been in there for about six months. I knocked away the fast-food bags and the crumpled beer cans and the CDs scattered across the seat and floor.

I'd probably get some kind of infection from being in such a nasty car so soon after my *procedure,* as the doctor called it.

I rolled that smelly jacket up as a pillow and lay down on the seat, trying to pretend like I was asleep as we headed home.

Something had changed inside me, and I knew those people with the signs were right. I probably wouldn't ever get over it.

TWENTY-SIX

They told me I would be over it in a couple of days, that the cramping would stop and I'd be as good as new. But the night of the abortion, I started feeling spacey and cold. I had dreams about my baby lying in the garbage bin behind the SOS Truck Stop where I worked and people throwing rotten food and broken glass on her.

And I dreamed about hell. It seemed like a place I recognized, a place where I could never really rest, where danger breathed down on me from every angle, where it was hot and smelly and I could hardly catch my breath . . .

I dreamed about a jury sitting in a courtroom, laughing at the idea that I deserved any kind of inheritance. Me, a dropped-out, used-up redneck tramp . . . trying to get money out of Amanda Holbrooke, who *seemed* so sincere.

You're so beautiful. Look at you! I love you girls.

I can't say why her voice was mixed in with the images of dead babies and hell and the laughing jury, but it kept coming at the strangest times.

Call me if you ever need me. I'll always be there.

I saw images of her stricken face in the football stands, her tears as she'd brought us presents on our tenth birthday, her warm eyes and the way she smelled when she bailed us out of jail.

Then I saw that jury again, full of mocking, cackling executioners, telling me I didn't deserve anything, nothing at all, just a life in Barton where I belonged . . .

I woke up in a shiver and drew up the covers around me. I was freezing to death, and my head hurt, and I was too weak to get up and try to find another blanket. My stomach hurt like I'd been kicked, and cramps doubled me up. "Lizzie," I managed to say. "Lizzie . . ."

Next to me, she stirred. After a second, she turned over. "Kara, are you okay?"

"C-c-c-old." I could hardly get the words out.

She sat up and touched my forehead. "Kara, you've got fever. You're burning up!"

"B-b-blanket . . ."

Lizzie disappeared, and I heard that jury again, laughing and mocking. I saw Crawley with his buddies down at the truck stop, cackling about how I'd acted today, making fun of my tears, telling everybody what I'd done.

I felt somebody lifting me off of the bed, carrying me out into the brisk night air, dropping me onto the backseat of the car. I pulled my knees tighter to my chest, trying to stop the cramping.

It's okay, sweetie.

The whispered voice whirled through my mind, calming me into a soft, surface sleep.

∽

I woke in a hospital bed, and the first person's face I saw was Amanda's. She stood over me, her face wet and weary, her hair messed up, as if she'd just gotten out of bed and hadn't bothered to grab a brush.

I was frightened at first. Then shame ached through me because, for some reason I couldn't pinpoint, I didn't want her to know what I had done to my baby.

Lizzie came up beside her and touched my forehead. "Your fever's down, Kara." I could see the relief and fatigue on her face. "How do you feel?"

I tried to sit up, but they made me lie back down. "What happened?"

"You were hemorrhaging and you got an infection. Eloise and Deke weren't home, so I got Crawley to come over and drive us to the hospital. But then I couldn't pay."

Amanda touched my hand. "She called me, Kara. I'm so glad she did. You might have died if they hadn't taken care of you when they did."

I sighed. It was so stupid for Lizzie to involve her. "I would have been all right. Lizzie, we didn't need her."

"Kara, they wanted insurance or cash. I didn't have it."

"Hospitals treat poor people all the time."

"Maybe so, but I didn't want to bog things down in paper-work. I wanted them to help you."

Amanda's lips trembled as she looked down at me. "Kara, why don't you want me here?"

"I just don't. I don't need you here. I know you don't really care about us. You just don't want us coming after your precious money."

"What?"

"I know all about you." I tried sitting up again. I had an IV attached to my arm and a clip thing on my finger. I was wearing one of those twisted hospital gowns that some genius designed to give you the least amount of dignity when you were at your lowest.

Lizzie touched my shoulder. "Amanda just wanted to make sure you were all right. She came the minute I called her and took care of everything. I sent Crawley to the Isle of Capri to find Eloise and Deke, but they still haven't come."

"That surprises you?" I felt about a hundred years old . . . nothing surprised me anymore, especially about Eloise and Deke. I slid my feet off of the bed and tried to get up.

"What are you doing?"

"Going to the bathroom. And then I'm going to get dressed and get out of here."

"They don't want you to go home yet," Lizzie said. "Kara, I'm not taking you home."

"Well, I'm not staying here, in the *enemy* camp." My feet

hit the cold floor, and when my knees almost buckled, I realized just how weak I was. I tried not to show it.

"The enemy camp? Kara, it's a hospital."

"*She's* here," I pointed out. "She's paying, and she's ordering . . ." I pulled the tape off my arm and slid the IV needle out. "You've got a lot of nerve, coming in here and pulling this on me when I'm sick . . ."

"Pulling what on you?" Amanda guided me back to the bed. "Kara, I'm not here to hurt you. What in the world have they told you about me?"

"That we're your biggest nightmare. That you want us out of the way, just like you wanted our father and our mother and our grandparents out of the way, so you could get their money."

"Those are *lies!*" She bit the words out. It was the first time I had seen her angry. "None of that is true! All I've wanted my whole life is to watch over you and make sure you're okay. And I'm counting the days until you turn eighteen and you can come and live with me, and I can restore everything that's yours. I've taken care of HolCorp, your grandfather's company, and I've saved the mansion for you, and everything that's yours will be—"

My hand started bleeding where I'd pulled the needle out, and I mashed it with my finger and started looking for my clothes. "What did you do with my clothes, Lizzie? Where are my clothes?"

Amanda started to cry, and finally, she started toward the door. "Look, I'll just leave. You don't have to run out of here because of me, Kara. I'm not going to force myself on you."

"Fine. Leave, then."

She stopped at the door, her face all twisted and tears on her red cheeks. "Lizzie, don't worry about any of the paperwork or money. I've taken care of everything."

"I can pay my own way!" I shouted the words as she left the room, but I knew it wasn't true. Even all the money I'd saved in the Secret Tree wouldn't begin to cover what a hospital bill would cost.

"You shouldn't have done that, Kara." Lizzie walked the line between anger and gentleness. "She came when I called, just like she said she would. She's always come. The things they've told us about her aren't true. They didn't come, but *she* did."

"Take me home, Lizzie."

I should have known better than to try and bully Lizzie. She crossed her arms and stood firm. "Not until the doctor comes in and releases you and gives you the antibiotics you'll need at home. You're not going anywhere until that happens."

I disappeared into the bathroom then and found my clothes folded neatly next to the sink. They had brought me here in my sleepshirt and a pair of white leggings, but that would do just fine. I got into them, feeling a little wobbly, and cursed the abortion doctor who'd done this to me, and the boy who'd impregnated me, and Eloise and Deke who'd raised me, and my father who'd abandoned me, and Amanda Holbrooke . . . who tormented me.

I hated everybody and everything. I couldn't think of one person in the whole world that I didn't hate at that moment. I even hated Lizzie.

Most of all, I hated myself.

TWENTY-SEVEN

I soon pushed my hatred of everything that breathed to the back of my mind and decided to exist in this sorry world, to just make the best of it. I counted down the days until I was eighteen and could get that lawyer and clean out Amanda Holbrooke's bank account.

Lizzie and I worked hard, trying to save up the money it would take to pay the lawyer when the time came. At night, we hung out with Crawley and the others in our group and took to using drugs. At least they spiced up our mediocre lives.

One night, Crawley and a guy named Pendergrast decided to hold up a liquor store with their hunting rifles, just for the excitement, and because they were trying to raise the money to buy a Harley that old Judd Sargent, the owner of the SOS Truck Stop, was selling.

They wanted me and Lizzie to drive the getaway cars. We thought they were stark-raving mad, but we both got caught up in the thrill of the planning, so we were going to go along with it. We figured we weren't really hurting anything since we weren't actually going to wave a gun ourselves or even go into the store they were robbing. And we knew they wouldn't actually *shoot* anybody.

But at the last minute, Caroline Harper and Milly Luckett, two of the other waitresses at the truck stop, wound up getting sick with some rough kind of stomach virus. So Lizzie and I were both called in, and Crawley and the guys had to find somebody else to drive their cars.

It was a real good thing, because they got caught the minute they came out of the place, and every one of them was arrested and locked in the Yazoo County Jail. Crawley and Pendergrast wound up pleading guilty since they had their faces plastered all over the store security tapes, and they wound up with seven years each.

The others got different length sentences, depending on the competence of their lawyers.

It gutted our group of friends and left me and Lizzie with a lot of time on our hands. We spent it getting to know some of the regular truckers who came through. We decided that one of these days one of them would ride up in a top-of-the-line Mack Truck, and strut inside like Richard Gere coming in to get Debra Winger. He'd pick me up, like a bride being carried over the threshold—or Lizzie, whichever one of us was telling the story—and carry us out to live happily ever after, just like in that movie.

Then, and only then, we'd tell him we were the Billion

Dollar Babies, and he'd help us sue Amanda Holbrooke until we had what was rightfully ours. Then we'd live happily ever after, even though neither of us could picture what that would be like exactly.

That dream trucker never did amble into the SOS. Lizzie and I settled for lots of others, though, and the closer we got to eighteen, the more nervous and restless I got. Eloise and Deke spent an awful lot of time planning out their strategy and explaining it to us. We would get a lawyer the week we turned eighteen. We'd file a lawsuit, and it probably wouldn't even go to court. Amanda Holbrooke wouldn't want the bad publicity, so she'd probably settle out of court and write us a check for a few billion dollars. They were quick to point out all the things they'd done for us, and how we would have to split the money with them since they were so willing to walk us through this process and find us the lawyer and everything.

But I couldn't remember the last time any of Eloise and Deke's plans had worked out like they'd said. Besides, I kept trying to push back my hatred of the man we'd had to lock out of our room at night. I couldn't imagine Eloise having the smarts to carry something like this through. Plus, I didn't want to give her part of my money, any more than I wanted to share it with Amanda. Paul Holbrooke was *my* blood grandfather. Amanda only knew him by marriage, and Deke and Eloise, as far as I could see, had no claim on him—or his money—at all, except through us. I figured blood must mean something to judges and juries, and Lizzie and I had paid our dues. We deserved our share of the Holbrooke fortune.

I was thinking those exact thoughts while I was at work on my eighteenth birthday, scrubbing up dried-egg crud from the counter where some slob had just eaten.

I heard a crash, and Lizzie cursed. She had dropped a plate, and it lay in fragments on the concrete floor, along with the eggs and biscuits and gravy she'd been taking to a customer.

Irritated, I went over to help her clean up the mess. "What happened?"

"Blake the Snake pinched me, and I dropped it. He thinks he's Mel Gibson, that I'm just floating around here waiting for him to show me a little attention."

"Just ignore him."

"I'm not gonna ignore him. If he does it again, I'll break his nose."

Blake spoke up then. "A person could starve to death waiting to get served around here!" He was a fat, self-important guy, who liked the sound of his own voice as he barked out orders to the girls. "Go get me some breakfast."

Lizzie looked at the soggy biscuit and egg yolks in her dishrag. In a quiet voice, she said to me, "Shame to waste all this good food. He wants breakfast? Let's give it to him."

I couldn't help grinning. I liked the way Lizzie thought when she was mad. "I'll have your breakfast right out, Blake," she said in a sweet voice. She hurried back to the kitchen, plopped the mashed, dirty food into a plate, and smothered it all in scrambled eggs.

I got the mop and followed Lizzie out with the plate, bracing myself for what would happen when he bit into the mix. But Blake didn't notice the mess she'd just served him right away, because there was some kind of commotion at the window. I went to see what everybody was gawking at and saw a black limousine pulling up to the front of the parking lot. A chauffeur got out and opened the door.

Lizzie spotted her before I did. "It's *her!* Amanda Holbrooke."

I groaned. "What is *she* doing here?"

Lizzie's eyes practically twinkled as she watched her get out of the car. "She looks like a movie star. Like Princess Grace or something. I love the way she dresses."

"You expect me to eat this slop?" Blake hollered across the room. "There's a piece of that broke plate in here!"

Lizzie swung around. "What's the matter, Blake? You were in such a hurry for your breakfast—"

He flung the plate off the counter, which sent it crashing onto the floor again. This time the plate didn't break. His face was mottled red, and I thought his blood pressure was probably around stroke level.

Lizzie bent down and started cleaning up the mess again. I grabbed a clean dishrag from one of the bus trays and stooped down to help her, but I couldn't help watching the front door for Amanda to come in. I figured she knew it was the day we'd all been waiting for. The day we turned eighteen, when we were old enough to file a lawsuit and take all her money. That was probably serious business to her, and she probably hadn't slept in days for worrying over it.

I couldn't wait to hear what she was going to do about it.

She stepped into the smoky place, and heads began to turn. A hush seemed to fall over the room, even though the country song blaring over the speakers kept droning on.

The intercom overhead momentarily cut the music off. "Number thirty-one, your shower is ready," Belinda, our cashier, crowed.

A big, burly man in a dirty black T-shirt that didn't quite cover his massive paunch got up, dropped his cigarette on the floor, and stepped on it as he started toward the back.

Lizzie had gotten to her feet, still clutching the offensive plate. She watched Amanda with as much interest as I.

Amanda spoke to Belinda, and the intercom crackled again. "Lizzie, Kara, come to the front, please."

Lizzie shot me a look. "Be nice, Kara. Maybe she just wants to wish us a happy birthday."

"She's up to something," I said through my teeth. But I followed her to the front, nonetheless.

Amanda stood there, all pristine and out of place, smiling as we came toward her. She took Lizzie's shoulders first and kissed her on the cheek. "Happy birthday, sweetheart."

Lizzie looked at me, and I stiffened as Amanda took my shoulders. "Kara, you're as beautiful as ever. Oh, you're both a sight for sore eyes."

I never could understand how she knew me and Lizzie apart, but she always had. She'd always called us by name with confidence, even though Eloise still got us mixed up at least half the time. I knew that my face was just the slightest bit rounder than Lizzie's, and I had a mole on my right temple near the hairline, but that wasn't enough to tip off most of the people we saw every day.

But Amanda always seemed to know.

"Your father would be so proud of you." Her mouth trembled a little as she smiled. "Please, would you mind sitting in my car while we talk? I have birthday gifts and some things to tell you."

Lizzie's eyes widened. "Sure. I've never been in a limo before."

"*I* have." I thrust my chin high. "I dated that limo driver who worked for the casino. It's not that big of a deal."

But I followed them out the door, anyway, if for no other reason than to leave Blake in there high and dry, and hungry to boot.

There was a chauffeur at the car door, and he waited as we got inside. It was like a mini living room, nicer than the one in our trailer. I tried to look unimpressed, but Lizzie glowed as she looked around her at the gadgets and furnishings inside.

Amanda just watched us, this nervous smile on her face. "Can I offer you something to drink?"

"A *drink?*" Lizzie was practically gushing. "You got a kitchen in here, too?"

She leaned down and opened a small refrigerator. "I have some bottled water and some soft drinks. What do you like to drink, Lizzie?"

"Water's fine."

I ordered a Diet Coke. I knew Lizzie was trying not to take advantage, but hey, I didn't ask to be lured into a limousine, so I figured I might as well make the best of it.

I expected a canned drink, but Amanda got me a glass, filled it with ice, and poured the fizzing drink. She handed it to me.

Then she looked at me for a long time as tears rimmed in her eyes. "Well, the day has come that I've waited for since you were three." She stopped and swallowed hard. "You're finally eighteen, and now you can live wherever you want and make decisions for yourself."

"Yeah, and one of those decisions is to go after what is ours," I said. "What you stole from us."

Amanda didn't look mad. She only regarded me with sad eyes. "Look, I know this is not easy for you. You've been told a lot of lies all your life. I don't blame you for not trusting me, but I've come to tell you that you don't have to hire a lawyer or let your grandparents manipulate you into suing me. I want to share all of it with you, just as if you were children from my own womb. When you were very little, I promised your father that I would always take care of you. I've tried to do that. I've tried to watch over you all your lives, to be there when you needed me. But now I want you to come live with me as my own daughters, finish your high school education, go to college, learn the business . . ."

I could see that Lizzie was buying into it, believing that this woman would come here and take us back with her and treat us like we were her own kids. Boy, I thought, she must really see us as a threat. And I started thinking that we must have a pretty good case if she would go to these lengths to distract us from it.

"People don't just ride into town in a limo and offer you all that unless they want something," I said. "What do you want?"

"I just want you home, where you belong."

"Home?" Lizzie's expression was soft. "What do you mean, home?"

"I have a beautiful house up in Jackson. It was the mansion your Grandfather Holbrooke built. I had your playhouse from our old yard moved there, and I've kept all the things that were in your room. I've saved all the presents I've bought you over the years, all the things that I got for you but couldn't give you. All the letters that came back unopened, because Eloise and Deke wouldn't let you have them."

"I don't believe you!" I stared at her, trying to see some evil in her face. "Eloise warned us you would do something like this. She said you would do anything to keep us from getting in your way. She said you killed everyone in our family for that money. I don't know how you got away with it, but she warned us that we were a threat to you."

Amanda's face changed, and I could see the anger hardening her face. "You would believe that woman who squandered the ten million dollars meant for you and Lizzie?"

Lizzie's mouth fell open. "Ten million dollars? *What* ten million dollars?"

"They won it in court when they sued me for the estate. Didn't you even know about that?"

Lizzie looked at me, but my eyes were fixed on Amanda. "We knew there was a check that came every year, but we didn't know how much . . ."

"And why do you think they want you to sue me now? They want to keep living off of you, squandering your inheritance. They don't want to be cut out, because the payments have stopped coming. Without you two, they have nothing."

I have to admit that her words *sounded* true, and I sure knew that Eloise and Deke were capable of what she was saying . . . but I couldn't be sure.

Amanda dabbed at her eyes and drew in a deep breath. She reached into a compartment and brought out two wrapped boxes. "Look, let's just calm down for a minute. It's your birthday, and I brought you gifts."

She handed one to each of us. They were wrapped in silver paper, like something a department store would have done, with skinny little ribbons ruffled up at the top.

"I hope you don't think I'm trying to buy your love." Her voice shook. "I just want to show you a little of what belongs to you. All of what I own is yours. If you come back with me, you can live in my house and eat at my table. I can show you your history, remind you of what it was like when we were a family and your daddy was alive—" Her voice broke off, and for a minute she even had me going. "I've missed you . . . ," she whispered.

We both just stared at the presents in our hands, and finally, she said, "Go ahead. Open the gifts."

Lizzie tore into hers first, and I fiddled with the tape and watched to see what she got. We hadn't gotten many presents in our lives. The last one I remembered was the one Amanda gave us on our tenth birthdays.

Lizzie got to a white box. "Go ahead, Kara. I don't want to open mine until you're opening yours, too. If I do, I'll ruin your surprise."

Slowly, I tore the paper off, and then we opened the boxes at the same time.

Lizzie gasped, and I just stared. Mine was an elegant string of pearls, like something out of a museum. It was something Julia Roberts or somebody would wear to the Academy Awards. No way it was real.

Was it . . . ?

"They belonged to your Grandmother Holbrooke," she said. "Your father's mother."

"It's so expensive," Lizzie whispered. "Kara . . ."

I couldn't seem to utter a word.

"They're yours," Amanda said, "and they're just a sampling of your inheritance."

My heart pounded out of control. "Our inheritance, huh? I thought you took that."

"The court awarded it to me," she said. "But you're not listening, Kara. I told you what's mine is yours."

"But why should it be yours?" I asked. "If you admit it should be mine, then why don't you just give it to us?"

"I'm offering to do just that. But on my terms. I'm not just going to hand that much over to you to squander. I want to take you home, nurture you, teach you. I want you to be educated, and I want to train you to take care of what is yours. Most of all, I want us to be a family."

I didn't like the sound of all that schooling and training. It sounded like a bunch of rules, and I was finished with rules. "There's something not right about this, Lizzie. It's a snake waiting to strike. We can't fall for it."

But I could see that Lizzie was already caught—hook, line, and sinker. "But, Kara, it's what we've dreamed of! We could get out of here. We're eighteen. We can leave this place!"

I finally realized that if I stayed in that car a minute longer, I would be duped, too. I set the box down on the seat and reached for the door. "I'm leaving."

Lizzie caught her breath. "Kara, we need to at least talk about this!"

"We're not talking here." I got out of the car.

Amanda took my hand to stop me. She didn't grab, exactly, just kind of touched me. "Kara, I don't want you to go. I don't want to lose you again. I've waited all these years . . ."

I looked back at her, and for a moment, I wanted to believe. But faith didn't come easy for me. "Lady, you can't lose something you never had." With that, I stormed back into the truck stop.

Blake was waiting to pounce. Thinking I was Lizzie, he lit into me about his nasty breakfast, but I just pushed through the swinging doors into the kitchen and locked myself in the bathroom until I felt composed enough to come back out.

I thought of calling Eloise and telling her to set up that appointment with that lawyer, that I'd seen a sample of what was mine and I was ready to claim it. But I knew she was probably already doing that. She hadn't talked of much else for the last few days.

After a moment, I heard a knock on the door. "Kara, it's me. Let me in."

I opened the door, and Lizzie slipped inside. For a moment, she just leaned back against the door, clutching that white box in her hand. I slid up onto the sink and looked down at my feet.

"She wants us to go with her tonight. She gave me this cell phone." She pulled the phone out of her pocket. "She programmed her number in and told me to call her when we're ready. She doesn't want us to tell Eloise and Deke, because they would try to stop us. And they would, Kara. She makes a good point about them using us. If we leave, they don't have a chance of getting any of that money."

I wanted to cry. "I can't believe you're buying into everything she's telling you."

"I can't believe you aren't! Look at our alternative. We can come to work here every day and keep hiding our pathetic tips from Eloise and Deke, because they've always stolen from us. We just didn't know how much until today. Or we can call Amanda and get into that car with her and let her take us back to the home she's got waiting for us. We can stop being Barton rednecks and turn into ladies, Kara. We'll have someone who loves us and wants what's best for us."

"She doesn't want what's best for me! If she did, she'd just write me a check. I didn't see her writing any checks."

"Why would she, when she wants us to have all of it?"

"Sure, if we fly right and do everything she says. And I'm still not convinced that she doesn't have some surprise accident waiting for us, just like she had for our mother and our father and our grandparents."

"I don't believe she had anything to do with that."

Lizzie's words rang of betrayal. "Well, I believe she did."

We stared at each other for several minutes, and finally Lizzie got this sad look on her face. "Well, I guess it all comes down to what we believe, doesn't it?"

For the first time in our lives, I realized with stark clarity that Lizzie and I didn't really share the same heart. We were separate, two different people with radically different ideas. She wanted to leave me . . . to join our enemy. "You're going to go, aren't you?"

"I'm thinking about it. Kara, we have nothing to lose."

"Nothing but our lives . . . or at the very least, our freedom. Eloise warned us. She said—"

"Why would you believe *anything* Eloise says now when she's told us nothing but lies? She doesn't *care* about us. She never has. She used to lock us in closets, Kara! Deke would have used us up if we'd let him! They've both treated us like trash. You believe *them* over Amanda Holbrooke?"

"*They're* what I know!"

Tears sprang to Lizzie's eyes, but she held her eyes wide to keep them from spilling. She looked down at a stain on the concrete, and I got off of the sink and turned to look in the mirror. I wasn't crazy about what I saw, but I didn't like the looks of her much, either.

When Lizzie spoke again, her voice was flat. "I'm tired of struggling, Kara. I'm tired of knowing that somewhere there's more, just not for us. I'm tired of dreaming about getting out of here. This is our chance."

I turned around. Those tears were rolling down her face. I couldn't remember the last time I'd seen her cry. "Lizzie, you'll fall for anything. Rich ladies don't drive up in shiny limousines and give us expensive necklaces and offer to take us back to their mansions. It just doesn't happen."

"She says it was ours all along. Our father married her. He must have seen good in her. She says we used to call her Mommy."

"Give me a break!" I slapped my hand against the sink. "Lizzie, don't you think we'd remember that?"

Lizzie wiped one of those tears. "Sometimes . . . I think maybe I do."

"Well, you don't. And neither do I."

"I'm going with her, Kara."

I felt the way I felt that day after the abortion, when my gut hurt like it had been kicked with a boot. "You can't," I whispered.

"I can." Lizzie stepped toward me, her expression pleading. "I'm going with her, whether you come with me or not."

I didn't answer, so she finally turned to the door and opened it. She scrunched up her face against the tears and leaned her forehead against the doorjamb. "Kara, please don't make me leave you."

I crossed the room and made her look at me. "Please don't go. You have a choice, Lizzie. You can stay."

"And you have a choice, Kara. You can come."

I started to cry then and I knew I couldn't go back into that smoke-filled dining room and work like nothing was wrong. So I pushed out the back door of the kitchen and took off running through the woods, crackling the sticks and sweeping through the leaves.

I can't explain the misery I felt. It was like somebody with a dull knife had cut me right down the middle. Lizzie and I were twins, but it seemed so much like we were one. I'd never been without her. Never.

But wasn't that what twins grew up to do? Some of them got married and moved on, had their own families, their own children . . . Some of them saw the vision of a new life.

And some of them stayed behind.

I got to the old trailer and stood in the trees, looking at it. Inside those dirty walls were dark memories of closets and whippings, of being cursed at and degraded, of being groped and afraid.

I admit, I was confused. Part of me wanted to let Lizzie have her own way, to get in that car and ride off into the sunset with her and Amanda Holbrooke.

But I knew better.

As I trudged around to the front door and went in the trailer, I felt as weak as I had that day when I woke with that IV in my arm.

Eloise and Deke sat at the sticky table, deeply engaged in some serious conversation. Two of Deke's hunting dogs slobbered over a couple of cans of tuna that Deke had put on the floor. The room smelled like Deke's chicken slime, tuna fish, and dog odor.

Nausea gripped my stomach and clawed into my throat. I fought it back and went to my bedroom, locked the door, and lay down.

Lizzie must have finished our shift, even though she planned to be an heiress by sundown, because she didn't come in until after three.

When she came in, I heard Deke calling for me to come out. "We need to talk to you girls. Come on out here now."

I would almost rather have been beaten, but I got up and took my time changing out of my waitress uniform. I pulled on a pair of jeans and a T-shirt and slipped my feet into my flip-flops, since I couldn't stand the thought of walking across that floor in my bare feet.

Lizzie already sat at the table, and she looked up at me. I avoided her eyes and cleared out a chair that was piled up with newspapers.

"It's your eighteenth birthday today," Eloise announced, as if we didn't know it. "Ain't that something?"

Lizzie's eyes were dull. "Yeah. Really something."

"We're excited for you." I wondered why Deke had chosen today to wear his work boots into the house. I felt like telling him to take them off and put them on the porch where they belonged. "And now it's time for you to come into your own."

I perked up. This was the part I was real interested in.

"We got you an appointment with a real good lawyer up in Yazoo City. We told him about your case, and he thinks it's a sure thing."

Lizzie slid her hand into her pocket, and I knew she was closing it around that cell phone. "Tell me something, Deke," she said. "Tell me why our inheritance is so important to you."

"Well, I'm not gonna lie to you. The truth is, we figure we're all in this together. We're a family, and families help each other. We took you in when you was nothing but orphans, and all these years, we've took good care of you. Now it's your turn to take care of us."

Lizzie's eyes flashed to mine. *See?*

I ignored her. "When's the appointment?"

"Two weeks from today, and you don't have to worry about a thing, because we'll go with you."

Lizzie's cheeks reddened, and I could hear her foot beneath the table, beating out a staccato beat. "What if we didn't have to sue her? What if this Amanda Holbrooke person just offered to give us the money?"

Deke and Eloise looked at each other, then Eloise pinned us with her glare. "Have you heard from that woman?"

Lizzie's face was flaming. "I'm just saying that maybe we don't have to fight for it. Maybe we don't have to spend money on a lawyer, or wait a long time, or split it with you, or do anything at all. Maybe all we have to do is just take it."

Eloise shot up. "You know more than you're telling. She *has* talked to you. What did she do? Call you at the SOS?"

I looked down at my hands. Maybe, if I told Eloise what had happened, she would be able to talk some sense into Lizzie. I drew in a deep breath and decided to go for it. "We talked to her today, Eloise. She invited us to live with her."

Eloise sprang up. "You can't listen to her lies! She's been

living high on your money since your daddy was laid in the grave. She knows you have a claim to it, and there's no telling what she might do to trick you out of it! She's expecting a lawsuit now that you're of age. She might even kill you to keep you from winning."

"If we have a claim to it, Eloise, then how come we grew up living here?" Lizzie's plans seemed to have given her a new kind of courage. "Amanda said you got ten million dollars to take care of us. So where is it? Did you gamble all of that away?"

Deke sent his chair flying back with a crash. "We didn't get that money all at once! The better part of it went to lawyers and taxes. The rest was eked out in payments, but it wasn't enough! You shoulda had the whole Holbrooke fortune, but that stupid commie judge gave it to her. She probably paid him off!"

Lizzie got up herself, facing off with him. "Then what makes you think the courts would give it to us now?"

"Because you're grown now. A good lawyer can find the right grounds for a suit. We can afford the best, 'cause he'll get a cut. This time we'll take a settlement. It could be huge."

"That's how I want it," I said. "I want it on my terms. I'm tired of depending on other people."

Lizzie just got up from the table and slammed herself in our room.

"You go talk some sense into that girl." Deke was as mad as I'd ever seen him sober. "Don't you let her mess this up now. We've waited too long for this."

I didn't feel like talking to Lizzie right then, so I left the trailer and went to sit by the Secret Tree. I sat there, thinking, until it started to get dark.

When I got back to the trailer, Deke and Eloise were gone. I went into my bedroom and saw Lizzie lying on our bed with her back to me.

"I'm still going," she said.

"Then you're a fool."

She flipped over and looked at me. "I think *you're* the fool."

"You're just lazy, that's all. You just don't want to do what it takes to get the whole thing, so you're willing to settle for a little bit on her terms. But it won't be any different than it was being here with Eloise and Deke. You'll be like a dog, slurping up the crumbs she throws you while she spends our inheritance on herself."

Lizzie shook her head. "That's not how it'll be."

"How can you think it's as simple as she said? That all we have to do is hop in the car with her and ride off into the sunset?"

"Maybe it just *is*."

"It's *not*, okay?" I started getting undressed, because I was feeling really tired and I wanted this day to be over. I guess I thought, too, that if I could just get Lizzie to go to bed, maybe she'd forget about that phone in her pocket and Amanda waiting with her engine running, and just go to sleep. Maybe she'd wake up tomorrow and forget we had a choice.

"I'm going to bed." Lizzie looked at me as I pulled my shirt over my head, threw it to the floor, and pulled on the grungy T-shirt I slept in.

"When you wake up, I'll be gone." She got off of the bed, and I got in.

I lay down, my face to the wall.

"I love you, Kara."

That made me madder than anything she could have said. I sat up and squinted at her. "Then why would you do this to me?"

"Do it to *you*? How could you deprive me of it if it turns out to be true? How could you want me to stay here in *this*? How could *you* want to stay?"

"I'll get out of here *my* way! I can wait until the money's mine. I don't need lies and promises. I don't need dangling carrots and magic carpets that can be pulled out from under me. I can get there on my own."

Lizzie started to cry, and she climbed up next to me and put her arms around me. I got stiff as a board, but she wouldn't let go. Soon the hardness in my bones seemed to melt, and I laid my head on her shoulder and cried like a little baby.

"Don't go, Lizzie. I can't stand to see you go."

"And I can't stand to leave you."

"I always envisioned us going together somehow, getting on that train and riding off into our future."

Lizzie's hold on me tightened. "We can do that tonight."

"But wouldn't it be better if we could get the money for ourselves, then go where we wanted, do what we wanted?"

"Where would we go, Kara? Amanda's offering us all of that. I believe that she loved our father. That he wanted her to raise us. I believe she's watched us from a distance all these years, waiting for us to come home. I believe that she has our best interests at heart. That my only future is with her."

I pulled away from her, weary of the fight, and lay back down, with my knees pulled up to my chest. She sat there, looking down at me, but I was finished.

"I'm going to sleep, Lizzie. Birthdays are hard on a person's soul."

"Kara, she said to call her tonight, before Eloise and Deke get wind of it. If they get to the casino, surely they're going to hear that she's here in town."

"I'm going to sleep now, Lizzie."

She sat there watching me. When I didn't turn back over, I felt her slipping away. I couldn't tell if she was sitting or lying down next to me, but I wanted desperately to know. If she lay down, maybe she would fall asleep and Amanda would leave.

But I couldn't look. All I could do was hope that she would still be there when I woke up.

TWENTY-EIGHT

A little while later, I heard Lizzie packing a few things into a Kroger bag. I lay still, pretending I didn't hear, but then she slipped out of the room and I couldn't pretend anymore. I got up and jerked on my jeans.

I heard her in the living room, talking on that telephone Amanda had given her. "Uh, Amanda? It's Lizzie. I've decided to come." Her voice was broken and hollow sounding, and I could tell she was crying. "But Kara won't come with me. I don't know how to convince her."

There was a pause, and I listened, hoping Amanda would say that it was a package deal. That she wanted both of us or neither of us could come.

After all, it made sense if it was her intention to get us both out of her way. Whether it was just to keep us under her thumb where we couldn't file lawsuits and take her money, or to kill us like she'd killed our parents, I didn't know. But if that was her intention, I figured she would want us both. It wouldn't work if only one of us came.

But she must have told Lizzie to come without me, because then Lizzie said, "I don't want you to come here. Eloise and Deke could come home, and there's no telling what they might do. There's a gas station about a block down from the truck stop. It's closed right now and doesn't open until seven. I'll be waiting there. It'll only take me about fifteen minutes to get there."

It was real. She was really going to go.

I stood there for a minute, feeling this awful sense of betrayal. I couldn't believe my Lizzie, who had lived the same life I'd lived, who had dragged herself through all the muck of our pasts, who had always been there for me . . . would leave me now. I tried to imagine standing on my own, drudging through this life without her.

And at that moment I hated Amanda Holbrooke more than I'd ever hated anyone.

I heard Lizzie slip out the front door, and my chest grew tight as panic shivered over me. I couldn't let her go the way we had left things. I stepped out into the night. I didn't see her from the porch, but I knew that if she was going to that gas station, she would have to take our path through the woods. I went around the house and saw the faint glow of her flashlight moving through the trees.

It was a full moon that night, and everything had a faint blue glow. The autumn wind had the slightest bite to it, and I shivered as I followed her.

I started to cry as I ran toward her. She must have heard me coming, for she turned around. I saw the tear stains on her face, the mascara smeared under her eyes, her pink nose, her purple lips.

We stood there among the trees, staring at each other as the minutes ticked by.

"You're really going?" I asked finally.

"I have to," she said.

I had already begged her to stay, given her all my arguments and opinions. Logic wasn't going to change her mind. Nothing was.

I smeared the tears across my face. "Well, I'll walk you to the gas station. We can say good-bye there."

"I'm going to miss you." Lizzie thrust herself into my arms and clung, like it might be the last time. I clung back, my face twisted as I buried it in her hair, finally letting all the despair of our separation wail out of me.

After a moment, Lizzie pulled back. "I'll get there and see whether it's better. And if it's true, I'll let you know. Then you can come."

I shook my head. "I'll never go with her. She stole my mother and then my father, and now she's stealing you. I hate her, and I don't want anything to do with her. Ever."

Lizzie started to walk, shining that flashlight ahead of her, and I followed behind. My legs seemed as heavy as steel beams, and my heart ached, raw and exposed. We tromped through the woods, winding through the path we knew so well, until the sleepy gas station came into sight. The limo was already coming off the highway, its headlights shining onto the small building.

I stopped at the edge of the woods, and Lizzie handed me the flashlight and gave me one last hug. Then I stood there alone as she headed toward the light. The limo pulled onto the pavement. Amanda got out of the car and threw her arms around Lizzie, rocking her back and forth, looking for all the world like a mother who hadn't seen her child in too long.

She didn't look dangerous or threatening, but I knew those were the worst kind.

"Where's Kara?" I heard her ask Lizzie.

Lizzie pointed to where I stood, but I stepped behind the trees and blended into the shadows.

Amanda got the box with the pearl necklace she had given me and set it on the pavement. "I know you're there, Kara. I love you and I want you, too. I'm leaving your necklace because it was a birthday gift, and I want you to have it."

She turned back to Lizzie. "Let me have the phone." Lizzie pulled the phone out of her pocket, along with its adapter cord, and handed it to Amanda. She set it on the box and stepped away.

"Kara," she called, "use this phone if you need to call. My number is programmed in. Just call, and we'll come back for you. Anytime, night or day."

I stood there, mute, without the heart to answer. Finally, I watched Lizzie climb into that limo. Amanda got in behind her.

I wept into my hands as the limousine pulled away, taking my sister with it.

For a minute, I couldn't think, couldn't move, couldn't do anything. I just stood there, feeling like an orphaned child who didn't know her way home. I cried for a long time, right out loud. If anyone had come along, they would have thought a wounded animal lay dying in the dirt.

Death would have been a relief.

I stepped across the pavement, feeling as if my tears had bled me dry . . . as if lead weights had been strapped to my limbs and I didn't have the energy to pick up my feet. I got to the box and the telephone and lifted them and started back through the woods.

Instead of going back home, I ventured from that dark path to the one leading to our Secret Tree. Holding the flashlight between my chin and chest, I moved aside the leaves that covered our treasures in the hollow and pulled out one of the Ziploc bags that still had some room. I stuck the necklace box and the phone inside it.

I don't know why I did it. I had no intentions of ever thinking of either of them again. If I'd encountered a garbage bin along the way, I might just as easily have tossed them in that. But I stuck the bag back down into the Secret Tree and covered it with the leaves.

I had stopped crying by that time. My nose was stopped up and my eyes stung and my head ached. I reached the trailer and went back in. It was desperately quiet.

I went to Deke and Eloise's medicine cabinet and found the pills he used for hangovers. I took two of them, then went back to my room. I kicked off my jeans and lay down on our bed.

Pulling her covers up to my chin, I felt something under there, pressing against my leg. I reached down. It was Eliza, Lizzie's doll.

She had forgotten it, and I knew she would be sorry.

I wished I could run after that car and give it to her, but it was too late. So I just held that doll close against me, the way she had done when she was little and we'd mothered our dolls together. Slowly, the drugs kicked in, anesthetizing my pain and drawing me into a shallow sleep. I dreamed of running through the woods, calling Lizzie, trying to save her, screaming her name.

But she didn't answer. She was already too far away.

TWENTY-NINE

About a week after Lizzie left, Judd Sargent, my boss at the SOS, brought me a letter from Lizzie. I was surprised that she had sent it to me there. I didn't want to read it in front of a bunch of gawking idiots, so I stuffed it into my apron pocket and waited until my shift was over. Then I went to the Secret Tree and opened it there.

It was written on pink stationery, with pretty little squiggly things in the margins and the name *Lizzie Holbrooke* embossed in gold at the top. It had a faint, sweet smell, not like she had doused it in perfume or anything, but like it had simply wafted on the air she breathed.

I wondered if my letters back to her would smell like the chicken plant.

I got comfortable against the stump of the Secret Tree and started to read.

Dear Kara,

I had to write to you at the truck stop because I didn't think you'd get the letter if I sent it to the house. Amanda told me she has been sending us letters and gifts for years, and we've never gotten any of them. The dolls—Eliza and Missy—were from her. I'm not sure why Deke and Eloise let us have them. The rest of the things she sent us either got thrown away or sold.

So I decided that I'd go through the truck stop, because I figured Judd wouldn't have any reason to keep your mail from you.

Kara, you should see this place. Everything she said was true. She lives in a house that's the closest thing to a palace I've ever seen, and she decorated my room like something out of a magazine. She has pictures all over the place of us when we were babies, stuff that belonged to our dad, and photo albums. We must have been the most photographed children alive back then. They must have recorded every move we made. Imagine being loved like that.

There's a little playhouse in the back that she moved here when she inherited our grandfather's mansion. She says that Daddy made it for us, and we sat inside it today and went through the photo albums. It all feels like another life, one I had no part in. But it's all there, in living color. You and me and Daddy and Amanda. And it's real. We looked like the happiest family.

I'm sending pictures of the playhouse, and the closeup of the wall is the one that we painted. Can't you just picture twin three-year-olds with paintbrushes? And you can see where we made a mess of the brush strokes. Daddy left it just like it was.

He didn't have much choice, because he died just days after we painted it.

It's weird how Amanda's waited all these years for us. She's never forgotten us, and she's always expected us to come back someday. In one room, she has gifts she bought us every birthday and every Christmas . . . the ones she didn't send. I opened mine today, and let me tell you, it was like no Christmas I've ever seen. I was overwhelmed at all of it. Yours are still in there, wrapped nice and neat, waiting for you.

She has a room decorated for you, too. It's a lot like mine, only different. I think you'll love it if you ever come.

She wants me to get my diploma, so she's hired me a tutor to help me get my GED. Then she says I'll go to college. She said I could take tennis lessons and learn to drive, and she's going to train me in the company. Next week I'm going to start working there in the afternoons, filing and stuff. She wants me to get good at the little things in the company, so I can someday be trusted with the big things. I'm nervous about it, but she says it will be fine.

It's not too late for you to come, Kara. She's still waiting for you every day, hoping that you'll call. All you have to do is punch one button on that phone.

If you came soon, you'd be here for the big reception party Amanda is throwing for me in a few weeks. Of course, it would be for us *if you were here. We've been shopping for cocktail dresses. I feel like Cinderella with her godmother. If you could just* see *some of these dresses. And I have this lady coming every day to work with me on manners and all. I don't want to embarrass myself or Amanda at the party, so I'm working really hard.*

I know this won't be easy. It'll be hard work to catch up on my education, since our Barton education wasn't much to write home about. But I'm willing to work hard. I want to please her and make her proud. And I want everything she has planned for me, because I just know it's for my own good.

It's kind of weird being an heiress, though. She says that our name makes us targets for all sorts of problems. She has a body-guard who takes me everywhere I go. He doubles as my chauf-feur. Can you imagine me riding around in a limo, with my own chauffeur/bodyguard?

Amanda gets tears in her eyes every time she talks about you, and I do, too. We can't understand why you could choose to live there, struggling every day, having nothing, working so hard, with Eloise and Deke treating you like you're trash. It's not the life for you, Kara. You could have all this with me. It breaks my heart that you refuse.

Why would you hold out for some crazy lawsuit when it's all yours, anyway?

Please come and at least see what you're missing. You'll understand that your suspicions are all wrong. We're waiting for you, Kara.

I love you,
Lizzie

I have to admit that I was jealous when I first read that letter. I sat there against that stump, reading the words over and over, and trying to imagine the things she described. I wondered if I was a fool, if I was just cutting off my hand to spite my face, as Eloise always said.

But it was too good to be true, and I knew from experience that things like that never panned out. It was like when you got a letter in the mail that said you'd won some giant sweepstakes—"Kara Holbrooke is the Winner Of Twenty Million Dollars"—only when you read the small print, you see that it also says, "if her name is drawn in our impossible drawing in which the odds of winning are four hundred million to one," or something like that. I figured that Amanda was still baiting Lizzie . . . or baiting *me*. That she had to make it look good for a while so that I would come, and then she could make her move.

And I started thinking about all the stuff Lizzie was having to do, and I didn't feel so jealous anymore. Teachers and tutors and lessons and rules? No, none of that was for me. You could say what you wanted about Eloise and Deke, but they had never had all that many rules. I'd been doing basically what I wanted for so long that I wasn't about to get locked up in a bunch of dos and don'ts now.

Besides, my appointment with the lawyer was just a few days away, and I had high hopes for that. Even though Eloise and Deke were furious at Lizzie for leaving the way she did, they were bending over backwards to be nice to me. They were as excited as I was about the appointment, and I knew they wouldn't be if there was any chance we would lose.

I folded the letter up in my pocket and told myself that I

was doing just fine without Lizzie, and I almost started to feel sorry for *her*. I hated to think how devastated she would be when she found out I'd been right all along.

But I knew that when that happened, she would be back. It was just a matter of time.

THIRTY

You might say I fell for Rudy Singer because I grieved over Lizzie, but the truth is I would have anyway. I noticed him the minute he came into the SOS just a couple of days after my first letter from Lizzie. He looked cleaner-cut than the guys around Barton, and he said he'd just taken a job as a dealer at the casino in Vicksburg, but had decided to live in Barton because his grandmother died and left him a house there.

It wasn't like I fell for every new guy who came on the scene. New guys were coming and going all the time at the SOS since we were a popular stop-off for every trucker on Highway 49. A lot of times they were married, but you couldn't tell it the way they hounded me. And it wasn't just the transient married ones who came after me, either. Even the married guys from Barton occasionally tried to get me into the back room.

Sometimes I went, just because I liked their attention. And

it depended on when they tried. If I was in a flirtatious mood, there was no telling what I'd do.

But that day I really was kind of sick of all of them, so when Rudy ambled in, looking like George Clooney with that amused grin on his face, I have to admit I got a little breathless.

Milly Luckett did, too, but she was married and overweight, so I quickly told her to get out of my way, that this one was mine.

He seemed fine with that arrangement, even though he didn't know about it, because his eyes were on me from the minute he walked in.

He ordered a beer and a cheeseburger, and every time I walked by him, he grabbed some part of me. Once he grabbed one of my curls and pulled it gently as I breezed by. Another time he grabbed the sash of my apron, untying it. Sometimes he just took my hand as he asked for ketchup or an extra napkin.

He was a toucher, all right. But that suited me fine.

"What's there to do around this town?" he asked me one of those times.

I flipped my hair back over my shoulder and smiled. "This is about it."

He rolled his eyes as if he couldn't believe my misfortune. "What about restaurants? A place where a hungry man can take an attractive woman out for a bite to eat?"

I hated to repeat myself, but I shrugged and said, "This is still pretty much it. For anything else, you can go to Yazoo City or Vicksburg. There's a lot around the casinos. Or you could go all the way to Jackson."

His eyes were a pale blue, and I thought he ought to be in

movies or something. "Where do your boyfriends take you on dates?"

"Dates?" I chuckled. "The men around here don't take girls on dates. They invite us to watch them get their hands greasy on a carburetor in their garage, or to sit on a dirt hill and watch them sling mud all over each other with four-wheelers."

"Then you need to broaden your horizons."

"Tell me about it."

"I will." He put his hand on my waist and pulled me closer. "What time do you get off?"

I grinned, though I didn't want him to see how thrilled I was.

"I get off at midnight," I said. "That is, if it's not crowded. That too late for you?"

"I think I can make it for a cute little redhead."

I flipped my hair over my shoulder again. I don't know why I kept doing that. I wasn't the hair-flipping type, but he was making me nervous. "All right. Hang around after I get off, and I'll show you around the town."

"I'd like to see those hills you were talking about where the men go four-wheeling."

"Well, they don't do it at night," I said.

"Of course they don't," he said with a grin, "but it sounds like a nice quiet place to sit and talk."

Right. I knew better than to think he wanted to talk. I got behind the counter and leaned over it, putting my face close to his. "It's private, all right. But I don't think I want to go there with a man I just met." I had just read in a magazine that guys liked it when women were coy.

"All right, then. We'll go to Vicksburg and eat at the Ameristar. How's that sound?"

"So you're gonna spend real money on me? Not make me pay my own way or anything?"

"I'm insulted. What kind of man would make a pretty lady like you pay her own way?"

"Just about every one in this town," I said. "And most want me to pay *their* way, too."

He gazed into my eyes then, and I had the thought that we must look like those posters of Clark Gable and Vivien Leigh. "I can see I'm going to have fun wining and dining you."

As I waited for midnight, my mind danced with the promise of being treated like a lady, and I decided that Lizzie didn't have anything on me. It was about the first time I'd felt good since she left.

I couldn't wait for my shift to end.

THIRTY-ONE

A couple of days later, I wrote Lizzie back.

Dear Lizzie,

I know things look good to you right now, but trust me, she's up to something. People don't ride into town in big old limousines and dangle a million dollars in somebody's face. Besides, it sounds like a prison to me, studying all the time, taking all those lessons, having all those rules. You know how I hate rules. When I get the money, I'll split it with you, and we won't have to do anything but drive around in our own limos and count our cash.

I've got all the freedom I want here, so I think I'll stay, thank you very much.

I met a new guy, and his name is Rudy Singer. He's tall and good-looking, and he works at the casino. He dresses real nice and talks smart and he beats the other men here in town hands down. He's got that movie-star charm that just melts my knees. It's a good thing you're not here, because you would have wanted him, too. He really seems to like me. You should see how he looks at me.

He's different than the other guys I've known, Lizzie. He has a respect for me that others don't have, and he cares what happens to me. He's always giving me advice about what I should do and where I should go, and I kind of like that. It's not like the rules you're under. More like just good suggestions. And it's fun to have somebody care that much. Maybe he's the one, Lizzie. And to think you missed it all.

Be careful now, because I think the other shoe is gonna drop any day now, and you'll wake up and find out that Amanda isn't such a fairy godmother after all. That Amanda's really the wicked witch, waiting to strike. I worry for you.

When you finally come to your senses, maybe you can come visit me and my good-looking husband and the little babies we're going to have together. We'll be sitting pretty with all my money, and probably move to New York and live in one of those fancy town houses. Maybe I'll get a job modeling for Cosmo or something. He seems like the type who wouldn't mind a girl having a career. He's been buying me things like jewelry and clothes, and plunking down his credit card like it was nothing. You gotta admire a man like that. I think this is the one, Lizzie. Keep your fingers crossed for me.

I miss you and wish you would come home. It's not too late.

Love,

Kara

My first appointment with the attorney was a colossal let-down. He reviewed the situation, then told me he didn't think I had a case. I figured it was because there was no money in it for him up front, and Eloise and Deke didn't exactly look like the kind of clients a man like him would want to represent.

But Eloise hadn't wasted any time in setting up a meeting with a different attorney in Vicksburg—the same one who had represented them in probate court fifteen years ago. They assured me he was the one and that he was familiar enough with the case to jump right in.

"Why wasn't he your first choice?" I asked.

"He was a little hard to find." Deke shrugged. "His firm closed down, and he's practicing by his self right now." I expected him to be practicing from a high-rise, air-conditioned office with secretaries and a big library of books. Instead, he had his office in a small strip mall situated between Sally's Beauty Supply and River City Liquor.

I followed Eloise and Deke into the stuffy office that reeked of cigarette smoke and body odor. No one sat at the cluttered front desk, but I could hear a phone ringing at the back and a man's voice from another room.

"Anybody home?" Deke called out as if he'd just walked into an old friend's house. In just a moment, a man emerged from the back, wearing a brown plaid blazer and wrinkled khaki pants with sneakers. His hair looked as if he had just walked out of a wind tunnel; he held a pair of glasses in one hand and a cigarette in another.

"Eloise, Deke!" He trod across the carpet to shake their

hands. "Good to see you. Sorry to keep you waiting. My secretaries up and quit on me." He turned to me, smiling. "You must be Kara Holbrooke."

"Yes." I shook his hand. It made me feel important. Most people either looked right past me or groped me in some way.

"It's hot as Hades in here," he said. "I'm having a little problem with the air conditioner. Come on back and we'll talk." He led us through a hall stacked with boxes and files, then to his cluttered office, which was a little bigger than the room out front. He rummaged around for a moment, trying to stack and restack things so that he could free up chairs. I took the one he motioned to closest to his desk. Deke plopped down in the next free one and set his feet up on the desk, as if he owned the place. I hoped this lawyer didn't think I was like that, all arrogant and rude. I sat up straight with my hands in my lap, trying to look a little more dignified.

Enos Wright took the chair behind the desk and leaned up, crossing his hands in front of his face. "Never thought I'd see you folks again."

Deke dropped his feet and sat up real slow-like. He looked around the office, rubbed his eyes. "You seem to have come down in the world since then."

Enos straightened in his chair. He cleared his throat and sniffed. "And so do you, for a man with ten million dollars."

I started to say that that ten million had been sucked down the casino's drain, but Enos was already explaining his own end of things.

"I had a few setbacks of the financial kind." He rocked his

executive chair back and forth as he spoke. "Sometimes we just have to adjust our standard of living to get through a bad spot."

"I hear you," Deke said.

Enos turned his attention on me. "So you want to sue again for the Holbrooke estate?"

My chair was about as comfortable as a granite block, so I crossed my legs, then uncrossed them again. Sweat prickled my skin under my clothes. "Well, yes. I mean, if the money was my grandfather's and then went to my father, it should have rightfully gone to me."

"But you realize it was resolved long ago in probate court, and Amanda Holbrooke got the bulk of the estate."

"I understand that, but Eloise and Deke thought that we could reopen it now that I'm eighteen."

"Well, whether we could or not," he said, "we could sure scare them, cause them enough hassle to make them want to settle." He looked down at his file, flipped through a few pages. "Where's your sister?"

I cleared my throat. "Uh, she won't be joining in the lawsuit."

"Why not?"

"Because she's gone to live with Amanda Holbrooke."

His chair snapped as he came to attention. "How in the world did *that* happen?"

I didn't feel like dredging the whole thing up again, but I figured it was necessary. "Amanda came and convinced my sister to come and live with her, like some kind of heir. But nothing is in writing, you understand. I think she was just trying to head off a lawsuit, but I'm not stupid enough to fall for it."

"Good for you." Enos leaned his chair back again. "I have to say, though, that it would be a much stronger case if your sister was involved. But we can do it without her."

Though I had fully expected to go through with the suit, part of me had some distant expectation that everything would fall through, since things rarely worked out the way I planned. I blew out a breath of relief. "How much do you think I can get?"

He shook his head, thought for a moment, and flipped through the file again. "How much were you hoping for?"

I grinned. "All of it."

He threw back his head and howled with laughter. "That's very funny." He glanced at Deke and Eloise. "She's a very funny girl."

I stiffened. "What's so funny about that?"

"You're not getting all of it," he said. "Maybe part of it. Fifty or sixty million dollars might be reasonable."

So much for pulling the rug out from under Amanda. And after all she'd taken from me. But fifty million dollars was nothing to sneeze at.

"Back when your father died, that estate was worth several billion dollars. By now I'd say it's doubled. Fifty million dollars isn't going to put a dent in Amanda Holbrooke's pocket."

Eloise cackled, and Deke chortled until he was overcome in a fit of coughing.

I had the strongest urge to jump up and run from the room,

to find a lawyer who'd never met Deke and Eloise. "So what do I have to do?"

"Nothing right now. You just leave everything to me."

"And how much will this cost?"

He shoved that cigarette back into his mouth and jotted something down. "I charge 40 percent when the case is settled," he said around the cigarette. "I don't anticipate we will ever go to court, so that money could come soon."

I wished I had finished school so I could figure up how much that was. But I knew it was less than half. That would still leave me with over twenty-five million. And then there was Eloise and Deke. They expected part of it, too. And I'd have to pay taxes.

The money was fast dwindling away, and I hadn't even gotten my hands on it yet.

He punched a few keys on his computer, puffing on that cigarette. In a moment the printer whirled to life. I watched as a document slid out of it. He snatched it up, slid it across the table.

"Now, if you'll just sign here."

I peered at it. "What am I signing?"

"It just says that you're hiring me as your attorney, that you're willing to give me 40 percent of the settlement amount, and that you will pay me a thousand dollars up front. You can make that check out to—"

"A thousand dollars?" I put my hands over my face. "I don't have a thousand dollars."

Deke shifted his slump. "Now wait a minute. The last time, you didn't charge us nothing until we collected."

"Well, the last time I was in a little better situation than I am now. Plus I *thought* I had a surer case. But you got to understand the estate isn't up for grabs. Amanda Holbrooke is firmly entrenched in that company and in that mansion and that money is all hers. That makes this case more of a long shot."

I leaned forward, trying to follow him. "But I thought you said it would be easy. I thought you said we would settle and it would be quick."

"Well, it will," he said, "but in the meantime, I have expenses. I have to keep my office running, pay a secretary, file court papers, make long-distance calls. There are just a million and one expenses that you don't even know about, and I can't do this unless I have some money up front."

I started thinking that it was all over, that I'd made a terrible mistake. I should have gone with Lizzie. I'd be sitting in some fancy Laura Ashley room in Amanda's mansion or shopping for a cocktail dress.

But I'd also be studying a bunch of worthless garbage, working in an office at her company where I probably wouldn't even get tips, and none of her money would be mine.

I looked at Eloise and Deke. Deke slapped his knees. "Well, I guess we'll get the money somewhere. But we don't got it today."

Enos leaned back hard in his chair, like *he* was the one whose time had been wasted. "Tell you what. I'll get the paperwork started and give you a couple of weeks to come up with the money. Sound fair?"

I couldn't believe how lucky I was. There I was, thinking it was all over, and now it would be okay. "Fair to me."

"Yeah, she can come up with it somehow," Deke said.

That stopped me, and I shot him a look. *She* can come up with it? Was he just coming along for the ride, with no intentions of helping at all?

"How's she gonna do that?" Eloise asked.

"Well, I don't know." He scratched his armpit. "But we'll figure something out. We always have before. This is too important to blow."

"But there are lawyers who would do this for free." Eloise crossed her arms and gave Enos a haughty look. "Only getting paid at the end, like he did last time."

Enos smiled and started rocking his chair. He took the cigarette out of his mouth and shoved his glasses on. "Look, I can see this is a problem. If I cut my down payment in half, would that make you feel better, Eloise?"

She thought about it for a moment, then frowned. "I guess so."

Enos turned to me. "Could you come up with that?"

This was getting better all the time. I knew I had some cash stashed in the Secret Tree. I wasn't sure quite how much, since I'd never thought of it as all mine before. But now that Lizzie was gone, I figured I could have mine and hers. If she'd wanted it, she would have taken it with her. "I think I can come up with it."

"How?" Eloise shouted again.

I started signing the sheet. "I've been saving, Eloise. I didn't want anybody spending it. It was my escape money."

Deke's voice was way too loud. "Escape from what?"

"From Barton," I said. "You didn't think I was going to live in that stink hole for the rest of my life. I was going to move somewhere and start over. But now I guess I can use it for this. And when I get the settlement, I'll be able to start over anywhere I want."

"You got that right." Enos grinned. "So you just bring the check by for five hundred dollars, and I'll file the papers."

I nodded. "It'll be a few days because I don't have quite five hundred dollars yet. Maybe I can get the rest by the end of the week."

He smiled and dropped both hands on the table. "Well, then, it looks like I'm your man." He got up and shook my hand again. His was soft and mushy, like that of some overweight woman. He patted Deke on the back as we all headed out of his office. "It's going to be a pleasure serving you again, and this time I think we'll all come out better than we did the last time. Miss Kara, you're about to become a millionaire. What do you think of that?"

It was about time, that's what I thought.

"Imagine me with money." I was already thinking of the things I was going to buy. A fancy red convertible, a mink coat, all the jewelry money could buy . . .

"What you going to do with it?" he asked.

I stopped for a minute and stared at the air as I thought of all the possibilities. "I'm going to move to New York and live in one of those fancy apartment buildings where celebrities live. And I'm going to shop and buy some clothes and go out every night clubbing. I might even go to Europe if I get the nerve up to fly on a plane."

"Good for you," he said, laughing. "And, young lady, I predict you're going to be able to do *all* of those things. No, Amanda Holbrooke hasn't seen the last of us."

That afternoon, as I went back to work at the SOS, I couldn't keep my good news to myself. I practically pranced around, feeling like I would wait on those idiots because I wanted to, not because I had to. But I couldn't get too proud, because I had gone by the tree on the way to work, and saw that I had exactly $350. I'd need another $150 before I could start this ball rolling and I was going to have to earn it through tips.

It was a hard thing, hustling to get the tips I needed while still floating around in the thrill of my millions.

Rudy came in a little while later and took his usual place at the counter. "So he thinks she'll settle out of court?" he asked me.

"That's right. He thinks she'll just write a check out to me on the spot, just to keep from having to go to court where I might get the whole thing."

Rudy pulled out a pen and started writing on his napkins. "So he wants five hundred dollars and 40 percent? You've got to be kidding me."

Rudy had on his casino uniform, which looked something like a tux. I couldn't take my eyes off of him. "What's wrong?"

"Honey, you don't pay five hundred bucks to someone representing you in a lawsuit like this. You shouldn't have any out-of-pocket expenses."

"Well, he gave me a deal. He cut it right in half. He asked for a thousand first."

"So you *paid* him five hundred?"

"No, not yet. I don't have quite enough. But I'm hoping I'll have good tips this week, and then when payday comes on Friday, I might have enough."

Rudy shook his head. "Who's this lawyer you're talking about?"

"Enos Wright. He has his office over in High Point Shopping Center in Vicksburg. He was real nice."

"Real nice? He's probably nothing but an ambulance chaser." Rudy stood up and reached across the counter for both of my hands. "Honey, look at me."

It always blew me away when he took my hands like that and made me look into his eyes. They were so blue that I started wondering if they were contact lenses, but then I decided that he was just one of those lucky people who'd been born with cobalt eyes.

"You can do better than a lawyer like this," he said.

I really liked it when he got all protective, so I smiled and tipped my head. "How? I don't have any more money than that."

"You don't *need* any money to file a lawsuit. Any decent lawyer with enough confidence in winning the suit shouldn't need any money up front. Besides, if Wright's practice is doing so poorly that he couldn't handle the expenses without it, then you sure don't need him. What did he tell you he'd do for you?"

"Well, he told me that he was going to get me fifty to sixty million dollars."

Rudy put both hands on my face and tipped it up to his. "Baby, you've got a lot to learn."

"Well, how can I learn it, Rudy? All I know to do is what Eloise and Deke tell me. If you've got a better idea—"

"I've got lots of better ideas. Girl, you could win that whole estate, snatch it right from under the woman who stole it from you, and who stole your sister and has been deceiving her all this time. You could have several billion dollars, be the owner of a major corporation with Learjets at your disposal, and live in that huge mansion."

I couldn't help being impressed at how passionate he seemed to be about my plight. "Well, why did Enos Wright tell me I couldn't have it all?"

"Because he wants to do this the quickest, easiest way. Going for the whole thing is going to take a little longer, but, baby, it'll be worth it."

"What do you think I should do, Rudy? Just tell me and I'll do it."

"I think you need to call this Enos Wright fellow and tell him to take a hike. And tomorrow I'll take you to see a friend of mine, another attorney. This one is legitimate and has a healthy practice. If anybody can win this case, he can."

"Really? How do you know him?"

"He helped me out of a few scrapes a while back."

"What kind of scrapes?"

He looked around like he didn't want anybody to hear. "Nothing big. Don't worry about it. But trust me. I won't let you down."

I started thinking how much better it would be to do this without Eloise and Deke. If they weren't in on the whole thing, maybe I wouldn't have to share any of it with them. It was *my* money, after all, and they'd already spent ten million of my money.

"All right," I said, "make me an appointment and I'll go."

"I'll drive you. And for Pete's sake, don't tell those parasite grandparents of yours. Those two lowlifes I see at the casino every night don't have any business getting their hands on your money. I don't care *what* they tell you. You need to make sure you do this by yourself."

"Okay, if you think I can."

"I *know* you can, honey. Just count on me. Now, I have to get to work. I'll call that lawyer from the casino and I'll let you know when he can see you."

He kissed me then, right there in front of everybody, and as he was walking away, I really felt like somebody. Like a *rich* somebody, with a good-looking boyfriend.

If only Lizzie could see me now.

THIRTY-TWO

Two days later, Rudy drove me to Jackson, where Bill Daniels's law firm was located. On the way, I tried to find out a little more about Rudy's relationship with him.

"So tell me about this guy," I said. "Did you go to school with him or something?"

Rudy laughed. "Hardly."

"Well, what kind of scrapes did he get you out of?"

"I had a couple of tickets, some DUIs. He was a public defender then. Now he's doing litigation. You know what that is, don't you?"

I had seen every episode of *LA Law*. "Yeah, I know what it is. I'm not stupid."

He reached up and slid his hand to my neck, and gently stroked it as he drove. "I know you're not stupid, baby. In fact, you're probably one of the smartest women in Barton."

Nobody had ever said that to me. Most people just thought

of me as a dropout loser. "Is that why you like me?" I flipped my hair. "For my brains?"

He had this lusty chuckle. "No. I can't lie to you. It was your looks that caught my attention. The brains are just icing on the cake."

That was okay with me.

When we got to the parking garage of the Deposit Guaranty Building, I was in a really good mood and looking forward to getting this thing underway.

We navigated our way up the garage elevator, then got out and walked across the walkway that crossed one of the busy streets in downtown Jackson. We rode the escalator down, then found another set of elevators. I wondered how in the world they did business here, when it was so hard to find anything.

But it was much more impressive than the hole-in-the-wall office of Enos Wright's.

Rudy got us to the right office, and we walked into a large waiting area with a busy receptionist, who smiled up at us as we came in. "May I help you?"

Rudy stepped up to the desk. "Tell Bill Daniels we're here, will you, please? Kara Holbrooke and Rudy Singer."

"Yes, sir, I sure will." She picked up the phone to let him know. "You can have a seat."

I took a seat on a couch that looked like something out of an Ethan Allen showroom, and Rudy sat down next to me. He took my hand in his, patted it, and said, "You don't have to be nervous. This is going to go real well."

"I'm not nervous," I lied.

He smiled. "Yes, you are. Your hands are shaking." He was real sensitive about my moods, and that pleased me. Most guys—Crawley, for instance—would have made me feel stupid for trembling the slightest bit. He probably would have told the receptionist and embarrassed me to death. But Rudy just closed his hands around mine to calm me down.

"It's going to be fine." His whisper was warm against my ear. "Wait and see. So did you tell your grandparents that they weren't going to be mooching off of you anymore?"

I almost had the night before, when they were riding me about getting that money to Enos. I noticed they weren't trying to raise it themselves. But I decided not to tell them until I saw how this turned out. "Not yet. I thought it was best if I just kept it to myself for a while."

"That's fine, as long as you don't start writing them checks."

A door opened, and a man in a dress shirt and tie stepped out and reached for Rudy's hand. "How's it going, Rudy?" He was polite, but I noticed an edge in his voice and strain on his face, like he didn't really like Rudy much.

"Bill, I'd like you to meet Kara Holbrooke."

Bill Daniels gave me a long, assessing look, then shook my hand. "How old are you now, Kara?"

"Eighteen."

He nodded. "Come on back to my office."

Rudy set his hand on the back of my neck, reassuring me that this was going to be easy. We got to the plush office. It looked like the Oval Office—or what I imagined it looked like: The paneling was made of cherry, matching a desk and tables. Several lamps sat at various locations around the room, and there was a sitting area with a leather couch and two plush chairs. I could have lived here very comfortably, I thought. I wondered where he'd gotten that couch.

Bill motioned us to that area and offered me the couch. Rudy sat down next to me.

"So . . . Rudy—" he took a seat facing us—"as I understand it, you wanted me to meet with Kara today to discuss suing Amanda Holbrooke. Is that right?"

"You got it," Rudy said.

Bill rubbed his forehead and shifted in his seat. "Kara, I did some research into this situation to prepare for this meeting. That case was settled about fifteen years ago. The only way to revisit it now is to open another suit that has nothing to do with the estate. The way I see it, if you had some kind of damages against Amanda Holbrooke, you might be able to take some civil action and win a settlement."

I sat up straighter on the couch, trying to follow the words. "What do you mean by damages?"

"Well, is there anything she's done to you that you could sue her for, anything that would give us a basis for taking her to court?"

"She stole my money."

He leaned forward. "But, you see, that's just it. She *didn't* steal your money. She was awarded it in probate court. She was the beneficiary in your father's will and the court upheld that."

"All these girls got was ten million dollars," Rudy said, "and, I might add, not a penny went to them."

"I understand that," Bill said, "but that's not the point. You see, Kara, the court did award you ten million dollars. Technically, you could sue your grandparents for squandering that money, but none of what happened to that money is the fault of Amanda Holbrooke."

Clearly he knew nothing about Eloise and Deke. "I can't sue them! They don't *have* anything."

"I realize that. But I'm just trying to explain that you do have a case against them, but not against Amanda Holbrooke."

I couldn't believe what I was hearing. I looked at Rudy. "I thought you said he was on our side."

Bill held up his hand. "It's not a question of sides. Rudy, I wish you would have explained to her that it's my job to figure out if we could win in court. And with the situation as it is, I don't see how we could. I'm going to have to refuse to take this case."

"You're what?" Rudy stood up, glaring at the man. "What do you mean, you refuse?"

Bill rose to face him squarely. "I mean what I said, Rudy. I won't take the case. It's not a lawsuit that can be won."

I felt as if my legs had been knocked out from under me. All this time I'd been so sure that this was going to happen. I thought of Enos Wright, telling me there was no way I'd get all of it, but at least he did think I had a claim to some. "Rudy—"

"Don't worry about it, baby." Rudy looked like he was about to knock out the lawyer's teeth. "Just because this goob won't take it doesn't mean we won't find a lawyer who will."

I got up, and Rudy touched my back as we moved to the door.

"Just one thing, Rudy."

Rudy turned around and glared at Bill. *"What?"*

"You need to watch yourself. One wrong move, and you'll be back in jail so fast your head will spin. I don't know what your motives are in helping Kara, but I'm warning you to be careful."

I looked up at Rudy. "Back in jail? Rudy—"

Rudy's eyes flashed. "Hey, I'm not doing anything illegal. I visit my parole officer once a week, just like I'm supposed to. Nobody can fault me for wanting to help a friend."

"Let's just say I don't trust your motives," Bill said.

I was sure that Rudy was about to break the man's face. "How *dare* you?"

Bill Daniels didn't seem intimidated at all, and I figured it was because he had a security guard somewhere real close by. "Kara, has he told you he was in prison for killing a woman?"

Rudy cursed and lunged at Bill, but the lawyer held him back.

I felt the blood draining from my face, and the room started to spin.

"You don't want to violate your parole, Rudy." Bill ground the words out through his teeth. "Step back before I have you dragged out of here."

Rudy finally stepped back, but I could see that he was seething as he turned back to me. I gaped at him, trying to see in his face if what the man said was true.

It was.

He grabbed my arm less gently then and marched me to the door and up the hall. The receptionist yelled, "Have a nice day!" as we made our way back to the elevator.

Rudy was muttering under his breath. "That sorry excuse for a human . . ."

"Why did you lie to me?" My throat was so tight I almost couldn't get the words out.

"Because I didn't want you thinking I was some kind of thug."

"Well, is that what you are? He said you *killed* somebody!"

"It was manslaughter, okay? I didn't put a gun to anybody's head. It was an accident, and I went to jail for it."

I stared at him. I don't know why it upset me so to know that he was some kind of convict. Some of my closest friends were in jail. Crawley was still in for his liquor store holdup, along with some of the other kids I used to hang around with.

The elevator came, and we stepped on. "How long have you been out of prison?"

He sighed. "A month."

I opened my mouth like I was going to scream, but it took me a minute to make a sound. "Why didn't you tell me that? There I was, thinking you were some real decent guy who'd blown into town like Prince Charming, when all the time you'd just got out of jail!"

"I didn't lie to you, Kara. It never came up."

"You *did* lie. You said you'd been working in Las Vegas, but that your grandmother left you that house, so you came here."

"The part about my grandmother was true."

I guess I was supposed to just forget about the part that wasn't. The elevator doors opened, and I stormed off, trying to remember which way to go. My head was starting to hurt, and

I was furious at myself for buying into Rudy's charm. I should have stuck with Deke and Eloise. At least I *knew* they were jerks. No surprises there.

He followed me to the car, the muscle in his jaw popping in and out, like *he* was the one who'd been lied to. We got to his car, and I plopped into my seat and slammed the door. I was so ready to go home.

He got behind the wheel and started the car, then drew in a deep breath and looked over at me. "Look, I'll tell you whatever you want to know. I didn't know that jerk was going to tell everything like that. Like he was protecting you from me or something. Like I'm going to get anything out of this."

"How long were you in, Rudy?"

"Ten years."

"Ten years." I bit the words out, amazed. "Were you paroled, or did you serve all your time?"

"Paroled."

I leaned against the window. How could I have fallen for some guy with a prison record? It was one thing to have the information up front . . . I still probably would have gone out with him, but I would have done it with my eyes open. There was nothing in the world I hated more than being lied to. "So how did you *accidentally* kill somebody?"

"It was a drunk-driving accident."

Things were coming into focus. "Don't tell me; let me guess. You were the drunk."

"Yeah, only it wasn't entirely my fault. She ran out in front of me when I had the green light. I had been drinking, but I wouldn't have run her over if she hadn't been so reckless."

I leaned my head back on the seat and wondered what Lizzie would say about all this. I didn't want her to know, because I'd played Rudy up so big. "So I'm going out with a killer."

"Hey, don't call me that! I don't deserve that." He started the car and pulled out of the dark garage.

The sunlight made me squint my eyes, and I just stared out the window.

"He's wrong, you know," he said. "You do have a case. He just had a chip on his shoulder and didn't want to do anything to help me. He didn't used to be like that. He was a decent guy back then when he was a public defender. But now he's sitting high in that big fancy office and thinks he's a big shot. I wouldn't be surprised if he knows Amanda. Maybe he's trying to protect her by talking you out of this."

I looked over at him. What he'd said made some sense. HolCorp was right there in Jackson, after all. Maybe this Bill Daniels did have some kind of connection to Amanda. Maybe he was holding out for a piece of *her* pie and figured it was a better bet.

That thought made me feel a little better.

"I'm not giving up," he said. "Why don't you let me take you out to lunch? And I'll call around and find another lawyer who'll see us."

I didn't answer right away. There were too many things whirling around in my head.

"What do you say, baby?" Rudy reached up and took a strand of my hair, twirled it around a finger. "Come on. You're not going to dump me over my past, are you? I thought a girl like you could overlook stuff like that. It's who I am now that's important."

He had a point. The truth was, I'd been arrested once, too, when Amanda had bailed us out. Who was I to judge?

Besides, a guy like Rudy was good to have around simply because he was shrewd and couldn't be snowed. I might need a guy like him when I got my money and didn't quite know what to do with it.

Like, for instance, where did you put that much money? Did you keep it in one bank account or a bunch of different ones, or did you spread it out over a bunch of different banks? I'd heard about Swiss bank accounts, but I wasn't sure why people used them. Maybe those were the only banks big enough to hold that kind of money.

And I didn't know a thing about investments or taxes.

But I was sure that Rudy would know all those things.

"All right, Rudy. We have to eat, I guess."

"That's my girl." He took my hand and kissed it.

I couldn't help thinking that he was still the best-looking man who'd ever darkened the doors of the SOS. I could break up with him now, but I'd only wind up going back with him when I got lonely. Besides, he was the only one I'd ever dated who knew how to treat a lady.

By the time we got to Dennery's Restaurant next to the interstate, I had stopped being quite so angry.

There was no use brooding when he was spending so much money on me.

THIRTY-THREE

While I ate my dessert, Rudy made a few phone calls from the pay phone. Finally, he came back to me.

"Good riddance to Bill Daniels, I say," he told me as he sat back down. "I've found another lawyer, a better one, and he's real interested in taking your case."

"Really? Where is he?"

"He's right here in Jackson and he can see us today. He's expecting us as soon as we can get over there." He grinned and leaned across the table. "He was almost giddy when I told him that Kara Holbrooke would like to talk to him about representing her in a lawsuit for the Holbrooke fortune. He's already seeing dollar signs."

I pushed my plate away. "Well, I guess I'm finished then. Let's go."

∞

I liked the new lawyer, Stan Mason, though his offices weren't as well appointed as those at Bill Daniels's firm. Still, it was better than Enos Wright's place. The attorney sat down with me and went over the case, trying to get a play-by-play of what had happened up to this point. Finally, he shook his head.

"Well, it's a long shot, but we can give it a try. The fact that she's taken your sister in indicates that she might want to settle this for your sake. There's no telling what kind of settlement that will be. Maybe a few million dollars."

Rudy shook his head. "No, uh-uh. She's not going into this for a few million dollars."

I thought Stan must not understand the situation. "Another lawyer I talked to told me that I could probably get fifty or sixty million."

Mason frowned. "That's not very realistic."

I was getting very tired. Nothing about this day had turned out like I'd hoped.

"She was just a baby when her father died," Rudy said. "Three years old. She never got a penny of the ten million her grandparents got to raise her. She was raised in a trailer, for Pete's sake! She was never properly represented in court, and her whole inheritance was stolen from her. You're telling me that that's not grounds for a lawsuit?"

"I didn't say we didn't have a case, but I'm not sure that this is a case I want to take."

I felt like screaming. Honestly, I did. I wanted to just jump out of my seat and let out a shriek that would shake the whole place.

Rudy could see how I was feeling, so he patted my knee. "Baby, why don't you let me talk to him alone for a minute? Just go sit out in the waiting room and leave this to me."

I didn't have a clue what he intended to do and I didn't much care. I'd just about had it with these losers telling me we'd lost before we'd even started.

I left the office and went back to the waiting room and thought about how much I could have made in tips today. If I hadn't taken the day off, I could have had the five hundred dollars by the end of the week, and then Enos Wright could file the papers. I should have just been happy with him in the first place. He knew what he was doing. He had gotten us ten million before, hadn't he? It wasn't his fault Deke had gambled it away.

By the time Rudy came out of the office, I had about decided the day was a complete washout, one of those live-and-learn kinds of days that made you want to break something.

But Rudy surprised me again. "He's going to take the case. Come on back in and sign the papers."

I got up and searched his face. "Why did he change his mind? What did you say to him?"

"I just explained how much Amanda had been trying to get you to come live with her, too, and how much she seems to care about you. That she'd probably write you out a settlement check without even batting an eye. And I told him we'd give him 40 percent."

I ignored the *we*. "You said 40 percent was too high to pay somebody. That's why you thought Enos Wright was a crook."

"I know, baby, but if you have to pay somebody that, it might as well be this guy. He's a more reputable lawyer. Trust me."

So I went back in and signed the paper to retain Stan Mason as my lawyer. Amazing how quickly everything changed.

I was giddy as we drove home. "I can't believe you changed his mind, Rudy. And to think I was going to pay that Enos jerk five hundred dollars!"

Rudy raked his fingers through his hair. "Oh, you still have to pay a retainer fee. Didn't I mention that?"

I frowned. "No."

"Well, yeah. He wants a thousand dollars up front."

"What? I don't have a thousand dollars!"

"Baby, that's just a drop in the bucket. You'll get millions out of this deal. He's the kind of lawyer who can get that for you. Now if we put our heads together and think, I'm sure we can come up with some way of getting that money."

I thought about that for a minute. I hadn't really come out any better than if I'd gone with Enos Wright. Enos was cheaper and he seemed to have more faith in my case. Still . . . this guy had admitted that he needed to do some research into Amanda Holbrooke's net worth before he could recommend an amount to sue her for. And Deke and Eloise weren't involved in this. That was a big plus. He seemed to know what he was doing.

"The thousand dollars is just in case you lose the lawsuit. He wants to make sure he comes out of it with something. People always skip town and forget they ever knew the attorney. When there's not a win, he has a hard time collecting. That's the only reason he takes it up front. Believe me, it's worth it."

I was really confused. "You said that wasn't right, that Enos Wright was an ambulance chaser, that he was only trying to milk me out of the money that I have."

"Look, this attorney is miles above Enos Wright. Did he have an office in a strip mall? Was he answering his own phones? No, he's in an important law firm that wins cases."

"Well, how will I come up with the money? I thought I could have five hundred dollars by the end of the week, but now you're talking about *another* five hundred bucks."

He considered that for a moment. "Didn't you say something about a necklace that Amanda gave you when she came to get you and Lizzie?"

I rolled my eyes. "Yeah, she gave me a stupid pearl necklace."

"Well, what's it worth, do you know?"

"I haven't got a clue."

"Maybe you could hock it. Just temporarily. You could buy it back later. But that could raise the money, if it was valuable enough."

I didn't think for a minute that the necklace was worth that much. But it was just sitting in a Ziploc bag in the Secret Tree, not doing anybody any good.

That necklace was like a sampling of my inheritance. That was exactly what Amanda had said. And now it could really be that, by giving me a head start on getting the rest of what was mine.

"All right," I said. "I'll get the necklace and I'll see about hocking it this afternoon."

"Good girl." He patted my leg, then he started singing "Money" by Pink Floyd, and I began to get in that rich mood again. I could almost see my ship coming in as we reached the turnoff for Barton.

THIRTY-FOUR

That afternoon before I went to work, I went to the Secret Tree and pulled out the plastic bag with Amanda's cell phone and the necklace box. I opened it and ran my fingers over the pearls. I had never put the necklace on, and I couldn't help wondering what it would look like on me. Oddly enough, as much as I hated Amanda Holbrooke, I didn't want to give it up.

But I had made up my mind. Rudy was right. The lawyer I'd visited that day was miles above Enos Wright, and it was worth extra money to get him to file my suit. Besides, cutting Deke and Eloise out of the picture sounded better all the time.

I closed the box, put the cell phone and my other childhood treasures back in the bag, and tucked it into the tree. Then I cut through the woods to the pawnshop near the strip mall.

The barred windows were filled with displays of guns and televisions and an old guitar in the hands of a chipped mannequin.

I stood out on that sidewalk, feeling like I'd been cut down the middle and left with half a brain, half a lung, half a heart. I had rarely been to this part of town without Lizzie. I missed her something awful and would have given anything to have her here with me. Was she wearing the necklace Amanda gave her? Had she found the right dress for that reception Amanda was throwing her? Had she realized yet that Amanda had ulterior motives? I hoped to heaven that she wasn't in any danger.

As mad as I was at her for leaving, I knew that the minute I got my money, I was going to try to lure her back. I would share it with her, no question. I couldn't picture a future without Lizzie, and I figured by then she would have seen Amanda for who she really was.

I went into the pawnshop and saw that Jason Pinkerton was talking to some guy at the gun side of the store. Jason was a huge guy who was always getting into fights at the local bars. He weighed about 350 pounds and had long, frizzy hair and a beard that needed trimming. He had tattoos all over his arms. It must have been his hobby or something. Tattoos with girls' names, tattoos of eagles and snakes and the American flag, tattoos with spiders and symbols of every kind you could imagine. You could hardly see his skin showing through on his arms.

He lived with the woman who owned the tattoo parlor in Pocahontas, so I guess she gave him a deal. He must have figured he'd get all the tattoos he could while he could get them for free.

I set the box down on the counter and looked around. He had several television sets lined up on a shelf, a DVD player, and a couple of computers. I wondered who they'd belonged to, or if someone had stolen them. After all, this was one of those places where crooks sometimes came to get rid of stolen stuff. Jason didn't ask questions. He just made the deals.

When the guy was gone, Jason came shuffling over to me. "You Lizzie or Kara?"

I got that all the time. "Kara. Lizzie moved."

"Oh, yeah, I heard that. Went to live with that rich woman, didn't she? How come you didn't go?"

"Because I don't need her." I lifted my chin like I was somebody. "I'm Paul Holbrooke's granddaughter, you know, and I've got a claim to that fortune. I've even got an attorney who's working on it right now. That's why I need to sell this." I opened the box and showed him the necklace. "It's real; you don't have to worry about that."

He kind of gasped when he looked at it. He took it out of the box with his big, tobacco-stained fingers. "Where in the Sam Hill did you get this?"

"It was my grandmother's. Not Eloise, the Holbrooke grandmother. It's probably worth a fortune."

He took a step back and peered at me as if seeing me for the first time. "Looks to be real," he said, fingering the pearls. "How much you want for it?"

"I need at least five hundred dollars."

"I can do that."

I quickly realized that I'd made a mistake setting the ceiling price. "If it's worth more, Jason, you could give me more."

"That's about what I'd say it's worth. Five hundred bucks."

I could see that his eyes were glowing. He thought he'd hit pay dirt.

He probably had.

As I waited for the money, I couldn't help wondering what the thing was really worth if he was that quick to pay. I took the money and stuffed it into my pocket. Now I had $950 to pay that lawyer. If I really hustled today, maybe I could make another $50 in tips.

I tried to forget about that necklace and just concentrate on my lawsuit as I walked to work. When I got to the truck stop, Rudy was waiting. "Did you get the money?"

"Yeah, $500. And I got the $450 in cash I had already. I should get at least $50 more in tips in the next couple of days. That'll make a thousand."

Rudy smiled and reached for my hand to pull me close. I practically forgot about his prison record and how aggravated I'd been with him earlier.

"Tell you what. Just go ahead and give me what you've got, and I'll put in the rest and take it to Jackson this afternoon so we can get this ball rolling."

I liked that idea, and I was impressed that he was willing to put in $50. I was really ready to get things started. The sooner that attorney filed the papers, the sooner I'd be rich. "All right." I pulled the money out of my pocket and put it into his hand.

"Tell you what," he said, "I'll come by and pick you up after you get off work tonight. I don't like you walking home by yourself."

It hadn't bothered him that much before, but I figured he was starting to have more tender feelings toward me. "All right. I get off at midnight."

"I'll be waiting," he said.

THIRTY-FIVE

Rudy was a dream for the next few days. He arranged his schedule at the casino so he could pick me up from work every night and drive me home. I started spending more and more time at his house. He used the word *we* a lot when he talked about the lawsuit and my future, and I started thinking that something might come of it.

I was feeling so good about Rudy that I wrote Lizzie again.

Dear Lizzie,

I just had to write and tell you all the exciting things that are happening here. The guy, Rudy, I told you about? I think I'm falling in love with him. Lizzie, he treats me like nobody else ever has before. He picks me up from work when I get off and he comes by several times a day and just hangs around. I can't stop thinking about him. It's driving me crazy.

I wish you could meet him. He's tall and good-looking and real self-confident. He makes a lot of money at the casino. He dresses nice, not like the bums in this town who walk around in greasy jeans and ten-year-old T-shirts. He's somebody, Lizzie, and when I'm around him, I feel like somebody, too.

You probably know by now that I've filed a lawsuit against Amanda. She may have gotten the papers by now. She's probably pretty mad, but, Lizzie, that money is ours, or it should be. We were the blood relatives of Paul Holbrooke, not her, and I don't know why you're not suspicious that she had anything to do with our dad's death. It all makes sense if you think about it. She would want to kill him just so she could get the money. And she did and now she's just biding her time with you.

Come back, Lizzie, and do this lawsuit with me. We can be rich together and go off to New York, just you and me and Rudy, and live in a penthouse condominium maybe in the same building that John Lennon lived in. Imagine Yoko Ono being our neighbor! I can't wait. Please think about it, Lizzie. It'll be more fun with you along. Besides, I miss you real bad. I can't believe you've stayed there that long.

Love,
Kara

When I went to see my attorney the next time, he told me that the prospects for getting a settlement from Amanda were good. He thought we would have an offer soon. As a precelebration, Rudy took me out to dinner at the fanciest restaurant in the casino. He had the band play Olivia Newton-John's "I

Honestly Love You," while he slowly moved me around on the dance floor like Prince Charming with Cinderella.

Then, between the third and fourth courses of our meal, he got down on one knee.

I thought he had dropped a contact or something and I felt a stab of disappointment that his eyes weren't really that blue. But he wasn't looking at the floor. He was looking up at me. He took my hands, and I noticed that a hush had fallen around the room. Everyone was watching.

I felt like I was the brunt of some kind of joke and I started to make him get up.

"Kara Holbrooke." He looked up at me with this look that said he was real serious. "You'd make me the happiest man in the world if you'd marry me." He said it real loud, so everybody could hear.

I caught my breath, and the diners all applauded. Aware that they were all waiting for my answer, I threw my arms around him and shouted, "Yes!"

The people applauded again, as if they'd just witnessed some grand Broadway performance, and the band struck up again.

I noticed there was no ring, but I told myself that I didn't need one. Soon I could buy all the rings I wanted.

Rudy was laughing when he sat back down.

"You're kidding, right?" I asked him. "That was just for show, wasn't it?"

"No, baby." He leaned on the table and put his face close to mine. "I mean it. I want to marry you."

"But isn't this a little quick? I mean, we haven't known each other all that long."

"How long do you have to know somebody? I knew the minute I laid eyes on you that you were the girl for me."

My heart was pounding, and I wished I could jump up and go call Lizzie. But the only number I had for her was on that cell phone in the Secret Tree. Anyway, I knew what she would say.

"You're not just doing this because I'm about to be a millionaire, are you?"

He looked wounded. "Do you really think that about me? Because if you do, maybe I've made a mistake—"

I took his hand, stopping him. "No, I don't think it. I just wanted to hear you say it."

"Because I liked you even before I knew about any stinking lawsuit, you know. Didn't I take you out the first night I met you? Didn't I?"

"Well, yes . . ."

"And haven't I treated you like a princess? Haven't I helped you?"

"Of course you have." He was so disturbed, I thought he might just cry.

"Then why would you ask me that? Why would you accuse me of something like that?"

"I'm not accusing you." He was really agitated, and the truth was, I didn't want him mad at me. Plus, I liked the idea of being his wife. I could picture us living our high life and traveling the country together. I really, really liked the idea of that.

"Kara, you're just about the best thing that's ever happened to me. You're the prettiest girl in Barton, hands down. Probably in all Mississippi, if you want to know the truth. How could I do better?"

He was a charmer, that Rudy, and my heart melted right to my toes.

"Come on, Kara. Marry me. And let's not wait a long time. Let's do it next weekend."

I caught my breath again. "Next weekend? Rudy! That's so fast."

"Well, what is there to wait for? We can't exactly afford a huge wedding right now, and we're not the church types. We can get the justice of the peace to do it, and take a little honeymoon in Vicksburg. The casino has a honeymoon suite, and I could get an employee discount."

"Next weekend . . ." The idea sounded good to me. I could marry him next weekend and leave Eloise and Deke behind. I could become Kara Holbrooke Singer, and then when I got the money, I would have somebody to share it with, even if Lizzie never came back.

Besides, I was so lonely . . . and I would have done just about anything to stop feeling so sad that Lizzie was gone. It was about time that something good happened in my life. I was long ready.

"All right." A thrill rose up inside me. "Next weekend, we'll tie the knot."

He pulled me to my feet then and started dancing me around again. People smiled and watched us, and I did a Lizzie wave. I laughed and laughed and laughed as he danced me around the dance floor to the sound of that big band playing Barry Manilow.

I didn't think I'd laughed like that for a very long time. And as he danced me around, I knew that my life was about to get drastically better.

I couldn't wait to tell Lizzie.

∞

Rudy got me home by midnight that night, since I had to get up early and work the next morning. Instead of going into the trailer, I ran through the woods with my flashlight until I got to the Secret Tree that had Amanda's cell phone in a Ziploc bag. I pulled it out and tried to turn it on, but the battery had lost its charge. Amanda had left an adapter cord with it, so I took it back to the trailer. Eloise and Deke were at the casino, so I had the place to myself.

I plugged the phone cord into the wall and waited a few minutes until it got a slight charge. I had played with some of the truckers' phones at the SOS, so I knew how they worked. I scrolled through the list for Amanda's number and hoped she meant it when she said that Lizzie would have that phone. I pressed *talk* and waited as it rang through.

After three rings, I heard Lizzie's sleepy voice. "Hello?"

"Lizzie, it's me!"

"Kara?" I could hear the excitement in her voice. "Kara, you finally called."

"Yeah. I figured if Amanda Holbrooke wanted me to use

her phone, I'd just use it. But I have some news I have to tell you."

"What? Tell me."

I could hear the anticipation in her voice, and I knew she was hoping that I was about to tell her I'd had a change of heart, that I was coming to join her. But my news was far better.

"I'm getting married!"

There was dead silence on the other end of the phone, and I started thinking that we'd been cut off. It wasn't that easy to get a good signal in Barton. The truckers were always complaining about it.

Finally, Lizzie spoke again. "Kara, you can't be serious."

"I am serious. I'm marrying Rudy. He took me out to dinner tonight at the bistro in the casino, and he had the band play 'I Honestly Love You,' and we danced, and he got down on one knee, Lizzie, and he asked me to marry him!"

"Don't do it, Kara. *Please* promise me you won't do it."

That set me off. I hated it when Lizzie didn't know the whole story, hadn't even *met* a guy, and started trying to change my plans. "Of course I'm going to do it. I've already told him yes."

"But, Kara, he's after this money that he thinks you're going to get. Only you're not going to get it. Amanda is not going to settle. You won't get any of it unless you come to us. It's *all* yours if you do that. You don't need Rudy or any bloodthirsty lawyer."

Now I was really insulted. "I *do* need Rudy. He treats me better than anybody in my life ever has. I'm going to marry him, and we're going to win this suit. I don't care what Amanda has been telling you. It's all lies. We've been told lies all our lives."

"Well, you're being told lies again. Kara, think about it. You don't know anything about him. Where did he come from? What's his background? Has he ever been married before? Does he have children?"

"I *do* know all that. He's never been married, has no children, and he used to live in Las Vegas." I left out the part about the prison sentence. That was really none of her business.

Lizzie got quiet again, and I started wishing I hadn't called her. She was really starting to bum me out. When somebody calls you up and tells you they're getting married, it's practically your *obligation* to act excited. I really resented that she couldn't do that for me.

But I didn't feel like getting into some big fight with her, so finally I said, "I want you to come to the wedding, Lizzie. I need for you to be here. It's next weekend."

"Next weekend? Kara, you're rushing into this. What's the hurry?"

"The hurry is that I want to marry him next weekend," I snapped. "I don't want to wait another day. Will you come or not?"

Lizzie thought that over for a moment. I could tell she was struggling with what to do. If she came, it was like she was condoning what I was doing. But if she didn't, she would really be letting me down.

Finally, she said, "Yes, I'll come. I know Amanda will want to be there, too."

I looked at the phone in my hand like I could see her crazy face. "You're nuts. I'm not inviting Amanda. I don't want her here. I don't want her anywhere near me."

"Why? What has she *done* to you?"

"She killed my father and she stole my sister. She took millions of dollars that would have been mine."

"She didn't do *any* of those things, Kara, and you know it. Our father died in a plane crash, and it was accidental. I've seen videos of newscasts when we were first taken away from Amanda. She even got arrested once for trying to run with us. She's nothing like you think."

"I don't want her here! Come by yourself or don't come at all."

The minute I'd said it, I started thinking that maybe she wouldn't come, and I couldn't stand the thought of getting married without her.

I knew Lizzie well enough to think she'd probably dig her heels in and spout off that she would miss it, then. I couldn't take that chance, so I said, "But I really want you to come."

Silence lingered between us. "I'll think about it," she said. "I'll need to ask Amanda."

"Right. Go ask the warden. See if she'll let you out for a weekend pass."

"It's not like that, Kara. Not at all. You don't understand. I just like to talk things over with her. She's wiser than I am."

"Well, that's *fine*. Knock yourself out. The wedding is going to be at seven Saturday night. We're getting married at the courthouse. The justice of the peace is opening it just for us."

"Justice of the peace? Oh, Kara, what happened to the beautiful wedding we used to plan? Ever since we were little we used to dress up with veils on our heads—"

"It's not the veil and the dress that's important, Lizzie. And that big storybook wedding doesn't matter. It's the man that counts, and I'm marrying the man I want."

I heard the phone beep and looked down at it. The battery was about to go dead again. "I've got to go. I think this phone is about to cut out. Come Friday, Lizzie. You can help me get ready."

There was another long pause, then, "Okay, Kara. I'll try."

The phone went dead before I could get a firmer answer from her. I sat there holding the phone, feeling as if my one lifeline had been slashed off. Despite my excitement over my wedding and my hopes about the future, I couldn't escape the feeling that something vital was missing inside me . . .

And I wasn't sure that even Rudy could fill it.

THIRTY-SIX

I didn't call Lizzie back, partly out of pride, and partly because I didn't want her trying to talk me out of it again. I figured by now Amanda had given her more ammunition for her arguments against Rudy, and I wasn't in the mood to hear them. I even worried that Lizzie might have found out about his record and start riding me about how I didn't need to marry an ex-killer and all.

I was having enough trouble with Eloise and Deke.

I hadn't expected a champagne celebration from them, but I didn't think they'd give my marriage much thought since they hardly knew I was there, anyway. Our paths didn't cross all that much since they spent most nights over at the casino and slept all day. I could have forgotten to tell them I was getting married, and they might not have noticed I was gone for months.

But the minute I told them, they started in on me.

"That man is out for one thing, Kara Holbrooke, and that's your money," Eloise said. "Don't you think it's not. He wants what you're gonna get, and then he'll probably clean you out and disappear without a trace."

Deke agreed, as passionate as I'd ever seen him. "You can't do this, girl! You wait until this lawsuit's settled, then you park it somewhere safe. If he still wants to marry you then, fine, but don't you do it before then."

"I'm marrying him next Saturday." I was getting good at standing my ground. "You can say whatever you want to about him, but he's going to be my husband."

"Kara, you're washing your future right down the toilet!" Eloise screeched.

I thought that was kind of funny since there'd never been any talk about my future before. "Seems like *everybody's* real interested in this money I'm gonna get. Seems like maybe you two are suspicious because you think this'll make your part smaller."

"We're looking out for you, girl," Deke said. "Don't you know that?"

I was so moved I wanted to gag. "You don't have to come to the wedding. I'm just telling you when it's going to be."

"Can't you at least wait until you've *filed* the suit?" A vein in Eloise's forehead looked like it might burst. "Just so's his name ain't on it, too?"

They didn't know I had already filed it. They still thought I was saving up the five hundred dollars so I could use their lawyer and that they would get a big hunk of whatever I won. I wondered how much they thought I would give them. Did they think I would just write them a check, out of the goodness of my heart?

I didn't bother to tell them any of that, though, because I didn't need any extra hassles before the big day. "I'm getting married next Saturday, and that's all there is to it."

Eloise started to cry then. I don't think I'd ever seen that before. She touched my hand in this real sweet, phony way, like it was just breaking her heart that she'd be losing me. "Well, you're just depriving me of all the stuff I've always wanted to do for you when you got married."

I moved my hand. "What would that be?"

"Shopping for a dress, a cake, decorating the church, looking for a wedding gift."

"Walking you down the aisle," Deke said, and I almost laughed. But I kept a straight face.

"We don't have any money, remember? I can't afford a cake or decorations. I'm hoping I can scrape together enough for a new dress. If you want to help me, you can help me with that."

"All right, sweetheart." Eloise sounded like she was auditioning for the role of a doting grandmother in some little theater production. "We'll start looking tomorrow."

I didn't think for a minute that she would keep her word, but she did. She took me to Vicksburg to the outlet mall, and we scoured the stores looking for something we could afford. I found a dozen dresses I would have loved to get married in, but quickly realized that I was going to have to settle for a stupid pale yellow sundress that cost twenty bucks. Eloise managed to shell out more for the dress she chose for herself, but I didn't say a word. I figured payback time would come soon enough.

She was syrupy sweet for the next few days as she helped me box up the things in my room in preparation for the big move. Every now and then, she'd come out with something like, "Don't you think you should call Enos and see if he'd come down a little more on your down payment? I bet he would, you know. Then we could get this thing started."

I'd be making a list of all I had to do—the blood test, the marriage license, the name change—when she'd pop out with, "Wouldn't it be nicer to get married after you had that money, so you wouldn't have to scrimp so?"

Finally, Deke called Enos up himself. I don't know what he told him, but the lawyer wound up lowering his price for fear of losing me entirely. He would take $350, Deke said. I just smiled and said that I'd let him know when I came up with that amount.

As good as they were treating me, I thought it was a shame I was leaving. I hadn't been treated that well in my whole life, at least not that I remembered. I'm sure my dad treated me well when we were living with him, but that wasn't anywhere in my memory.

The only bad thing about that week was that I had so much flying through my head that I needed to talk about, but Lizzie was off living her new life, and I didn't even know if she'd be coming to the wedding. I was really lonely for my sister that week. I'd imagined my wedding so many times in my life, and

Lizzie was always right there, standing up beside me. It was just too depressing for words not to have her there now. All I had was Eloise and Deke, doing their phony slobbering all over me for fear that I was going to cut them out of my life and doom them to a life of poverty.

When that Friday came, I was real jittery, wondering if Lizzie would come. I didn't have that much left to do. We'd had our blood tests and gotten our license, the justice of the peace was booked, and my few belongings were boxed up and ready to be moved.

I was home alone that day, and thankfully so, since I thought I might just snap if I had to listen to much more from Eloise and Deke. I kept going to the window and looking out, hoping I would see Lizzie driving up. I didn't know what she'd be in. She couldn't drive when she left, and I doubted she had learned this quickly.

Then I saw the limousine pulling into my driveway, and I let out a scream and ran out the front door. Lizzie jumped out of the car and ran into my arms, and we held each other, squealing with laughter, as the chauffeur got out and stood by the car door.

"Lizzie, you're a sight for sore eyes!" I clung to her as if I could pull her inside myself. "Oh, Lizzie, you *came!*"

"Of course I came. You didn't think I'd miss it, did you?"

She looked different, much more groomed and poised than she had before. She smelled like Amanda, and her hair was softer than mine. I figured she'd been using some expensive conditioner on it. She didn't look at all abused or mistreated. She looked like her new life was doing nothing but good for her.

But I knew better.

I took her hand and led her into the house. She held back at the front door, like she dreaded coming all the way in. "I never thought I'd come back here."

"Trust me, once I'm gone, I'm not coming back, either."

"The whole town smells." She wrinkled her nose. "You have to be gone from here to realize it, but it does. It's an awful smell. I can't believe I lived in it all those years. I can't believe you'd want to stay in it."

"I'm used to it." I pulled her inside. "It doesn't bother me."

She got a pinched look on her face and looked around at the dirty living room. "It smells in here, too. Smells like Deke's slimy shoes and those dogs."

I was getting aggravated. "It won't kill you to come in for a minute."

"So where are Deke and Eloise?"

"They won a little money last night so Eloise is out trying to find me a wedding gift."

Lizzie looked at me like she didn't believe a word. "No way."

"Oh, yeah. You should see how they're treating me. It's just sickening. It's like they think I'll forget the past fifteen years and only remember that they were nice to me the week of my wedding. They're scared to death I'm going to leave them out when I get my money. And just between you and me, that's exactly what I plan to do."

Lizzie swallowed, and I knew she was holding back her lecture about the lawsuit. I was thankful.

"Want to see what I'm wearing?" I have to admit I asked mostly for a distraction. I knew my dress wouldn't impress her. The dress she was wearing was nicer than my wedding day dress.

"Show me," she said.

I led her into the bedroom we had shared for so many years. It was just as she'd left it. The sheets hadn't even been changed.

I pulled my dress out of the closet and held it up to myself. "It was all I could afford."

She didn't look impressed. "It's pretty, Kara . . . but didn't you want a real wedding dress?"

"Well, yeah. I wanted a honeymoon in Paris, too, but I'm not gonna get it." I put my hands on my hips. "I hope you haven't turned into a snob, Lizzie."

She looked downright insulted. "I haven't. I just want you to have the best. So I brought a few things you might want to consider. I brought my evening gown that I wore to my reception last week. It's ivory. Maybe you could wear it."

I knew in that moment how Cinderella must have felt when her fairy godmother had come to save the day. "Oh, let me see!"

Lizzie opened the door and stepped out on the rickety porch. The chauffeur immediately emerged from the front seat. "Could you bring my suitcase in, Charles?"

I had to laugh as I leaned against the post, my arms crossed. "Charles?"

"He doubles as my bodyguard and chauffeur. He's a nice guy. Amanda really trusts him."

"A bodyguard? Isn't that a little extreme?"

"No. Amanda says we're targets because of the Holbrooke name. She insists I be protected wherever I go. Besides, he's gotten to be a good friend. If you came, she'd make sure you had one, too."

"I'm not coming. I'm *never* coming."

Charles brought in the suitcase and put it in the living room. "Anything else, Miss Lizzie?"

She shook her head. "Thank you, Charles."

I was watching him go back to his car, when Rudy's dusty Volvo pulled in on the gravel. "There he is." I turned to see her face. "That's Rudy. Are you ready to meet him?"

Lizzie got a little pale, but she looked out the door.

"Isn't he handsome?" I hugged myself. "Just look at him. Can you believe I'd get a man like that?"

"Kara, you could have had any guy you wanted. You weren't limited to Barton, Mississippi."

I grinned. "You won't say that when you meet him." Rudy got out of the car. He had dressed nice for this visit, and I knew Lizzie would be impressed. I went down the steps and out to him, took his hand, and led him back up.

His step slowed as he reached the porch, and he started to laugh. "I feel like I'm seeing double."

I had forgotten that he'd never seen the other half of me. "We get that all the time," I said. "Lizzie, meet Rudy. Rudy, Lizzie."

Lizzie's eyes were cold as she shook his hand. "Nice to meet you." She was polite and all, but the tone of her voice made it clear that she wasn't that glad to meet him at all. I decided that she *had* turned into a snob, and I didn't like it.

Rudy held on to her hand. "Just when I thought Kara was the most beautiful girl in the world, I find out there's another one just like her."

"Not just like her," Lizzie said without a smile. "Kara's one of a kind."

I wasn't sure what she meant by that, but from her voice, I knew she didn't mean it in a bad way.

Rudy put his arm around my waist. "So what do you think about our plans?"

Lizzie was barely able to force a smile. "They're a little surprising, but Kara knows I wish her the best."

"Come in, Rudy," I said, "and help us decide what I should wear tomorrow."

"I thought you'd already gotten a dress."

"I did, but Lizzie brought some other things. She said she had an ivory dress. Can you believe it, Rudy? I might actually get married in white."

He followed us in and took his place at the edge of the couch, as if he didn't want to get his clothes dirty. I didn't blame him. Nothing in the house had been vacuumed in about a year, and the dogs came in often and napped on that couch.

He couldn't seem to tear his eyes off of Lizzie as she stooped down at her suitcase and opened it. I almost got jealous, but then I realized that he might as well be looking at me. Guys had always had trouble telling us apart, and it was a common problem to have one of them fall for me, only to have his eyes stray to her when she was around. I didn't like it much, but I knew it was normal.

Lizzie unfolded the suitcase divider panel and slid out the dress that had been carefully strapped in. The dress looked just like the one I had imagined I'd get married in, with a scooped neck and a full chiffon skirt.

"We used to draw a dress like this." She held it in front of her. "Remember, Kara, all those times we dreamed about our weddings?"

I could hardly speak as I took the dress. It was the most beautiful thing I'd ever seen in person. "Lizzie," I whispered reverently. "It's gorgeous."

"I bought it because it reminded me of what we always wanted. Amanda said it was appropriate for my reception. Who knew that you would need it for your wedding so soon?"

Tears stung my eyes, and I held the dress high to keep it from touching the dirty floor. "Oh, Rudy, isn't it just the best thing you've ever seen?"

"It's pretty, Kara, but don't you think it's a little dressy?"

He just didn't get it, and that frustrated the life out of me. "No. It looks more appropriate for a wedding than that stupid sundress. I'm wearing it."

"We could fix your hair up," Lizzie said, "like we used to do when we were little. Remember, we'd put a doily on our heads and prance around like we were princesses?"

I hung the dress over my arm and hugged her. "I'm so glad you're here," I said. "This is the best day of my life."

She wiped a tear. "Here, go try the dress on. I want to see it. I brought shoes, too." She dug those out of the suitcase and handed them to me.

I was so full of emotion that I went over and kissed Rudy on the cheek. "I'll be right back."

I closed myself in the bedroom and started changing. I couldn't wait to feel that dress against my skin and watch Rudy's face light up. I couldn't wait to see *myself* in it.

I heard them talking in low voices and I pressed my ear to the door.

"You don't have to stand up," Rudy said. "Come sit down and we'll talk."

I heard Lizzie's footsteps as she crossed the room. "I want you to tell me something honestly. I want to know why you're marrying my sister."

He let out a laugh, as if he couldn't believe she'd ask such a bold question. Truth was, I couldn't believe it, either. "Why *wouldn't* I want to marry her? She's beautiful. You see that."

"I asked you a question. Why now? What's the rush?"

"She's the love of my life. My soul mate. She's just the one, that's all."

"It wouldn't have anything to do with that lawsuit she's got going, would it?"

I almost came out of the bedroom then, but I had already undressed. I slipped the white dress on and zipped it up, still listening through the door.

"I'm just helping her out with the suit, that's all. Whether she wins or loses, it's all the same to me."

"So you don't care if she makes minimum wage or wins fifty million dollars in court?"

"No difference to me."

I heard her walk across the room again, and she closed her suitcase. "I want to tell you something, Rudy. If you hurt my sister, you'll be sorry. She's vulnerable and she'll fall for anything right now. But I better not see you breaking her heart, especially when she loses that suit."

"She's not going to lose," Rudy said.

"Amanda has no intention of settling out of court. She's not going to do it, Rudy."

"Watch," he said.

"I live with her." Lizzie's voice got louder. "She's told me what she plans to do. She knows if she gave Kara the money it would be squandered. She doesn't trust you or Deke and Eloise. She doesn't even trust Kara to know what to do with that much money."

"Well, your Amanda may not have a choice." He sounded cocky, challenging. "I don't see any way a judge is going to turn Kara down, a young girl who was tricked out of her family's fortune. No way. She'll get hers."

"And you'll get yours. I can promise you that."

Silence . . . then, "You talk big for a little thing."

I knew that would set Lizzie off. I quickly slipped the shoes onto my feet.

"If you hurt her, I'll find out," Lizzie said.

"Are you threatening me?" Rudy's voice sounded just like it had when he'd gone after Bill Daniels.

There was a long pause, then Lizzie said, "Yes, I think I am."

I opened the door then and stepped into the living room. I looked from one of them to the other . . . Lizzie didn't know I'd heard any of their conversation, and a smile lit up her face. "Oh, Kara, it's *you*. It looks so much better on you than it did on me."

"Rudy," I said, my voice barely audible through the emotion in my throat. "What do you think?"

He hardly even glanced at me. "I'm with Lizzie. It's gorgeous on you. I'd marry you right this minute if we had a judge around."

I was satisfied with that answer, so I nodded and went back to the bedroom. Thankfully, Lizzie came with me this time.

"Take it off and let's hang it up. We don't want it to get dirty on this filthy floor." She closed the bedroom door, locking Rudy out.

I just looked at her. "Oh, Lizzie, you'll warm up to him. You just don't know him, that's all." I slipped the dress off of my shoulders, and Lizzie unzipped it.

"I want to spend time with you tonight," I said. "Rudy has to work. I want you and me to go to the casino and talk over drinks."

"Kara, we're not of age to drink at the casino. What are you talking about?"

"Of course we are. Rudy'll get us anything we want."

"I don't want to go to the casino," Lizzie said. "How can you even walk into that place when you know how much money Eloise and Deke lost there? Don't you realize that Eloise and

Deke got over $300,000 a *year* for fifteen years for the sole purpose of taking care of us, and we didn't get any of it? We lived in this dump and ate dry cereal and wore clothes that we dug out of Goodwill bins. And the worst thing, Kara, is they kept us from Amanda, who loved us and would have done anything for us."

"Boy, she's really been filling your head, hasn't she?" I slipped back into the jeans I'd been wearing and pulled my T-shirt back over my head. "If she loved you so much, why doesn't she just write you a check and give you your share?"

"She wants a relationship with me," Lizzie said. "She wants me to have a good life. There are things I have to learn. I'm way behind, Kara, and I want to be everything she wants me to be. I'm going to have a lot of responsibility ahead of me someday and I have to be ready."

"Do you really think she's going to hand that company over to you? If you do, you're more naive than I thought."

"I'm not naive." Lizzie's eyebrows arched as she tried to make her point. "She's an amazingly good person. She's going to leave it to me in her will. And you, too, if you come, Kara. She wants to train us, groom us to take it over. And we can. I already see that I have a good business head. I'm not stupid like they told us in school, Kara. I'm smart, and so are you. By the time Amanda retires, we'll be ready to do it."

"By the time Amanda retires, I might own that company myself. And, Lizzie, you could do it with me. The two of us in this lawsuit would make it even easier. We could get the whole thing from her and kick her out of that mansion and take over the business. And all of that would be ours without any of the schooling and hassles."

"I don't want it that way!" Lizzie looked at me like I was just too dense to grasp what she was saying. "It gives me peace knowing it's all Amanda's right now, that she's taking care of it, keeping it safe. I'd make a mess of things. Whoever is telling you that you can have it on your own is lying to you. It's not going to happen that way. Amanda has no intention of settling out of court, and there's no way a judge is going to reverse the decision he made when he gave her the estate, especially not when I'm there and she's showering me with all this goodness."

"Well, you're not going to testify against me, are you, Lizzie?"

Lizzie stared at me for a moment, and her eyes misted with tears. "If it's necessary, I will, Kara. If they ask me questions, I have to tell the truth, that Amanda offered you everything she has and you refused it. It's not going to look good, Kara. You won't have a leg to stand on."

"Well, Rudy says she's going to settle out of court, and I believe him."

Lizzie sank down onto the mattress. "You're so deceived. You believe so many lies."

My heart beat so hard in my chest I thought it might burst through. "I believe him more than I believe you. You rushed off and left me here."

"You could have come with me." Grief twisted Lizzie's face. "I begged you to."

"You *left* me, and *he* didn't! He's here for me, and you're not. You're just jealous. You think I'm not special enough to win somebody important like Rudy. You just can't imagine him falling for me."

"I know you can do better," Lizzie cried. "You could meet a man your own age—a *decent* man—and marry him and have children. We've been told all our lives we were nothing but trash, Kara, and *you* still believe it. But whether you believe it or not, Rudy's still *treating* you like trash. He wants the money he thinks you're going to get. That's why he's in such a rush to marry you."

"Hey, he didn't even know who I was before he met me. He fell for me before I told him the first thing. And it wasn't his idea for me to file the suit. I started that whole thing with Eloise and Deke."

"You see?" Lizzie said. "You've been manipulated by somebody all your life. Why don't you start thinking for yourself, Kara? Start using some of your common sense. I know you have some."

I couldn't believe she was attacking me this way, on one of the happiest days of my life. "I wanted this to be a special weekend, but you're ruining it for me. Why do you have to come here and do that?"

Lizzie got quiet. "I don't mean to do that, Kara. I do want you to be happy. I want that with all my heart. But I don't see it coming this way."

"Well, this is the way I'm going to get it. Like it or not. Now, I appreciate the dress and everything, but if you're going to just badger me the whole weekend, you can leave right now."

I could tell Lizzie struggled to hold back the tears overcoming her. "All right, Kara. I won't say any more about it."

"Fine." I sat down on the bed and laid the dress over my lap. Lizzie smeared a tear across her cheek. Rudy had probably heard every word from the living room. I almost hated her for doing that to him.

"So . . . are you going to stay here with me tonight or—"

"I'm staying in a hotel," Lizzie said quickly. "Amanda got me a suite in a hotel in Vicksburg."

"At the Isle of Capri?" I raised my eyebrows. "That's where we're honeymooning tomorrow night."

"No, not the one at the casino. It's down the block a little. She said it's an exclusive little hotel called the Simmons Suites. I was hoping you'd stay there with me."

"Really?" I perked up at that. "Oh, Lizzie, that'd be fun. We could stay up all night and talk, just like old times."

"The old times weren't all that good, Kara."

"I know, but they're about to get better. I promise, Lizzie. Trust me, okay?"

"I hope you're right, Kara. I really do." She got up from the bed, took the dress out of my hands, and hung it back up. "We can take all your things and get ready over at the hotel tomorrow if you want to. That way you don't have to do it here."

"Okay." I was already starting to forget how angry I'd been. Excitement was creeping back in. "I'll get my stuff. But don't you want to stay and see Eloise and Deke?"

Lizzie considered that for a moment. "No, I'd really like to be gone when they get home."

"Fine by me. I can't put this place behind me fast enough."

THIRTY-SEVEN

That night, we sat up late into the night, talking and catching up.

Lizzie couldn't stop talking about Amanda and the house she lived in and the family they'd forged there and how wonderful it all was.

I wasn't buying any of it, but I was curious enough to listen.

"You should have seen me that day when we got to her house." Lizzie's eyes widened, as if she was reliving the whole thing. "You can't even see it from the street. It's real private, down a winding road with these beautiful oak trees on either side, making a canopy over the road. Even the ride up to it was peaceful and beautiful. It would have been perfect if you'd been there."

"How did *she* act on the way there?"

"She talked all the way there, telling me about when we were little. How she met our father, and how she fell in love with us, and how she loved taking care of us."

"Nothing that can be proved," I pointed out.

"No, I guess she can't prove her feelings for us back then. But I believe her."

"Well, that's just crazy."

"Not to me." She sat on the hotel's king-sized bed, her legs crossed Indian-style. She had pulled her hair up in a ponytail, and she looked more like her old self. "But when we got to the gates of the house, I just couldn't believe my eyes. It looked like a big, white palace. Like something right out of the movies. I figured it would be all cold and untouchable.

"But the minute I got out of the car, the huge, massive front door flew open, and this group of people burst out, acting all excited to see me."

"Who were they?"

"Practically family, though none of them are really related to us. See, years ago, Amanda moved into the mansion because her life had become a security nightmare. After she got the inheritance, no one would leave her alone. She decided to move into the mansion, even though she couldn't imagine living in a place like that, because she wanted it to still be there for us when we grew up."

"Yeah, right."

"But she didn't want to live there alone, with just the staff. And she didn't like the butler. He was this snobbish jerk who looked down his nose at her and made her feel creepy, so she fired him and all of the staff who acted like that and hired up people she liked. Instead of a butler, she hired her father's best friend, Mack, to move in and help oversee the staff. He's a sweet old man, just like a grandfather ought to be. Nothing like Deke . . . Mack is sweet and plump and keeps hugging me and telling me how thrilled he is that I'm finally home. He was the first one out to greet me that day. You would have thought I was really his family. He even had tears in his eyes as he hugged me."

I tried to imagine it, but all I could picture was some guy working up a lot of fake emotion.

"Who else?"

"Joan, of course. She's Amanda's best friend. When Amanda inherited HolCorp, Joan became her assistant. You never met a more efficient person. Joan can do *anything*. She lives in the mansion, too. Amanda invited her to live there with her and Mack and the staff. And then there's Sarah, the head maid who raised our dad. She's old now, but she's sweet and Amanda loves her. Amanda doesn't let her do much work. She's even given her her own set of rooms and she treats her like a mother or something. Sarah's always telling me stories about when Daddy was little. I can almost picture him bouncing a basketball on the marble floor, sliding down the banister, playing hide-and-seek in those huge rooms."

"Is it like a museum?"

"No," Lizzie said. "It's warm and cozy in every room. Amanda redecorated completely so it would look more like a home. There's not a room in that house that I don't feel comfortable in. But it wasn't like that at first." She got up, standing on the bed. "When I got there, they took me into the ballroom where the staff, about two dozen people, were lined up, all dressed in crisp black and white." She demonstrated. "I thought I was going to faint. But then someone blew one of those curly horn things that people have at parties, and all of a sudden everybody started clapping for me, like I was a movie star or something. And they surrounded me and we had this big party." She bounced back down on the mattress.

"That's weird."

Lizzie frowned. "Why?"

"I don't understand what they want."

"Nothing. They just want to restore me to my home and my family. The weird thing is that they knew everything I liked, without my telling them. Amanda had kept such tabs on us growing up that she knew our favorite foods, the colors we liked, the kind of decorations we'd want in our rooms."

"*Our* rooms?"

"Yes, Kara. Yours is there, just waiting for you to come. It's decorated like a dream. Bright floral prints and beautiful curtains and polished cherry furniture. I have a fourposter bed that's high off the floor, Kara, and it's so beautiful. You have one, too, with a green-and-white canopy and lace curtains draping down."

I got up and went to my suitcase, then rummaged around like I was looking for something. I have to admit I was confused. It didn't sound like Amanda was mistreating her. It sounded like everything she'd promised was true.

But I still couldn't believe it.

Lizzie jumped off the bed and stood at the center of the floor, waving her arms, as if to show me all the things she described. "From my room, I can look out the window onto the back lawn. It's brimming with flowers in every color. And sitting right in the middle of the garden is the little playhouse I told you about in my letter. Amanda had it moved there from the little house we lived in. Daddy built it for us. We even helped. You can see where we painted and hammered."

I looked up at her then. "*That's* got to be a lie. I would remember something like that."

"I don't remember it, either," she said. "But it's all true. There are pictures. When she took me out there for the first time, we went inside the playhouse. There was some little Fisher-Price kitchen furniture in there, and she said it was what we used to play with. She brought a photo album, and we sat out there and looked at pictures of our family."

"What pictures?"

She gave me an *aha* smile and rushed to her suitcase. "I'll show you."

She pulled out a wrapped gift and set it on my lap. "This is kind of my prewedding gift to you."

I sucked in a breath. "My first gift." Grinning, I tore into the paper, opened the box, and pulled out the photo album decorated with pearl beads and gold plating. I ran my fingers over it. "I've never seen one this fancy," I whispered.

"Open it," Lizzie said. "Look at the pictures."

I flipped back the cover and saw the pictures of a woman holding two little red-haired babies, just hours old.

"That's our mother." Lizzie's voice was laced with reverence. "She died when we were just weeks old."

I turned the page. A man who looked strangely familiar, though I didn't think I'd ever seen him before, sat grinning, two tiny babies in his arms. He had red, curly hair like ours and big, friendly eyes. "We look like him," I whispered.

"Yes, we definitely have our father's eyes," Lizzie said wistfully. "And his hair, of course. But I think we have our mother's chin."

I turned a couple of pages and found another snapshot of our mother, holding us.

"That one's you." Lizzie pointed to the one that was yawning. But my eyes were on my mother, who was blonde and thin and prettier than Eloise and Deke had ever told us.

"And look at this." Lizzie turned the page and showed me another one of our father, holding me in his arms, and leaning down to put a kiss on my round little cheek. I'd never been all that sentimental, but my throat got all choked up. I had to close the book. "I don't think I can look at this right now."

"That's fine." Lizzie laid her hand on my arm. "I got real emotional the first time, too. You can look at it when you're ready. There are lots of pictures of us with Amanda when we were three, before they took us away from her. When you see them, you'll realize how much she loved us."

Silence fell over us, and Lizzie got down on her knees in front of me. She looked up into my face and pushed my hair behind my ear. She was different than she'd been just weeks ago. She was sweeter, more sensitive.

Nothing like me.

"Kara, I feel like I was in a prison for most of my life, with cruel, greedy people lying to me and making me think that it was my fate to be there. They kept us down, Kara. They controlled us. They made us into people without hope. And it was a life sentence. You're accepting that sentence, Kara, when the doors to that prison are open now. But you won't walk through them. We can go back to the family in the pictures of this photo album. We can know peace and joy."

"On *her* terms!"

"Yes, on her terms. They're good terms, Kara. I've never felt more free in my life. The whole world is open to me now. I have hope and a future. Things are happening to me that I never even knew to hope for or imagine. For the first time in my life I feel like I'm standing on steady ground. And I feel strong, because it's not just me, Deke and Eloise's tattered granddaughter. I have all of Amanda's resources behind me, and she's there rooting for me and guiding me. It's all about love, Kara. Not money."

"Love is always about money."

"No, it's not! That's a lie you've been taught!"

I bit my lip. Maybe I was just messed up. Maybe Lizzie had it right. After all, Rudy *might* be in this for the money, just like Eloise and Deke were. I started wondering what it would be like to get into that limo with Lizzie tomorrow and let her take me to Amanda's with her.

But those thoughts felt like self-betrayal. Lizzie was playing with my emotions, luring me with these pictures and all the stuff she'd told me.

But it was going to blow up in her face before long. It was too good to be true. Too easy. Nothing was that simple.

"I brought you more gifts," Lizzie said, and I looked up at her.

She got out a flat box wrapped in white, and another small box.

I felt the shadows in my heart lifting. I smiled as I took the boxes.

"The big one's from me," Lizzie said. "The small one's from Amanda."

"Yours first." I undid the bow. "It looks so pretty. I hate to mess it up."

"You *have* to mess it up to see what's inside."

I grinned, then tore into the paper. I got down to the white box, pulled it open. An ivory veil lay folded there, with a band made of inset pearls. I pulled it out and settled my astonished eyes on it. "Oh, Lizzie."

"I couldn't let you get married without a veil, after all those times we played—"

I threw myself at her, and she laughed and hugged me. Tears started to make their way down my cheeks. I couldn't believe how lucky I was.

Lizzie shook the long netting out and slid the comb into my hair. "I tried it on myself at the store. I pictured you in it."

Wiping my eyes, I floated to the mirror. "I'm a bride," I whispered. "A real bride."

Lizzie stood back and watched me go to the dress hanging in the closet. I quickly undressed and slipped the dress back on, then spun around in front of the mirror. "Look at me, Lizzie. It's just what I always imagined."

"Except for walking down the aisle of a church."

"Well, I don't have a church. Anyway, could you just picture Deke giving me away? No, walking up the courthouse steps is just fine."

I didn't want to take the dress off, so I just sat there in it. I couldn't stop looking in the mirror.

"Don't forget Amanda's gift."

I hated to tear myself away. "I don't really want anything from her."

"You'd be silly not to take it. Trust me, you'll love it."

I took the package she handed me and tore into it with less excitement. "Looks like jewelry," I said when I got to the box. I took off the lid and gazed down at the pearl bracelet, exactly made to match the necklace I had hocked.

"Pearls again."

"Where's your necklace?" Lizzie asked. "Are you going to wear it in the wedding tomorrow?"

I swallowed. "No."

"Well, you should. Do you know how valuable this bracelet is? It's probably worth thousands of dollars. The necklace is worth even more."

I felt a little sick. "Thousands? Over at the pawnshop they only gave me five hundred!"

Lizzie looked crestfallen. "Kara!"

I jumped up and backed across the room, lifting the skirts of my dress as I moved. "I shouldn't have told you that. I knew better."

"You *hocked* it for five hundred dollars? Kara, how could you?"

"I needed the money! I had to have it to pay my attorney."

"That's just like you, Kara. Trading your birthright for a bowl of stew."

A bowl of stew? I stared at her like she was nuts. "What are you talking about?"

"It's what Esau did in the Bible."

"The Bible? Since when have you read the Bible?"

"Since Amanda got me interested in it. It's good, Kara. Better than any novel I've ever read. But that's not the point. The point is that you don't even understand the value of the things Amanda has for you."

"I guess not." I looked down at the bracelet. "But I won't sell this."

Lizzie looked as if I'd insulted *her* when I sold the necklace. "At least not for five hundred bucks," she said. "If you do sell it, at least get what it's worth."

"Well, how do you do that? The pawnshops don't give you that much."

"Take it to a jeweler," Lizzie said. "I'm not telling you to sell it, but for heaven's sake, if you're going to, just do it right."

"All right, I will. But you can tell Amanda that she doesn't have to keep sending me fancy jewelry. I'm not going to wear it. Soon I'll be able to buy all the jewelry I want."

I could tell that Lizzie didn't want to fight with me, so she bit her tongue and didn't mention it again.

We slept for a few hours, and when I woke, I jumped out of the hotel bed and cried out, "This is my wedding day!"

Lizzie didn't say much. She just ordered up room service

and set about getting ready. She was quiet as she fixed my hair and helped me into the dress and veil. Then she took a bunch of pictures, probably to take to Amanda.

When we got to the courthouse, I could feel Lizzie bracing herself as Eloise and Deke arrived in their gaudy new clothes.

"Well," Eloise said when she saw her, "imagine you lowering yourself to join us."

"We thought you was too good to come back to Barton," Deke added. "In your ritzy clothes and that limousine out front. You really think you're something, don't you?"

Lizzie didn't flinch. "I know who I am."

But she looked miserable a few minutes later, standing there with me gushing about how good Rudy looked, all dressed up in a black suit and a white shirt and tie.

I noticed her wiping her tears as the judge conducted the no-frills ceremony. It was over almost minutes after it got started, and I felt a little let down. But then Rudy kissed me, and I realized I was Mrs. Rudy Singer, that I never had to live in that filthy house with Eloise and Deke again.

When it was all over, Lizzie hugged me tight enough to break me. "Kara, promise me you'll call me if you need me. Anytime. Keep that phone with you. Do you hear me?"

"Of course I will." I almost laughed. You would have thought I was heading off for the jungle or something. "Don't worry. He's going to take good care of me."

I could see that she didn't believe it.

As I got into Rudy's car to head off to the Isle of Capri

where we would spend our wedding night, Lizzie got into her limousine. She was crying as they drove off.

I didn't let it bother me this time. I was too excited about my new life.

THIRTY-EIGHT

I had never been treated like an adult before, not in any real way. But now that I was Rudy's wife, I felt I was a full-blown grownup. I ordered drinks in the casino that night, and they actually brought them to me. They brought a few too many to our table, as a matter of fact, because Rudy threw down drink after drink, getting louder and more boisterous as he did. I laughed out loud as he twirled me around the dance floor and pranced me around the game room, showing me off to his coworkers. It was the most fun I'd ever had.

But sometime after midnight, he seemed to turn a corner. His eyelids grew heavy, and he started to stagger instead of walk.

When I finally suggested that we go up to our room, he was all agreement.

They had given us a suite. It wasn't quite as nice as the one Lizzie and I had stayed in the night before, but it was miles above where I'd lived before. He kicked off his shoes as we came in, and he pulled off his tie and plopped down on the bed.

I slipped into the bathroom to change into the gown I'd bought with last week's tip money. I looked good in it and I knew it was going to knock his socks off.

But as I walked back into the bedroom, I heard a snore. Rudy was lying on his back, his mouth open, sound asleep.

It wasn't exactly my idea of a perfect wedding night, and I wasn't about to accept his snoozing off without any romance at all. So I nudged him slightly. "Wake up, Rudy. You're not supposed to fall asleep on your wedding night."

He cleared his throat and turned away from me.

"Rudy." I shook him harder. "Come on, honey." But he was out.

So this was how it was going to be . . .

I sat down on the bed and watched him for a minute, trying to decide whether to hit him with a pillow or just let him sleep. It wasn't as if it would have been our first time. I guess Rudy didn't feel the sense of anticipation that I had felt.

I finally told myself that it was okay. I couldn't judge our whole marriage on one night. Besides, being here with him was so much better than living in that trailer without Lizzie around. I started to feel cold lying there beside him, so I got under the covers and moved up next to him.

And as he resumed his rhythmic snoring, I drifted into a light sleep.

∞

He woke me up the next morning as he stumbled out of bed.

I smiled. "Morning, *husband.*" I loved the sound of that word.

He didn't even look at me, just headed for the bathroom. I decided I must look pretty awful for him to ignore me like that, so I got out of bed, brushed my hair, and straightened my gown. I didn't want him to think he was going to wake up to a hag every morning for the rest of his life.

When he came back in, I sort of sashayed toward him. "You fell asleep last night—"

"Food." He pulled on his clothes, his features grim. "I need food and coffee, and a couple of aspirin. Get dressed," he said. "We're going down to eat."

His tone shattered my anticipation, but I told myself not to be offended. He didn't mean any harm. I'd seen Deke and Eloise suffering through hangovers for most of my life, and I knew that it would pass and he would feel better soon.

I gathered up my clothes and changed into the sundress that I had originally planned to wear in the wedding. It was cheap and inferior to the dress I'd gotten married in, but it was fine for today. Pleased at the way I looked, I came out and spun around.

"Do I look anything like a married woman?" I asked playfully.

"Nice," he muttered.

Well, he wasn't exactly waxing poetic, but it was something. I followed him out of the suite, rode down in the elevator in silence, then waited as he ordered coffee and eggs over easy. When he'd finally gotten food in his stomach, aspirin in his bloodstream, and caffeine in his brain, he started to look a little more like himself.

"I'm sorry I passed out last night." He rubbed his eyes. "I sure didn't intend to do that."

"It's all right. You're supposed to party on your wedding night. It's a law or something."

He forced a grin and looked at his watch. "What time did I say checkout was?"

"Eleven, but I love it here. Can't we stay another day?"

"No. My boss gave us one complimentary night for a wedding gift. After that, they make me pay."

"But don't you have any money?"

"Not enough for this place. If you hadn't spent all your tip money on clothes . . ."

My mouth fell open. "Now, wait a minute. I hardly spent anything at all, but what I did spend I spent because I wanted to look pretty for you."

"You look pretty no matter what you wear."

That helped a lot. I smiled again and took his hand, but he pulled it away and looked at his watch. "I guess we'd better go on up and pack. We'll need to get you moved into my place."

"When the money comes in, Rudy, let's leave this place. Let's just put Barton behind us and go to New York. I've always wanted to live there. We could get jobs there and start over. Heck, maybe we shouldn't even wait until the suit is settled. Maybe we should do it now. I can get a job as a waitress. I've got plenty of experience. I know there's something you could do there."

He leaned back on the booth and shook his head hard. "We're not going anywhere until that lawsuit is settled."

"But we can be in touch with the lawyer from there." I was getting all excited, really thinking that we could pack up and leave for the Big Apple today. "We could go ahead and start our new lives. We don't have to live anywhere fancy. Something like what you've got now is fine. But we'd be out of here."

He leaned up on the table, resting on his elbows. "We need all our money right now to get through this lawsuit. Where's that bracelet she gave you, by the way?"

"Upstairs in my suitcase."

"Good. When we get back to Barton, I'm going to take it and hock it."

I shook my head. "No! I wanted to keep it."

"Why? You don't need jewelry from that woman. You said so yourself."

"But Lizzie told me it was stupid to hock it at a pawnshop, that we could take it to a jewelry store and get a lot more. Anyway, I like it. It's pretty. I kind of thought I'd hang onto it until I really needed the money. Let me keep it. Please?"

He breathed out a sigh as the waiter brought the ticket to

the table. I watched him scowl as he read it, then he slapped down the cash and got up. He didn't look like he was going to wait for me, so I got up and followed behind him.

"We have to hurry," he said. "I've got to be back here for work at three this afternoon."

"You have to work today?" I stared at him. "Rudy, it's our *honeymoon.*"

"Somebody's got to pay some bills. Life isn't free."

"But I took the next couple of days off," I said. "I can make it up later."

"Well, you shouldn't have. Things are going to be tight until we get that settlement."

I was glad Lizzie wasn't here to hear that. As we drove back to Barton, I started hearing her voice, telling me that she was right, that Rudy only married me for the settlement, that it was more important to him than I was.

But it wasn't true! He *did* love me. He would have married me if I was going to be dead broke for the rest of my life. I told myself that over and over until we got to his house.

The house his grandmother left him was old and decrepit and leaned so badly that, if you dropped a marble, it would roll all the way across the floor. And it was almost as dirty as Deke and Eloise's place. I had never cleaned up at home, mainly because nobody else cared if it was filthy or not, but this was going to be my own home, so I decided to make the best of it. I figured I'd clean up his house and try to make my feminine mark on it. Rudy wouldn't be back until midnight, and though that was a long time, I figured when he did come, he'd be surprised at the changes I'd made.

I started by unpacking my suitcase and finding a place in the closet for my things. I had so little that I didn't need much room. I pulled out my underwear and found a space for it in a drawer, then put away my makeup and a few earrings I had bought at Walgreens.

I had finally gotten everything out of the suitcase when I realized that I hadn't come across the box with the bracelet in it. I searched through my shoes to see if the box had slipped inside one, then the pockets of the suitcase, then the underwear drawer where I'd put my things.

The bracelet was gone.

Had Rudy gotten it when I wasn't looking?

I knew without a doubt that he had. Again, I heard Lizzie's voice chiding me, telling me that he'd stolen from me now, that it *was* all about money. But wasn't I the one who'd said it always was?

I don't know why I was so surprised.

My face was hot as I hurried to the phone and dialed the number where Rudy worked. It took a few minutes for them to find him, but soon he came to the phone.

"Yeah, what is it?"

"Rudy, it's your wife." I liked the sound of that, even though I was mad.

"Yeah?" There was nothing but cool impatience in his voice, probably from guilt.

"Rudy, I was looking for the bracelet. It's not in the suit-case."

"I took it with me. I ran by a jewelry store before coming to work. I got a thousand bucks for it."

"*What?* That wasn't right, Rudy. I told you I wasn't ready to sell it."

"Well, I was."

I couldn't believe his attitude. He hadn't acted like this even once when we'd been seeing each other. But I tried to keep my voice level. "Well, what are you going to buy with the money?"

"Just a few of the things we need. It'll be fine. Just trust me."

"But, Rudy, I asked you not to sell it. I told you I wasn't ready. That just wasn't right."

"Kara, when you don't use common sense, I'm always going to override you."

"But it *was* common sense. Why are you treating me like this? Ever since last night, you've acted like I'm just a lot of trouble to have around. You're starting to make me wonder if Lizzie isn't right."

"Oh, that's just beautiful! What did she tell you?"

"She told me you were after the money, and I said no, that can't be right. Not Rudy, sweet, loving Rudy, the man of my dreams." I started to cry, and I hated myself for it.

His voice instantly softened. "Hey, it's not like that. It's going to be all right."

I had just about had it. "Bring that money home, Rudy. If you spend it, so help me, I'll have this marriage annulled and

I'll go live with Amanda just to show you." Then I slammed the phone down.

When it didn't ring right back, I threw myself on his bed and cried my heart out.

∾

He came home at 7:30 that night, surprising me. I was still brooding and angry, but he held a bouquet of roses and wore that same old smile that had won my heart before. "I asked them to let me off so I could spend some time with my bride," he said. "I made dinner reservations at Delta Point."

I looked up at him with wet eyes, wanting to believe that things were really okay. But I couldn't help remembering the threat I'd made to him, that I might have the marriage annulled and run off to live with Amanda. I didn't want to think it had taken that bluff to change his attitude. "Where's the money, Rudy?"

He took it out of his pocket and laid the cash on the table. "There, now. See? It's all there, every penny of it."

I counted out the thousand dollars. "I'm still mad at you for doing that."

"Honey, I didn't do it for me. I did it for us, so we could get a good start. But I do intend to use part of it to take you to dinner tonight."

I looked up at him, searching his face. "Did you really tell them you wanted to spend time with me?"

"Of course I did. I said that they could dock my pay if they wanted, that my little wife was sitting at home alone, and I wanted to be with her."

I felt better as I tried to picture him saying such a thing to his bosses. "All right I'll go get ready." I put the sundress on that I'd worn that morning, since I didn't have anything else for a place like Delta Point. He kissed me when I came out of the room and told me I was beautiful, and he held my hand as we drove out of Barton to the restaurant near the casino.

As we ate prime rib and lobster next to a window that over-looked the Mississippi, he started to dream with me about the penthouse condominium we were going to get in New York City, in the high-rise building with a view of Central Park.

"I'll take you for a cruise around Hudson Bay," he said, "at least once a week. And we'll see every Broadway show in town. And we'll hobnob with celebrities."

Mesmerized, I hung on every word. I wished Lizzie could hear this. She'd be happy for me then.

"Rudy, Kara, how are you?"

I looked up and saw Stan Mason, my lawyer, the one who was filing my lawsuit. Rudy got up and shook his hand. "We were going to call you Monday. Kara and I just got married yesterday."

"Really?" The lawyer looked taken aback by that news. "Well, congratulations."

"Have you filed the suit yet?" I asked him.

"I expect to serve Amanda Holbrooke in a few days. I'll be getting in touch with you to go over a few more things before we do that."

It was finally going to happen! I clapped my hands together.

"Well, it was great seeing you. I'll let you two get back to your meal."

We watched him return to his table, where several men in business suits were talking.

"We're so close!" I said. "Rudy, just think of it."

"Gonna be rich, baby."

After dinner, I got up and went to the ladies' room to freshen my makeup and fix my hair. I felt like I was already some rich millionaire as I came out. Stan Mason was getting ready to leave and he crossed the room to me.

"It was good to see you, Kara."

"You, too. I'll tell you what: I couldn't wait to raise that thousand dollars so we could get this show on the road."

He frowned then. "What thousand dollars?"

"The thousand-dollar retainer fee."

He shook his head, then looked toward the dining room. Rudy was sipping on his wine and looking out the window. "Kara, did Rudy tell you that I was charging you a thousand dollars?"

My heart took a nosedive, right into my stomach. "Well, yes. Are you telling me he didn't give it to you?"

"No, he didn't. We negotiated a commission for me, but I didn't ask for anything up front."

I felt like an idiot, standing there with that stunned look on my face. But I couldn't think of another word to say. I looked toward the dining room again. Rudy looked so content.

I'd been robbed—not once, but *twice*. And I heard Lizzie's

voice again, chiding me, reminding me that I didn't know Rudy that well and that I could do better.

"I'll talk to you next week," the lawyer said, but I didn't reply. Finally, he headed out.

I went back into the bathroom and pushed into a stall. I stood there a moment, trying to get my bearings. The lawyer wouldn't have lied, which meant Rudy had to be the liar. I felt dizzy and thought I might throw up, but I had to pull myself together. Slowly, I went back out to the table.

"Rudy, I'm ready to leave." My voice came out hoarse and raspy.

"But you didn't order dessert."

"I'm really not feeling well. Can we just go?"

He flagged down the waiter and handed him a hundred-dollar bill. When he'd paid the bill, we hurried out to the car. We were both quiet as we drove the thirty minutes back to Barton, and I used that time to try to sort out what I knew. If Rudy had deceived me, stolen the down payment money *and* the bracelet, then what did that mean? Was Lizzie right? Had he married me for the money?

I was shivering by the time we got back to the house, but I didn't want to make a scene out in the yard and let everybody in Barton find out that our marriage was already falling apart. I held myself together long enough to get inside. But the moment the door was closed, I turned to him.

"What happened to my thousand dollars, Rudy?"

He looked at me like I was crazy. "It's right here. We spent a hundred tonight, but the rest is—"

I slapped it out of his hand. "Not *that* thousand dollars! The money I gave you for the lawyer! Where is it?"

"I gave it to him, just like I said."

I got up in his face, my teeth gritted. "You're a liar, Rudy. Lizzie was right."

He looked startled, caught . . . *busted.* Then slowly, his lips tightened into a snarl. He came toward me, a murderous look in his eyes.

He showed me what he thought of my defiance with a backhand across my face.

If he'd thought that would turn me into a purring kitten, he was wrong. I lunged at him, my own fists flying. I was ready to kill him if I had to.

He balled his hand into a fist and hit me again, cracking my jaw. I rolled on the floor, clutching my face. "I hate you!" I cried, trying to get up.

He kneed me in the nose, and his fist pounded my face again. Blood dribbled from my nose and mouth, and one of my eyes started swelling.

I should have shut up then, but I had never felt such burning, lethal rage in my life. "You're a liar and a thief!" I staggered to my feet.

I grabbed the telephone and started dialing, but he jerked the phone cord out of the wall and threw it down with a clang.

I spun around and grabbed for the lamp on the table. I was ready to use it in any way I had to, and he knew it. I waved it over my head, waiting to strike, as I backed toward the front door.

He inched toward me, his eyes wild. I knew if he reached me, he'd kill me. There was no doubt in my mind.

"Don't you come near me or I'll crack this over your head," I said in a voice that didn't even sound like mine.

He came at me anyway, not showing one ounce of fear. He grabbed my arm, but I jerked away. Pulling my last bits of strength together, I crashed it over his head. He fell back, dazed, and I took the opportunity to bolt out of the house.

There was no time to get to the street or flag down help, so I headed for my woods. I stumbled through vines and tripped over branches, knowing that it was *my* territory, and he wouldn't be able to navigate his way through. I came out at the railroad tracks and ran across ties and ballast, fleeing for my life.

I was gasping for breath by the time I got to Deke and Eloise's trailer, but I fell onto the porch steps and banged on the front door. "Let me in! Please, let me in!"

Deke swung the door open and gaped down at me. "What the devil happened to you?"

I fell inside the door. "He beat me! He's a thief and a wife-beater and a liar."

"Girl, what happened?" Eloise had her wig off, and her hair stuck to her scalp like a greasy cap.

"I just need to lie down." I stumbled toward my room. "Let me just stay here for a few minutes until I figure out what to do."

"Sure, sweetie," Eloise said. "You go lay down, and we'll take care of everything. Deke, you have to call the police."

They were only being nice to me for the money. I knew that. No one was ever decent for any other reason.

I headed for the bedroom I had hoped never to sleep in again. But here I was, back with the couple that had held me hostage when I was too young to defend myself. It was all about money. It was always about money.

If I was worth so much, why did I feel so worthless?

I closed the door behind me and crawled onto the bed, curling up and swallowing the blood in my mouth. I was pretty sure my jaw was broken, and several of my teeth were loose.

"Lizzie," I whispered, wishing she were here beside me. I thought of calling her, but Deke and Eloise didn't have a phone, and the cell phone was at Rudy's house with my things.

Then I heard a car door slam, footsteps banging on the front porch, a fist hammering on the door.

"Let me in!" Rudy's voice thundered through the walls. "I want my wife!"

To my horror, Deke opened the door. The money, I thought. Deke would defend me because of the money. He wouldn't let Rudy come in because of the money. Surely he could muster some courage because of the money.

I heard words exchanged. Then that stomping across the floor again, and the door to my room flew open. I covered my head with my arms and screamed as I scooted back against the wall.

"You little witch! You thought you could get away from me, didn't you?" He grabbed me up and lifted me off of the bed. I fought like a madwoman, but he was stronger than I was.

He carried me out past Deke, who just stood there like the

coward that he was, and threw me into his car. I screamed and wailed and cussed, but Rudy twisted my arm behind my back.

"You shut your mouth or I'll break this arm," he said through his teeth.

I had no choice but to shut up. I hoped he would release my arm before it did break. It felt like it was going to snap right out of the socket. Every time I tried to squirm out of his reach, he jerked it harder, making me arch and yell out with pain.

"Why are you taking me back?" I asked him. "Why wouldn't you let me leave? You got what you wanted from me. You have my money."

"Not all of it. I'm your *husband*, and I'm going to get that estate when you get it. We're in this together. After that, you can go anywhere you want to, but the money is *mine*."

We got back to his house, and he dragged me out of the car and up the porch steps, threw me onto the living room floor, and bent down over my broken face. He squeezed my broken jaw with deadly fingers, and I thought I was going to pass out. I hoped I would. He was going to kill me anyway, and I wanted it to be quick.

But it wasn't. There was just more riveting, stabbing, nauseating pain, and he was enjoying it. I tried to fight my way up, but he wrestled me back down and hit me again. "Are we clear on the lawsuit?"

"Yes." I sounded like a wimp. I hated myself for not standing up to him, but the pain was making me weak.

"Good." He got up, and I thought he was going to let me

go. I struggled to get to my feet, but before I could get upright, he kicked me in the side, crushing my ribs.

I fell back to the floor, hugging my ribs and screaming.

He dragged me back into the bedroom and threw me into the walk-in closet. I hit the floor, and the door slammed.

A key rattled in the lock. I got up and flung myself at the door. "Let me out of here! I'll do whatever you say . . . Please, Rudy. We can work this out!" I screamed until my voice was shot, and finally I collapsed on the floor. My side felt crushed, and my jaw was swollen and locked. My teeth hung loosely in my tender mouth, and my eye had swollen shut.

The television came on at top volume, and I knew it was no use screaming anymore.

At that moment, I thought it was over. I was as good as dead. I wished I could leave a note for Lizzie and tell her that she was right, that I should have listened, that she was the smart one.

I knew he would hold me here until the lawsuit was settled and the check was deposited, and then he would kill me and bury my body in some hole in the ground, where no one would ever find me.

Lizzie would never know.

I was wrong . . . so wrong. I could be living in that mansion with Amanda, in that room she'd prepared for me. I could be learning and growing. I could be loved . . . and maybe it wouldn't all be about money.

But I had chosen the lie.

As I lay there, waiting for Rudy to come back and finish

me off, I started thinking how great it would be if I could get out of here. If I had just one more chance . . .

I knew I'd insulted Amanda, shamed her, and she had probably washed her hands of me. I knew I couldn't expect her to sweep into town in a limo to pick me up again. But maybe I could get to *her*. Maybe I could go to her and offer to work in that house and pay my way. If I earned my keep, maybe she would take me in. Maybe she would forgive me then.

I sat up and took trembling inventory of my wounds. I got my feet under me and staggered up. I found the light switch, and the yellow bulb lit the closet. Frantically, I searched for escape. I caught my breath as I saw the small, narrow window at the back of the top shelf. I hadn't noticed it before. Rudy hadn't lived here long; he probably hadn't noticed it, either. He never would have thrown me in here if he'd known.

I looked around for something to stand on, and my eyes scanned the clothes hanging there. My own few things hung beside his . . . two waitress uniforms, the dress I'd married him in, a couple of pairs of jeans.

My heart stopped as I saw the cord dangling out of the pocket of one of my aprons, and I remembered that I had left the phone there. Almost weeping in gratitude, I grabbed it out.

I punched the power button, my hand trembling, but there was no charge.

It was worthless unless I could get to an electrical outlet.

I looked on the top shelf, saw a hard suitcase and three boxes. I took a coat hanger off of the rod and, reaching the suitcase, slid it quietly off of the shelf until I could grab the handle.

The TV still blared in the bedroom. I got the suitcase to the floor and set it under that window. Trembling, I stepped up onto it, then reached for those empty boxes. They weren't heavy—they held only a few items of clothing that Rudy hadn't unpacked after he moved in. I pulled them down, then stuffed them with clothes from the hangers so they would bear my weight. I stacked one on top of the other, then put the suitcase on top.

Slowly, gritting my teeth against the agonizing pain, I climbed to the top of the suitcase, balancing by holding on to the shelf. I slid prostrate onto that shelf, biting my lip to keep from screaming out. Breathing hard, I rotated the handle until the window levered open. But it didn't open all the way.

It didn't leave room enough to get through, so I knocked it up with the heel of my left hand, breaking the frame.

I froze. Had Rudy heard the noise?

The television still blared, and I prayed he had fallen asleep. Beating your wife half to death does take it out of you.

I threw the phone out, heard it thud lightly onto the grass.

Gritting my teeth, I slid my feet through the window's opening, then scooted my body down until my rump rested on the sill. It was like being reborn, pushed into a new world, frightened and damaged, but I managed to slip the rest of the way out and dropped to the ground.

I didn't wait to see if Rudy had heard me. With life-or-death determination, I grabbed the phone and cord, clutched my side, and ran again toward the safe haven of the forest that had always sheltered and hidden me.

In the darkness, I strained to see the landmarks that told me where I was. The fallen tree, the thornbush growing out of a stump, the path that Lizzie and I had used so often. My breath whistled as I ran, and I knew that my rib had penetrated my lungs. I couldn't gasp enough air in, and I was growing weaker as I went.

I managed to trudge on, across the railroad tracks this time, deeper into the woods.

The old gas station from which Lizzie had left with Amanda was lit up on the highway, and I stumbled out and headed toward it. It was closed, so no one was there, but I found an outdoor plug in the front of the building. Shaking, I plugged the phone in.

Gratitude gushed through me as its light came on.

I found Amanda's number, pushed *talk* . . . and waited for my sister to answer.

THIRTY-NINE

Lizzie answered after the first ring. "Kara?"

Her voice sounded frantic, breathless, like she already knew why I was calling.

"Lizzie!" I knew I didn't sound like myself. I was hoarse and couldn't catch a breath, and my jaw would hardly move.

"Kara? You're hurt, aren't you? The pain . . . it woke me up. I knew you were in trouble . . ."

As sorry as I was that she felt this pain, it gave me hope to know we were still connected. "Lizzie, he beat me."

"Rudy beat you? Are you all right?"

"*No!* You were right, Lizzie. You were so right. I should have listened to you."

"Kara, tell me where you are."

"I'm at Zeke Stafford's gas station . . . but I can't stay here in the light . . . the phone doesn't have a charge." I couldn't breathe. "He'll find me and drag me back."

I heard a commotion on the other end, other voices, then Amanda took the phone. "Kara, I want you to wait there for the police. Do you hear me? I want you to—"

I saw headlights coming up the road and I knew it was Rudy. I jerked the cord out of the jack and hid behind the building. I sat there in the shadows, trembling and watching. I was right. Rudy knew I was gone and was searching for me. His car slowed down . . .

"Please, Lord . . . Oh, please, please let him pass."

I'd never had a prayer answered before. In fact, I didn't remember ever praying. But I was overcome with gratitude when I looked again and he was gone.

I had to get out of town. I couldn't let him find me.

I put the phone in my pocket, along with the adapter cord, and made my way to the SOS. It was still open, though a skeleton crew worked in the dark hours of the morning.

I went between eighteen-wheelers parked in the lot behind the building, then reached the back door. I stumbled into the kitchen. Andy Yarbrough looked up at me and swore under his breath. "What in the blazes happened to you?"

"Andy, I need money," I managed to say. I tried hard to get a breath, but my lungs just weren't taking it in. My side hurt so bad that I wanted to die. "I need it quick. Please. You've got to help me."

"How much you need?"

"Enough to buy a train ticket. Please. I have this phone I can sell you if you could just give me forty or fifty dollars."

"Are you kidding? I ain't got that much on me."

"Please. Get it out of the cash register. The phone's probably worth a hundred bucks. Come on, Andy. You're saving a life. I've got to get out of town."

He narrowed his eyes. "Did your new husband do this to you?"

"I don't have time to go over this! Please. You've got to help me."

He drew in a deep breath. "Well, all right. Just a minute. I'll be back with the money." He left the kitchen, and I stepped into the pantry, out of sight, and waited for him to come back. In a moment, he returned with two twenties.

"You give me that phone," he said. "When the boss comes in in the morning, I don't want to have to explain why we're short. At least he'll have this."

I thrust the phone at him. "Call the police for me. Tell them Rudy beat me and locked me up. And if he comes, don't tell him I was here. Say you haven't seen me. *Promise me!*"

"All right," he said, already heading for the wall phone.

"And then call my sister," I rasped out. I tried to get my breath. "Number's on the phone, under *Amanda.*"

"Okay, okay."

I bolted out the back door, wondering if he'd really do any of what I'd said. Agony almost paralyzed me, but I made myself move. I headed for the train station as fast as my feet would carry me, but it was a long walk that seemed to take hours. My lungs seemed like a balloon with a gaping hole, and I kept stopping to rest. I feared I would collapse in the middle of the woods, only to be found days later when some nasty hunting dog smelled my decay. I made myself trudge on, soaked in sweat and whistling each breath. I made it to the depot just as darkness had begun to lift.

I checked the parking lot for Rudy's car. It wasn't there, so I went in and leaned against the counter. "What's the next train out of here?" I asked the depot manager through my teeth.

He regarded me with alarm. "Girl, you need a hospital."

"I don't have time for a hospital. Hurry. What's the next train?"

"Well, we have a seven o'clock headed for Dallas. Where you trying to go?"

I burst into tears and covered my face. "I just want to go to Jackson. Is there a train to Jackson?"

"Not until ten o'clock."

"I can't wait. I have to get out of town now. What's the next train out?"

"Well, you could take that train headed for Dallas and change trains in Monroe. That'd get you out of town. Then you could head back to Jackson."

"I only have forty dollars. Please. It has to be enough."

He took the two twenties, punched some numbers into his little computer, then nodded. "Forty bucks is just right." I doubted that was true—maybe one person in this sorry town had some kindness in him, I thought. "But you'll need more when you get there."

"I'll worry about that then." I took the ticket and held it against my heart. "Please. If a man comes in looking for me, just tell him you haven't seen me. You'll be saving my life."

"Do I need to call the police for you?"

I thought of Andy at the SOS. "They've already been called."

I headed into the bathroom and went into a stall. I sat there, waiting until I heard the train pulling up. Then, when I was sure it was time to board, I rushed out, still soaking with sweat and struggling to breathe.

I climbed on the train and limped from car to car. I found a seat at the very back and lay down, just in case Rudy got on and looked across the heads to see if I was there. I curled up in a fetal position, groaning at the pain. I started to cough and put my hand over my mouth to muffle it. The blood was still wet on my face.

"Help me, Jesus," I whimpered. "I'm dying in a sticky, stinking seat in the back of an old train." It was appropriate, I thought. A horrible end to a terrible life. "Please, Lord, get me to Lizzie . . . I'm so sorry for all I did. Let Amanda give me another chance."

The train had pulled away from the station, and I realized I had escaped. But I couldn't breathe, and the pain was more than I could bear.

I lay there, trying desperately to breathe, but I felt my life beginning to fade. And as the sun began to come up and shine through the windows, darkness fell over me.

FORTY

While unconscious, I dreamed of Amanda and Lizzie searching for me, running from house to house in Barton, scouring the woods. I dreamed they were crying, and the tears on Amanda's face were real. It wasn't about money.

It had never been about money.

Even in my unconscious state, I knew that I was dying—and I was fully aware that I'd brought it on myself. I deserved to drift away in the backseat of a train, beaten up by the man I thought I loved.

I deserved to have Amanda laugh at my funeral. How absurd that I refused the free gifts she offered me . . . and for what? To keep wallowing in the slime of my childhood? How ridiculous that I would choose the familiar, when I had so much more waiting.

I curled into a tighter ball as I felt the train slowing to a stop. I tried to open my eyes, tried to pull myself back to consciousness, but I hovered in some netherland between sleep and death.

I dreamed I heard the sound of a helicopter, voices shouting in the other cars, my name being called, feet running . . .

I tried to open my eyes, to sit up, to call out that I was here . . . but I couldn't seem to move.

But the voice sounded like Amanda's. *"Kara! Kara!"* I knew it had to be a dream. Amanda hadn't come for me. She didn't even know where I was. I had insulted her, practically spit in her face, and she had probably written me off.

But then I heard it again . . . closer now.

"Lizzie! There she is!"

I heard Lizzie then, crying out as if *she* was wounded, and I wondered if Rudy had gotten to her . . .

I managed to slit my eyes open enough to see her fall to her knees beside my seat. "Kara, wake up," she sobbed. "Please wake up. Don't leave me now, Kara. Please wake up!"

I garnered all my strength and forced my eyes to open wider.

"Kara, it's me." Lizzie touched my bruised, swollen face. "Amanda and I came for you. Kara? She's awake, Amanda."

Amanda called out, and paramedics came running up the aisle. I felt her lifting my head and putting it on her lap, and she stroked my hair with gentle fingers. "Be careful with her," she told the medics. "That's my daughter. She was lost, but now she's found. She's very special."

Her tears dropped onto my face.

I looked up at her and tried to open my mouth. My jaw was too frozen, but I managed to get out three words. "I'm so sorry."

"It's okay, sweetie, it's okay. You're going to be all right. Welcome home, sweetheart."

∞

They managed to get me to an ambulance.

I heard them radioing the hospital that my lung had collapsed, my jaw was fractured, and several ribs were crushed.

I don't remember much else about that day, except that hours later I woke with wires and monitors attached to me, stitches across my face, and an IV in my arm. Amanda and Lizzie sat beside my bed and took care of my every need. They brushed my hair, nursed my wounds, talked to me about my past and who I really am . . .

This time I listened.

A few days later, they took me home.

∞

I eventually recovered from my injuries, and Rudy was locked up for forty years for violating his parole by beating his bride to a pulp.

Even now, months later, as I sit on the balcony of the room Amanda prepared for me, as I look down at the gardens flowing over with color and a sweet breeze blows through my hair and calms my regrets . . . even now, the beauty of this life makes my heart ache.

I know I don't deserve it. Amanda should have left me to wallow in my own mess. But that's not how she works.

As long as I live, I will never understand the undeserved grace that she brought to my life, even after I treated her with such contempt. I'll never grasp exactly why I didn't have to buy a train ticket and make my way to her. She came the moment I called, without a moment's hesitation.

I hear her footsteps across the plush carpet, and she steps out to join me. I smile up at her, and she sees the tears on my face.

"What's the matter, sweetheart?"

My heart is so full that I can hardly speak. "I'm just trying to figure myself out, that's all."

She sits down next to me, her eyes adoring my face.

I look down. "I can't understand why I waited to come to you. I *chose* poverty instead of paradise. I created my own prison, thinking it was freedom. Some of the things I did . . . I don't even know how you can forgive me."

"Forgive you for what, honey?"

I screw my face up with shame. "For who I was."

"But that's not who you are anymore." Her words have the sure sound of truth, and that truth radiates through me. "You've been washed clean of your past. And all I see now is my beautiful, sweet daughter."

I weep against her as she holds me, stroking my hair, rocking me from side to side.

"Shhh," she whispers again. "It's okay, sweetie . . . I've loved you since you were three . . ."

I know she means it with all her heart. And it isn't because of money. It never was. It's because of a promise made to a man I don't remember . . . by a woman I thought I hated.

A promise I didn't deserve. A promise that meant new life, undying love, and redemption from the bondage I was in.

After all the broken promises of my life, it was the one kept promise that finally changed everything.

DISCUSSION QUESTIONS

The following questions may be used as part of a Book Club, Bible Study, or Group Discussion.

1. This story is told from Kara's perspective. Kara is a perpetual skeptic—an unbeliever, if you will. Lizzie, on the other hand, is a believer—able to embrace her inheritance without hesitation. Which one are you?

2. Was there anything about Lizzie that made her more suitable for the inheritance than Kara, or was it equally accessible to both of them?

3. What were the conditions—if any—under which Amanda would take Lizzie into her home? What did Kara imagine the conditions would be? Do unbelievers ever have wrong ideas about the Christian life?

4. Why did Amanda watch over the girls all those years? What did her promise to Jack have to do with her commitment to the girls?

5. God promised Abraham that through Abraham's seed, all the families of the earth would be blessed (Genesis 12, 15, 17). Galations 3:16 tells us that the promised "seed" was Jesus Christ. How are you a child of that covenant? Discuss the parallels in this book to the promises that God kept on your behalf when he sent Jesus Christ.

6. Eloise and Deke deceived the girls all their lives. Then Rudy came along and told Kara further lies. How may you have been deceived about your own "inheritance"?

7. What is your inheritance in Christ (1 Peter 1:3-5)?

8. Has there ever been a time when lies kept you from entering the kingdom of God?

9. Why did Kara choose her poverty over her inheritance? Discuss ways that we choose our spiritual poverty over the inheritance God offers us.

10. Discuss ways that you have extinguished the power of the Holy Spirit in your life, or insisted on living a bland and useless life instead of the abundant life Christ offers.

11. When Kara finally realized the truth, what did she do? Have you ever tried to work your way to God?

12. Is it possible to come to the Lord on our own terms? What are His terms?

    (See Romans 10:9-13.) Why are God's terms better than ours? Read Jeremiah 29:11.

13. Read 1 Samuel 18, 19, and 20, about the covenant David made with Jonathan. Jonathan extended that

covenant to his "household" or his descendants
(1 Samuel 20:15-16). What did this covenant obligate
David to do?

14. Jonathan and his father, Saul, are killed on the
    battlefield. Opposition forces come into the palace and
    begin wiping out the entire family of Saul. Read
    2 Samuel 4:4 about Jonathan's five-year-old son,
    Mephibosheth.

15. Now read 2 Samuel 9. Why did David invite
    Mephibosheth into his home? What was
    Mephibosheth's self-image?

16. Do you see parallels between the story of David and
    Mephibosheth, and *Covenant Child?* How does this
    biblical story effect us as believers? Can you see any
    parallels between your own life and Mephibosheth's?

17. If we are children of God, members of His family, and
    fellow heirs with Christ, do we ever have reason to feel
    lonely or helpless? (See Romans 8:15-17.)

18. In Luke 12:32, Jesus said, "Do not be afraid, little flock,
    for your Father has chosen gladly to give you the
    kingdom." Is there anything we can do to earn the
    grace Christ gives us when He invites us into His
    family? What does Christ require of us?

Now that you've finished this study, I challenge you to make the
next "novel" you read the Old Testament. It happens to be true,
but it's more exciting than any fiction you could read! Then follow it up with the New Testament, and see how you are the
Covenant Child who is constantly on God's mind.

WOMEN OF FAITH
fiction

Additional books in the Women of Faith Fiction Series

When PanWorld flight 848 crashes into Tampa Bay killing all 261 people on board, journalist Peyton MacGruder is assigned to the story. Her discovery of a remnant of the tragedy—a simple note: "T—I love you...All is forgiven. Dad."—sends her on a quest to find its owner and the story behind it. In the process, Peyton uncovers lessons about love, forgiveness, and herself.

After 23 years of marriage and raising their family in the same lakeside home, John and Abby Reynolds are getting a divorce. But before they can tell their family, their daughter makes a joyous announcement of her own: She is getting married. John and Abby decide to postpone their news until after the wedding, but as the big day approaches, questions continue to haunt them. Can they find once again what they've been missing for so many years, the joy of magnificent love, the time...to dance?

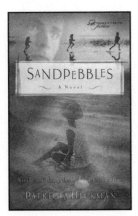

Recently-widowed March Longfellow efficiently commandeers the lives of her son, Mason, her pastor father, and the staff members of the small-town newspaper she owns, all the while grappling with grief and issues unresolved before her husband's fatal boating accident. When a new pastor comes to town and his family's lives become intertwined with her own, March finds her life thrust into a new direction—one she cannot control. As March begins to release the things of the past, God rekindles her faith and her joy and offers her renewed hope for love.

Visit *www.wpublishinggroup.com for discussion guides
to these and other W Publishing Group novels*

W PUBLISHING GROUP™
www.wpublishinggroup.com
A Division of Thomas Nelson, Inc.
www.ThomasNelson.com